D0122077

The Odds of Lightning

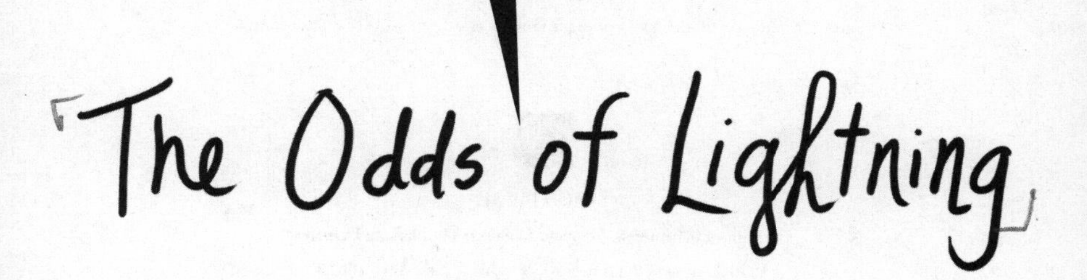

JOCELYN DAVIES

SIMON PULSE

NEW YORK DELHI

SIMON PULSE

An imprint of Simon & Schuster Children's Publishing Division

1230 Avenue of the Americas, New York, New York 10020

First Simon Pulse hardcover edition September 2016

Jacket design and illustrations by Karina Granda

Interior designed by Steve Scott

The text of this book was set in Bulmer.

Manufactured in the United States of America

2 4 6 8 10 9 7 5 3 1

This book has been cataloged with the Library of Congress.

ISBN 978-1-4814-4053-0 (hc)

ISBN 978-1-4814-4055-4 (eBook)

TO BEST FRIENDS EVERYWHERE, ESPECIALLY MINE

As far as the laws of mathematics refer to reality,
they are not certain; and as far as they are certain,
they do not refer to reality.

–Albert Einstein

And if I ever was myself, I wasn't that night.

–Wilco

The Odds of Lightning

NOW

Eventually, there would be lightning.

Not the kind of lightning that's over before you know it, that flickers briefly in the space between two tall buildings and leaves you wondering if it was ever there at all. But the kind of lightning that cracks with a vengeance. That rips through your soul and sends your heart knocking along your spine for luck. The kind that brings with it a courageous, unpredictable magic, a feeling that time—and certainly the present—no longer matters.

The kind that keeps you up all night.

This isn't a story about superheroes, even though that's how we felt sometimes. It's not about extraordinary creatures. It's just about us, and the extraordinary things that happened to us when we were least expecting them.

We were smart kids. We were friends once, but the four of us hadn't been friends for a long time. Now, we knew *of* one another. We saw one another in the halls. We heard one another speak in class. One of us had been in the school play that the rest of us had been forced to go see. One of us had written something for the literary magazine. The byline read "Anonymous." We'd wondered who had written it.

But sometimes to be super—to be more than ordinary, greater than the sum of our parts—it takes doing something you didn't think you had in you.

If we hadn't gone to that party, none of this would have happened in the first place. We never would have found one another again.

We never would have been struck by lightning.

Friday Night

8:00 p.m.

(12 Hours Left)

If It Was the End of the World, Would *You* Stay at Home?

Tiny stood in front of the bathroom mirror. She opened her eyes.

Still there.

She tried to see herself as someone else might see her.

Her hair was a nothing brown.

Her eyes were a nothing brown.

Her skin was pale and freckled. Her cheeks were a little too squishable. Her nose unremarkable. Her lips totally unkissable.

It was amazing anyone saw her at all.

The box of hair dye on the sink promised to give her multifaceted blond hair. If the model on the front was any indication, it would also give her a great complexion and a carefree attitude toward life.

That would be nice.

She was going for something cool and fun, something that would get Josh Herrera's attention. She and Lu had it all planned out.

Tiny and Josh would lock eyes on the bus the next morning. And instead of ignoring her like he always did, this time he would smile. He would say hi. He would brush his hair out of his face and ask her if she wanted to go to a reading sometime at Housing Works Café. They'd sit together, sharing one of those giant chocolate chip cookies, and every so often their knees would bump into each other. They'd sit there even after the reading was over, talking about their favorite authors and how they wished the school English curriculum let them read better books. They'd sit there for hours. Outside, the rain would come down and they would sit there until it had stopped enough for them to run to the subway.

That's where they would kiss for the first time.

But so far Tiny hadn't even worked up the nerve to open the box.

She hadn't always been like this. But things had changed.

Sometimes she was afraid she was the kind of person who would always be stuck, holding the box of hair dye, wondering if she even wanted to open it.

One subway stop downtown from where Tiny was staring into her bathroom mirror, Lu was procrastinating.

She drummed her fingers restlessly against the scenes she was supposed to memorize for that fall's drama department production of *A Midsummer Night's Dream*, even though a voice—a small one in the back of her mind—was urging her to study for the SATs instead. One of the reasons Lu loved acting was the complete and glorious feeling of pretending to be someone else. Getting to escape into a character's life. She could say anything she wanted, do anything she wanted, and there were no consequences. It was the best feeling in the world.

If her mom weren't out teaching a class for her psychology postdoctoral students, she would say it was Lu's *choice* whether she wanted to study or not. Her mom was all about *choices*. She respected Lu's sense of *agency*. Her mom had said to call her cell if she needed anything. But she hadn't come home when the news reports had gotten worse. Some parental figure. Her dad would never have let that happen. Even when he was sick, Lu was the one to remind her mom to make the doctor's appointments and the pill charts and the organic recipes. Maybe if her mom weren't always doing stupid, flighty stuff like this, her dad wouldn't have left them for the nurse at the hospital as soon as he got better.

Outside the windows of the small apartment Lu now shared with just her mom, the wind was kicking up, howling through the slats of the creaking rusty fire escape, and she could hear thunder rumbling up from the depths of the earth. All people were talking about online was how the news had predicted that what was supposed to be just your typical, run-of-the-mill thunderstorm was actually part of a larger storm pattern rolling up from Florida, where it had left a trail of flooding and devastation in its wake. The city was suspending bus service and said it might suspend subway service if the storm got bad enough. They were urging people to stay indoors.

By four o'clock the Duane Reade on her corner was completely out of bottled water, granola bars, and D batteries, which Lu knew because she'd popped in for a pack of gum and a magazine on her way home from school. Staring at the surge of people stockpiling for the apocalypse, she wondered if they would cancel the SATs, but she didn't get her hopes up. They never canceled stuff like that. Her school had only had one snow day in her entire life, when she was eight. School hadn't closed for any reason since, including the 3.0 earthquake she'd thought was just the coffee grinders at Starbucks on full blast.

She couldn't imagine some rain was going to stop the SATs.

Lu smiled.

If there was one thing she'd always loved, it was a good thunderstorm. She couldn't wait for the rain to start. How could she possibly be expected to study on a night like this? It was too dark and stormy to do anything practical.

Lu turned up the moody indie rock wafting out of her computer speakers, and pulled her knees into her chest.

When her phone buzzed on the desk in front of her, her first thought was that it was her mom, texting to say she'd changed her mind and was coming home after all, or her dad, coming out of months of hiding to say he would never leave her all alone when the sky looked like it was about to fall and smoosh them all and the biggest test of her life was the next morning.

But it was not her mother and definitely not her dad. It was Owen.

HEY, WE SHOULD TALK.

The thunder outside seemed to rattle her bones. Nothing good ever started with those words.

CAN YOU COME TO THE SHOW TONIGHT? HURRICANEFEST. CENTRAL PARK. MIDNIGHT.

A weird feeling stirred in her chest. Something restless and uncomfortable was beginning to build. The sensation was physical. It grabbed at her heart and squeezed.

He was about to break up with her. The night before the SATs!

I'LL BE THERE.

Lu wrote. And she meant it. Like hell she was about to let that happen. Lu didn't like whatever this was that she was currently experiencing—this feeling of being raw and cracked open. Vulnerable. Screw the SATs. Screw the storm. She'd get to that show in Central Park if she had to swim there. Getting dumped was for the weak of spirit. She'd never been dumped, and she wasn't about to start now. She imagined a force field surrounding her. Fortress walls that no mere mortal could penetrate.

She texted Tiny.

WE'RE GOING OUT.

At that same moment, across Central Park, Will Kingfield had just gotten off the phone with his parents, who were stuck in an airport in Spain. Flights in and out of all New York–area airports were canceled. It hadn't started raining yet, but pressure systems were intense, the wind was wild, and visibility was low.

"We're trying to get on the next flight we can," his dad said. "Just stay put, okay, my man? Study. Watch a movie. Call your grandma. Do *not* go out in the storm."

"Whatever." Will rolled his eyes. He didn't plan on it.

His phone pinged with a message from Jon Heller, his soccer co-captain.

LET'S GO OUT. STORMPOCALYPSE!!

NAH, DUDE, Will wrote back. STORM + STUDYING = STATIONARY

LAME.

IF YOU WANT TO GET RAINED ON, Will wrote, BE MY GUEST.

IF IT WAS THE END OF THE WORLD, WOULD YOU STAY AT HOME?

IT'S NOT THE END OF THE WORLD. IT'S JUST A BIG THUNDERSTORM.

The little ellipses at the bottom of the conversation stopped and then started again. Will watched them like a Magic 8 Ball.

YOU NEVER KNOW WHEN A BIG THUNDERSTORM WILL TURN INTO THE END OF THE WORLD.

More ellipses.

LIVE IT UP WHILE YOU CAN.

Will didn't write back. He threw the phone onto the bed. Jon didn't need to worry about the SATs because his mom was a legacy at Cornell. Will's parents were rich like Jon's, but unluckily for him they hadn't gone to college anywhere his guidance counselor thought he should go. So he actually had to work.

But it wasn't like he was about to sob on about being nervous for the big test or anything. He'd get Nathaniel to come over and help. Will grabbed his phone and called him.

"Dude," Will said. Nathaniel was such a nerd. They'd had that in common once. They'd gone to nursery school, elementary school, and middle school together before high school. They'd gone to math camp together every summer. At least, they had until freshman year, when Will joined the soccer team and Nathaniel started spending all his time in the science lab after school like he was working on a cure for cancer or something. Now they only hung out when it was convenient, like when there was a test the next day, or there was no one else around to see.

If Will knew Nathaniel, he was probably studying away in his bedroom, the door closed to keep his parents from barging in to check on him every five minutes, and a lifetime supply of Cheez-Its to snack on. Maybe he was doing that thing where he took the hardest test first and then worked his way backward to the easiest one. Will idly picked a Nerf basketball up off the carpet in his room and tossed it at the mini hoop above his closet door.

"If you come study with me for like, two hours, I'll play you in Playstation Golf as a reward for being exceptional and focused on our futures." He held his breath. Will still always felt vaguely guilty when he suggested they study together, like it was a business transaction or something. He got the feeling Nathaniel didn't love it either.

The Nerf ball circled the rim.

"Yeah," Nathaniel said after a pause. "Sure."

Swish. Will hung up. "Whattup?" he said to no one.

Will took a few more shots (*swish, swish, swish*), then opened a practice test book and chewed on his pencil eraser. It tasted salty and kind of satisfying. He didn't stop chewing right away.

His phone pinged again.

PARTY was all Jon said this time. YOUR PLACE.

Will chewed on the eraser some more. If he said no, the whole team would be mad at him.

JUST THE GUYS? Will wrote back.

TOTALLY. AN INTIMATE PRE-STANDARDIZED-TEST AFFAIR.

OKAY, SCREW IT. LET'S HAVE A PARTY.

PARTY!!!!!!!

Will took a deep breath. He was doing this.

PARTY!

He wrote back.

Will chucked the phone back onto his bed and rubbed his face.

He changed out of his Daybrook Athletics sweats and tried not to think about how much he'd changed since he and Nathaniel had been friends. Real friends.

And how different he was now. Unrecognizable, even.

He barely knew who he was anymore.

Nathaniel hung up the phone and looked down at his bed. His practice books were all laid out the way he'd arranged them half an hour before, in an arc from hardest to easiest so he'd end the night on a note of confidence. His box of Cheez-Its was waiting for him on the desk.

But he hadn't looked at any of the books since he'd finished arranging them. Instead he kept folding and unfolding the Anders Almquist Earth Science Scholarship application.

For the past three years Nathaniel's dream in life was to follow in his brother's footsteps and win the Anders Almquist and get into MIT's EAPS program—Earth, Atmospheric and Planetary Sciences—to study geophysics. As far as Nathaniel was concerned, space got all the credit for being mysterious. Like, do wormholes exist? Are there other universes besides our own? What happens if you get sucked through a black hole? But if Tobias taught him anything, it was that there were enough mysteries within the Earth itself to occupy the rest of his life. The shifting of tectonic plates, electromagnetic currents crashing together in clouds, the kinetic energy of falling objects, the inescapable gravitational pull of the Earth's core. And how each of those mysterious forces conspired to control our lives. The spin of the Earth might cause a car to crash, for instance, or a bicycle to spin out of control on a humid late-summer night.

Tobias taught him that everything was connected.

The application for the Anders Almquist Earth Science Scholarship had been due on his adviser's desk no later than eight a.m. that morning.

Nathaniel had stayed up until three, working on it. His parents had warned him not to save it all for the last minute. But they were so used to Tobias, perfect Tobias, who never saved anything till the last minute. And, of course, Nathaniel had lied. Every time they checked in, he said he was fine. He was almost done. So they went to bed, and before he knew it, he stopped hearing cars on the street below and started hearing the clanking of predawn garbage trucks, and then the next thing he knew he was starting awake and it was 8:05 and the sun was streaming in through his window and there was a puddle of drool on his computer keyboard. On the screen, the cursor was blinking in the middle of an unfinished sentence.

He made it to school, disheveled and disoriented, the printed-out unfinished application clutched in his hand.

But he was too late.

Tobias would never have let something like that happen. He would have finished it early and he would have gone to bed early and not slept through his alarm and he would have made it to school in time to hand it in and he would have done it all without breaking a sweat.

Nathaniel had been sweating.

He unfolded the application again and smoothed it out on top of the first test book (the hardest one). It had four distinct lines creased into it, from being folded into quarters in his pocket all day.

Because he knew, deep down, that he would never be up there onstage presenting his paper like his brother once had. Not now and not ever. He would never be as good as Tobias. His brother was, like, a superhero. And Nathaniel was just so . . . not.

The creases were really ugly. He folded the application up again and stuffed it into his back pocket in disgust. That was one dream he could give up on. He shoved the books on his bed into his backpack, knocked his cell phone off the desk, and into the front pocket, and crashed out the door.

As he left, his backpack hit the desk chair, sending Cheez-Its cascading across the carpet.

Tiny slid to the floor, leaning her head back against the cool tile.

She opened the box. Did the tube in her hand have life-changing properties? Would she look cool? Would she look stupid? Would anyone notice? Was it worth the risk to find out?

She twisted off the cap. Some of the hair dye dripped into a puddle of water on the tiled floor, making crazy patterns before turning the entire puddle a muddied brown. Tiny stared at it. She wished she could be a drop of dye swirling in water, twisting and unfurling in clouds and billows and patterns like there was no stopping her.

Lu sat at her computer, repeating Hermia's lines over and over, resolved that it didn't matter one zillionth of an ounce what she got on the SATs if she wasn't going to college. In the middle of shouting "What, can you do me greater harm than hate?" Will Kingfield popped up in her news feed.

STORMPOCALYPSE PARTY! COME OVER IF YOU DARE.

Lu suddenly got quiet.

Josh Herrera would be at that party.

She and Tiny didn't go out a lot together these days. Tiny would want to play it safe and stay home. Lu would need a great reason to convince her to leave the apartment during a storm like this, especially with the SATs the next day. And now she had one. Kissing Josh.

That, and Lu *always* accepted a dare.

The party wasn't Will's fault, really. Or that's what he was telling himself.

It wasn't his fault that he had trouble concentrating. It wasn't his fault that he could never say no to his teammates. It wasn't his fault that Nathaniel took his sweet time getting there. It wasn't his fault that Jon Heller, standing over his shoulder while Will typed, pushed *post* and made the most epic status update ever official.

By the time Nathaniel got there, the guys were already in the den playing Golf on the Playstation, drinking Will's dad's Bud Lights, and texting the girls to come over.

"SATs!" they shouted every time they swung.

Nathaniel stood in the doorway and looked from the TV to the guys to Will.

Will didn't want to be taken on a guilt trip.

"Dude." He smiled, knowing Nathaniel wouldn't argue. "Early study break?"

There were so many things Nathaniel should have been doing instead. He should have been studying. He should have been sleeping. He should have been relaxing and letting his brain rest the night before the biggest test of his life, as his parents had advised him to do. The voice in his head was telling him to go home. But he couldn't go home. Now that he was no longer working toward the Anders Almquist Earth Science Scholarship, Nathaniel didn't know where he was supposed to go anymore.

The first flash of lightning lit up the sky outside Tiny's window. Her mind filled with images she couldn't control and couldn't stop: the churning black water of the East River, the shimmer of heat lightning above the skyline, the sound of crunching metal and shattering glass.

The memory of her first kiss and everything that came after.

All she wanted was to forget. But lightning would always make her remember.

Come over if you dare. Lu picked up her cell phone and speed-dialed Tiny's number. Whatever—there was no one home to stop her.

Will took the six-pack and cracked open a beer. He tossed one across the room to Nathaniel.

Nathaniel looked at the blue can in his hand and then back at Will. He thought about the books in his backpack on the floor by the foot of the stairs.

Tiny's phone rang in the bedroom. Without another thought, she pulled the curtain closed and went to get it.

It's not like my mom would even notice if I tanked, Lu thought.

"Here's to tonight!" Will boomed, raising his can. "Carpe fucking diem!"

"Here, here!" Nathaniel heard himself shout.

There comes a time in your life, Tiny realized as she answered the phone, *when you just have to say—*

At a certain point, Lu thought as she heard Tiny pick up—

"Because sometimes," Will said to the group, "everyone knows you gotta just—"

"What the hell?" Nathaniel said, taking a sip.

"Fuck it."

THEN

The Last Day of Summer Before High School

Three Years ago

8:00 a.m.

Cumulonimbus Clouds

Tiny

There were some things you just couldn't put into words.

"Tell me again how you got your nickname," Luella said through a mouthful of Lego candy.

It was the last day of summer, and Tiny and Luella were sitting outside the Guggenheim Museum, contemplating their futures. They wore shorts and flip-flops and tank tops, and still felt overdressed. It was the hottest day of the year by far, and the entire city was engulfed in a sticky, thick, edible humidity. The heat was a tangible, visible, moving thing, rising up off the sidewalk as if it were alive.

Tiny just hoped they could get everything on their Last Day of Summer Itinerary done before the skies opened up on them. It was eight in the morning. They had the whole day in front of them, and there was a lot they still had to accomplish. Traditions were important. They gave your life purpose and structure and meaning. When the world got crazy and nothing felt permanent anymore, they helped tether you to the ground. They helped you remember who you were.

Tiny felt like she'd hardly seen Luella at all this summer, which is why today's traditions were extra important.

Tiny and Luella—Tlu, as they called themselves often, or Talulah when they didn't feel like abbreviating, or Tine or Tine-O or Loozles when they referred to each other individually—met at eight in the morning on the first and last day of every summer. They walked through Central Park to the Guggenheim, by far the coolest building in New York, and sat on the wall out front, watching the tourists. Luella would eat candy. Tiny would eat normal breakfast foods. It was always the same. It was comforting. Some things between you and your best friend should never have to change.

Other traditions on the last day of summer were:

Meeting Will and Nathaniel for a picnic lunch at the Alice in Wonderland statue by the boat basin.

Getting gelato that night, and everyone had to pick the weirdest flavor possible.

Doing one thing you've never done before.

The last one was Tiny's favorite. She looked forward to it every summer. She made lists throughout the year, saved up all of her firsts for that one special day, to keep the tradition intact.

"Tell me again how you can eat candy for breakfast?"

"It's just one of my many lovable quirks." Luella grinned. Her teeth were pink with melted candy. "Now tell me."

"You know how I got my nickname," Tiny said.

"Yes, but it's hot and I'm bored and I want you to *tell* me."

Tiny put her notebook down.

"Once upon a time, there was a girl named Emma. She lived in New York City, the biggest, craziest, best city in the world. She wanted nothing more than to grow up into a strong, well-respected cultural icon. But one day, she angered a vengeful troll. And so he cursed her. With tininess. In perpetuity." She picked her pen up and started writing again.

"Hm," said Luella. "That's not how I remember it."

"I took some storytelling liberties."

"Good job, Sister Grimm." Luella squirmed, trying to see over her shoulder. "What are you writing?"

"A poem."

"What's it about?"

Tiny flipped the notebook closed. "I can't tell you." It was a love poem, kind of. Luella would make so much fun of her if she found out.

As always, the real story of how Tiny got her nickname was less epic than the fairy tale she'd made up about it.

It all started when Tiny was little, in nursery school, or maybe kindergarten. Nathaniel had made up a game called Science Club. The four of them—Tiny, Nathaniel, Lu, and Will—used to huddle over Nathaniel's kitchen table after school, pouring different ingredients into glass jars and documenting the results.

Salt + Water = Salty Water

Vinegar + Baking Soda = Frothy Bubbles

That was back when Tiny went by the name Emma. Because that was the name her parents had given her, and no one had ever called her anything different. Even at five, Luella was always the dramatic one, and Nathaniel was the smart one, and Will was the funny one. Emma was just . . . Emma. The quiet one.

Until the day everything changed.

It was the day Tobias walked into the kitchen, carrying a robotic hand made of balsa wood. Four years older, Tobias was the real scientist. He won the science fair every year and always had the coolest project in the class. He had curly dark-brown hair and wire-rimmed glasses, and was wearing a T-shirt with Han Solo and Chewbacca drawn in the style of Calvin and Hobbes.

"Greetings, earthlings," Tobias said. He pulled a rubber band at the base of the hand, and the fingers contracted in a wave. "Nathaniel. William. Luella." Luella snickered. Tobias stopped on Tiny. The hand reached over and patted her on the head. "Tiny," he said. She was at least two feet shorter than he was.

"Am not," Tiny said.

"Are too."

Tiny felt her cheeks turn pink.

"Am. *Not.*"

Tobias laughed. "Bye, Tiny!"

"Shut up, Tobias!" Nathaniel called after him.

But it was too late. Her head wasn't the only thing Tobias had held in his robotic hand. He had plucked her from obscurity. He had noticed something special about her—even something as dumb and insignificant as not growing as fast as the others—and he had shone a light on *her.*

He was now holding her heart, too.

"Are you going to submit it to the lit mag?" Luella was still trying to read the poem over Tiny's shoulder.

"I don't know. Probably not." Tiny blinked. It was amazing how much of your life could be defined by one singular memory. Ever since that day, she had been Tiny.

"You totally should. How cool would it be to write this amazing poem and have everyone know it's yours?"

"This one's private. The only way I'd submit this is if I did it anonymously."

"If you say so," said Luella. "I love being the center of attention. I'd want all that glory." Luella smiled to herself and hummed under her breath.

"Luella," Tiny said. "What's up with you today? You are acting like you do when you have a secret."

"I don't have a secret," Luella said, and kept humming.

"Uh, yes, you totally do!"

"Do not." Luella stuffed a piece of candy into her mouth and crunched down audibly.

"Okay, weirdo." Tiny nudged her with her elbow. "You always hum when you have a secret." They sat in silence for a minute or two. Well, silence, except for Luella's crunching and the sound of heat thunder rumbling in the distance.

"Hey," Tiny said, swinging her feet out. "How are you and your mom doing? With the move-out and everything?"

"Fine," Luella said absently.

"Fine?"

"Just trying not to think about it."

"Oh," Tiny said. "Yeah. Okay." She struggled to think of something else to say. Luella was clearly done with the subject. "So, I have an idea about tonight. It combines two of our traditions: meeting up for gelato, and the thing I've never done before."

"Oooh." That got Luella's attention. "Tell me."

"Well, okay. Tobias leaves for Boston tomorrow and has to get some final data to submit with his interdisciplinary course proposal for EAPS. Something about climate change and cities and electrical energy. Nathaniel asked if we wanted to go with him to the Brooklyn Bridge and watch. It'll be very Benjamin Franklin."

Luella looked skeptical.

"Yeah, okay. Maybe."

"Luella! You mean no, don't you?"

"I mean maybe. But, Tiny, here's the thing. We start high school tomorrow. Tobias is going to college. Isn't it time to get over him? Put him behind you and start the year fresh?"

Tiny frowned. "I'm fine. I don't need to put him behind me."

Luella grabbed the notebook. "What's this? I see his name! In your di-a-ry." Tiny grabbed the notebook back.

"It's not a diary. It's a poetry *journal.*"

"Whatever. Well, then maybe just bite the bullet and tell him you like him already and want to have ten thousand of his little genius babies." Luella bit down on a piece of candy. Hard. It broke in half.

"Er. Maybe," Tiny said, meaning no. But Luella was getting excited.

"Yes! *That's* the thing you've never done before! I'll go tonight if you do that!"

"I'm not going to do that."

"Then my answer is still *maybe*."

Tiny eyed her. "Why are you being so mysterious? Do you have other big plans tonight that you're not telling me about?"

"No."

"Is that why you're acting all weird?"

"*No.*"

"Because we have to check off all of our traditions! If we don't, life will have no meaning!"

Luella snorted. "I thought I was supposed to be the drama queen."

"Luella, pleeease. It's the last night of summer. Tomorrow is high school. It's not going to be like this forever. Tonight is, like, pivotal. I need you! *Promise!*"

"God, Tiny, yeah, I promise."

Maybe Tiny would tell him tonight. Maybe it was her last chance before he went away to college and she started high school and everything in her life changed.

Luella

Luella walked back across the park, thinking about what Tiny said. *Tomorrow is high school. It's not going to be like this forever.*

If you took away traditions, did life really have no meaning? Were things supposed to stay the same, always? Was she supposed to want them to? Tiny clearly did, but Luella wasn't so sure. She was excited about making way for the new. She was ready to let go of some things from the past.

Suddenly, the way one memory will sometimes flash at you while you're trying to remember something else, a scene from finals week popped into Luella's head.

She and Tiny had been sitting cross-legged in the fifth-floor hallway, their backs up against the lockers, working through some geometry study sheets.

"I don't get this," Tiny muttered, frustrated.

"Oh, hey," Luella said. "So, my dad is leaving."

Tiny didn't look up. "Where's he going?" she asked, erasing something and then blowing away the eraser shavings. "Somewhere on business? Anywhere cool? You should get him to take you."

"Actually," Luella said, "he's just leaving." Tiny stopped scribbling and looked at Luella. Luella nibbled on her lip but didn't look up from her homework. "He's leaving us."

"Like, moving out?" Tiny said quietly.

"Yeah."

"Oh my god, Luella." She put her arm around Luella's skinny shoulders, but Luella pulled away.

"No, whatever, it's cool," she said. "It's fine. He's probably taking all the dude stuff, so Mom and I are, like, excited to redecorate, and—"

"Luella," Tiny interrupted. "How could it be *cool*?"

"It just is," Luella said, looking past Tiny's shoulder down the hall, as if someone more interesting were walking up.

"Luella, how can it be? Your dad's leaving. It's, like, anything but!"

"Tiny," Luella said sharply, suddenly, turning back and focusing her green eyes on Tiny. "It just *is*."

"But—"

"Because if it weren't, things would be so, so, so the opposite of cool. So it has to be cool. Okay? It has to be." Tiny was looking at her like she wanted to say more, so Luella cut her off before she could. "Geometry is so fucked up," she said. "How is this going to be remotely useful in my life? Why don't they teach us anything useful here! What about some real-life skills for a change!" She threw her notebook across the hall, where it slammed into the row of lockers, and a few people turned to look at the noise. Then Luella got up, picked up the notebook, shoved it into her backpack, and stalked off down the hall without saying good-bye.

* * *

Luella didn't know why she was thinking about it now, as she walked back across the park on this last day of summer. A lot had already been changing this summer for Luella. Things had been happening that she didn't tell Tiny about. It's not that she didn't trust her best friend. It's more that she didn't know how to put them into words. Tiny was a words person. She valued strong communications skills.

Luella was not especially strong at communicating. Or so her mother told her all the time.

She'd lied to Tiny. She did have a secret.

She kept it inside of her for now.

It had started like this.

Back at the beginning of the summer, Luella had been standing outside the Kaye Playhouse at Hunter College trying to get cell reception on her phone after her summer acting class, when some boys in glasses walked past her.

"Keebler?" She looked up, then immediately kicked herself for responding to that stupid nickname. Will had peeled off from the group and was walking toward her, grinning.

"Hey, Will."

"I knew that name would catch on," he said. "How could it not?"

"Beats me," said Luella. "It's so flattering and complimentary."

"Whatcha doing? Are you done pretending to be someone else for the day?"

"Hmm? Oh yeah. Acting class just finished. I gotta go somewhere and memorize these." She held up a stack of pages. "I'm auditioning for the summer play."

"What play?"

"*Cat on a Hot Tin Roof*. You know it?"

"No."

"Oh."

Will shuffled his feet.

"Do you, like, play the cat?"

Luella squinted at him. "No."

"Oh."

There was a pause that lasted a few seconds too long. Will pushed his glasses up on his nose.

"Hey," he said. "I have some homework and stuff too. Want to join forces and do our work together? I know somewhere quiet."

Luella didn't say anything right away. She and Will had been friends since they were kids, but they usually hung out in a group with Tiny and Nathaniel. They had never hung out one-on-one before. Will blinked, waiting for an answer.

"Look, if you don't—I mean, if you're busy, it's—"

"Okay," Luella said. She slipped her phone into the pocket of her bag.

"Really?" Will beamed.

"You don't have to throw a parade or anything. It's just homework."

"Surly," Will said, then turned and began walking. Luella stepped out into the glaring sun and walked quickly to catch up to him. She held her arm in front of her eyes.

"Here." Will handed her a pair of knockoff Ray-Ban Wayfarers.

"Did you get these at Rachel's Rockin' Eighties Bat Mitzvah?" Luella said dubiously, looking at the writing on the sides.

"You should know," Will said. "You were there, remember? Look, is the sun in your eyes or what? Just put them on, you vampire."

Luella put them on. "They're huge on me."

"They're fine."

"I feel stupid."

"You look cute." Luella stopped in her tracks, but Will kept walking on ahead. "Come on, Keebler! Time waits for no man. Or elf." She felt her cheeks turn pink, and hoped the sunglasses were big enough to hide it. She hurried to catch up, muttering under her breath.

"You know," said Will, "maybe if you got more vitamin D, you wouldn't be so mean."

"If I were being mean, you'd know it."

"Fine, then maybe you'd have a boyfriend."

"Ew, that is a totally sexist thing to say. Like having a boyfriend is the pinnacle of accomplishment? The bar to which we all must strive? Listen, Kingfield. I'm going to win an Oscar one day. And a Golden Globe. And the goddamn Nobel Prize for drama. And you"—Luella paused to breathe—"will be begging to accompany me down the red carpet." Will held up his hands in surrender and kept walking.

They took the bus across the park at Sixty-Sixth Street, and then walked up Central Park West. Luella had to admit that it helped to have the sunglasses, but she wasn't about to say anything. Will was wearing cargo shorts and a baggy T-shirt with a linocut of some guy's face on the front.

"Weird shirt," said Luella. "Who is that?"

"Who *is* that? Do you seriously not know who Bill Murray is?" Will looked aghast.

Luella shrugged. "No."

"Oh my god," Will said, slapping his forehead. "Oh my god. *Saturday Night Live*? *Groundhog Day*? *Ghostbusters*?" Luella shook her head. "Just . . . watch *Caddyshack*, please. Please just watch it. It is one of the greatest films of all time."

"Wait," Luella said. "Was he the old guy in *Lost in Translation*? I love that movie."

"I'm going to cry," said Will. "You are such a girl." Luella stopped and stared at him, her mouth gaping.

"That's not an insult, Will!"

"Catch up, Keebler," he said, smiling. "We're here."

Luella looked up and realized they were standing in front of the Museum of Natural History.

"The museum?" Luella asked.

"It's my secret study place. Come on."

They sat in a corner of the Milstein Hall of Ocean Life. Growing up, Luella had always been secretly afraid of this room. There was a humongous to-scale model of a blue whale suspended from the ceiling, and she was always afraid that if she walked under it, the giant thing would fall and crush her. Usually, she had never gotten farther than the fake firefly display outside. It was a favorite spot for her and her dad, but even her dad knew never to try to force Luella into the whale room.

But she didn't mention any of this to Will. He looked so sure of himself as he breezed past the fireflies and into the massive hall. She closed her eyes when she saw the whale, but she didn't want Will to think she was some kind of wimp. She insisted they walk about the edges of the room instead, so that they didn't have to walk directly underneath it.

They made their way past the life-size dioramas of dolphins and sea lions, manatees and jellyfish and octopi, suspended in fake time in the fake ocean, until they found a dark corner of the room where the whale probably wouldn't fall on them. They sat down.

"This should appeal to your vampire nature," said Will. "Nice and dark. You can give the glasses back now."

"Shut up." But she handed them over.

They sat in silence, except for the sounds of Will typing away on his calculator, and Luella muttering words out loud every now and then.

Will looked up.

"Is there even a cat in that play at all?"

Luella rolled her eyes. "Haven't you ever heard of a metaphor?"

"I think they should call it something else. That title is so misleading."

"I'll e-mail Tennessee Williams and tell him you think so."

"What kind of a name is Tennessee?"

"What is your *obsession* with names?"

Will seemed to consider this. "I don't know," he said finally. "Maybe because Will is so boring?"

Luella reached into her bag. "Here," she said, shoving something into his chest. "You need to read more books. Broaden your mind. Try this one."

"*Hedda Gabler*? What the hell kind of a—"

Luella clamped her hand over his mouth.

"No," she said. "Do not make fun of *Hedda*. *Hedda* is a brilliant feminist play that was way ahead of its time."

"Yay," said Will. "Sounds fun."

"Just read it."

He read the back cover, then looked at her. "I think I'll just get back to my problem set."

"Wuss."

"Unless you want to switch?"

"What's wrong with the name Will?" Luella said suddenly. "Don't you like it?"

"Is it a big deal if I don't?"

"Well, yeah," Luella said. "It's *yours.*"

"So? Do you like *your* name?"

"Luella? I don't know. It doesn't feel very *me.* I think I sound like a debutante."

"It's unique. Let's look up what it means." Will pulled up a name meanings website on his phone. "Oh. No. Way."

"What?" Luella cried. "Let me see!"

"No." Will held the phone away from her.

"Why not? Let me see!"

"I'll never hear the end of it."

Luella pounced on him and tickled him.

"Stop. That's not nice."

"Let me see what my name means!"

"Fine. Fine. Stop tickling me!"

Luella grabbed the phone from him. She smiled.

"*Renowned warrior.*"

"I told you." Will snatched his phone back.

"That is the most badass name ever!" Luella put her hands on her hips. "Renowned warrior."

"I had a feeling you would like it," Will said, rolling his eyes.

Luella was floored. She always thought Luella was some family name she didn't really feel any connection to. Her grandma was Luella—not her. But *renowned warrior.* Luella liked the sound of that.

She was. She would be. She'd get through this stuff with her parents. She had to.

"Will," she said, "there are maybe a handful of things in this world that are truly yours, and your name is one of them. You have to, like, *own* it. Besides, you should feel comfortable being yourself."

"Do *you* feel comfortable being yourself?"

"That's not the point."

"Well, I think that's bullshit advice," Will said, picking *Hedda Gabler* back up and paging through it. "Who wants to be themselves? No one *I* know."

Luella was smiling just thinking about it.

On the west side of the park, she passed two kids, a guy and a girl who were both kind of hipster and did theater at her school, as they performed a scene on the street from *A Midsummer Night's Dream*. On her corner, she stopped to get a dark roast French press from her favorite coffee shop. (She'd gotten into dark roast French press last year, and loved how mature and sophisticated it made her feel to drink coffee out of a white paper to-go cup while walking down the street in sunglasses, like an actress in *Us Weekly*.)

The moving van was just pulling away when she made it to the front of her building, a five-floor brick walk-up with a front door that was painted a crisp white.

Inside, their apartment looked like it had been robbed. Half their stuff was gone. Everything that was left belonged to either Luella or her mom. It was a lot of plants and floor poufs. Her dad's stuff was gone. Vanished, like some sick magic trick.

On the coffee table there was a note. Luella wasn't in the mood to read it.

She texted Will, and went to meet up with him instead.

NOW

9:00 P.M.

(11 Hours Left)

The Intricate Parabolic Equation of Life

Tiny

The wind whipped fiercely as she and Lu made their way across Park Avenue toward Will Kingfield's brownstone.

Tiny was wearing high-rise cut-offs and a black crop top, neither of which was hers. She kept pulling down the hem of the top, which was starting to drive Lu crazy.

"Leave it!" Lu yelled. "If you got it, flaunt it, Tiny. At least you *have* boobs. I'm basically, like, a stick insect." As Tiny was still vaguely uncomfortable with the boobs that had popped up, seemingly overnight, this was not a fair comparison.

Tiny had come over wearing a navy blue T-shirt dress and floral Vans, but Lu said you could hardly see her awesome bod under it, which was kind of the point. Lu had found the cuts-offs and crop top in her closet and decided that Tiny had to wear them to the party, and if she even thought for a minute about wearing something else, it would have been the greatest tragedy known to man, and the universe as they knew it would disintegrate into gazillions of miniscule dust particles and get sucked into, like, a black hole, or something.

"You can kind of see my butt cheeks though," Tiny had said, inspecting her reflection from the rear.

"You'll thank me for doing this," Lu said now as she dragged Tiny across the street by the elbow, freshly painted *Poor Li'l Rich Girl*–red nails scratching lightly against Tiny's goose-bumpy skin. It was October, and even though the weather was still sort of warm enough for them to go jacketless, their wardrobe choices involved some wishful thinking. "You didn't want to study for the SATs, anyway," Lu informed her. "You've been studying all year—what more could you possibly fit in there?" She poked Tiny's temple affectionately. "You'll reach your parents' target score, easy. I'm the one who has to worry about not bombing." Lu linked her arm tighter through Tiny's, and grinned like the devil. "Lucky for me, famous actresses don't need to go to college. Besides, what if the world ends tonight? We're going to live a little."

"It's not the end of the world," Tiny said, struggling to keep up with Lu's manic pace, and leaning into the wind. "It's just pressure systems colliding." The wind blew her hair into her face, and she pushed it back. "Just . . . really big ones. How did you convince me to do this again?"

"It wasn't that hard." Lu snorted. "I lured you out with the prospect of seeing Josh, like, outside of school property." She fluttered her eyes and clasped her hands to her chest. "Oh, Joshuwaaa, read me *The Waste Land* again while we talk about fear in a handful of lust!"

"Dust."

"Whatever."

"According to the news," Tiny said, ignoring her, "we should be inside right now with our windows taped up and our bathtubs filled with water, just in case."

"Tiny." Lu turned to her. "Do you know what a storm is? Do

you? It's *water*. Are you going to let a little water stop you from making *memories* you'll have *forever*?"

"I guess when you put it that way . . ."

"Besides, you're a great swimmer. If I start to drown, you could totally save my life."

"But what if *I* drown?" she said under her breath. Lu didn't seem to hear her.

"I don't get why I have to convince you to go to a party where you're going to see the guy we've been planning your first kiss with for months," Lu muttered. "He's almost definitely going to be there. He's such a floater."

It was true. Josh was equally at home with the arty lit mag crew as he was at a party thrown by the soccer team. He was liked and accepted by all. It was part of his alluring mystique.

"Tonight could be the night!" Lu sang. "The night you swap spit with Josh Herrera!"

Tiny's heart muscles tensed up.

According to Lu, the following truths were held to be self-evident:

1) Tiny had a massive crush on Josh Herrera.

2) Tiny wanted to get Josh Herrera alone and smoosh her lips against his.

And those two truths were built upon a third piece of relevant information Lu believed was true:

3) Tiny had never been kissed.

But Tiny was lying. She *had* been kissed once. A perfect kiss. Her first and last kiss. The kind of kiss she sometimes wished could be her only kiss, for the rest of her life, because there would never be another one as perfect as that.

She had never told Lu.

And she still wasn't over it.

The thing was, Josh was cute. If Tiny had a crush on anyone, it would be Josh. He was coeditor of the school lit mag, *Calamity*, with Malin Kopparberg. He was into books and poetry. He was someone she *should* like. She wished she had a crush on Josh. But when Lu talked about Josh, Tiny was still thinking about someone else.

And she had to kiss Josh. She had to get him to notice her, somehow. It was the only way to forget that other someone. It was the only way she'd be able to move on.

Part of her felt guilty. But was it really so bad to want someone to see her again, the way she was seen the night of her first kiss?

So she bought the hair dye. She came to the party. She had a plan, and she was going to stick to it.

Lu was reapplying bright-red lipstick, using a car window as a mirror.

"Trust me," she said with a smack of her lips. "You look hot. Very Lana Del Rey meets Taylor Swift. Josh will love it." She turned to Tiny and grinned. "Maybe this is what you'll be wearing when you have your first kiss."

Tiny sighed and tugged her shirt down again. "I hope so." Lu batted her hand away.

"You have to stop hoping for things, Tiny." Lu stopped in the middle of the dark street, and instinctively Tiny looked both ways. To their left, a pair of headlights loomed large and bright.

"Car," Tiny said, and they stepped out of the way as the dark shape of a car swished past.

"Hope is how you get yourself into trouble," Lu continued, standing still in the middle of the street, even though more cars were probably going to come along any second. "When you hope for things, you only get disappointed. But when you *know* something will happen, you *will* it to. Come on. Say it with me: I *know* so."

Tiny smoothed her hands over her hair. "How could I possibly *know* when it hasn't happened yet?"

"Because you can't know anything until it happens. But you can believe it will. It's all about attitude." Lu took a deep breath, closed her eyes, and centered her hands over her heart. Then she cracked one eye open. "Come on. Live a little."

This was something Lu told her to do at least once a day. If life were a movie, there would literally be a montage of clips set to music, just of Lu telling Tiny to live a little.

They started walking again at the same time, as if they'd planned it.

Sometimes Tiny thought she'd never have the guts to do anything if she didn't have Lu there by her side. When it was the two of them, they could do anything. They could go to parties to which they weren't technically invited. They could do the unthinkable and go out on the night before the biggest test of their lives. They could talk about kissing Josh like it was something that might really happen.

It was too bad they didn't hang out as much as they used to.

Out of the corner of her eye, Tiny snuck a glance at Lu's outfit again. She was wearing black skinny jeans and a tight T-shirt that said PROSE BEFORE HOES in gold glitter, under an etching of Shakespeare. Her blunt black bangs were flat-ironed stick straight, and thick stripes of black liner extended out at least an inch past the outer corners of her eyes. It was a look Tiny could never pull off, but she couldn't help admiring Lu's effortlessness at that kind of thing.

She tucked her own brown hair behind her ears, but the wind whipped it right back.

Stupid wind. Stupid hair.

She wondered if Josh would notice. She wondered if he would say something about the poem she had submitted anonymously to *Calamity*. The committee had discussed the poem at this afternoon's meeting. People had taken its anonymous moniker as a free pass to analyze away, tearing it apart, using words like *trite* and *structurally unremarkable*, and saying things like, "I'm pausing on the part where . . ."

Jordan Brewster got all twitchy. "On a technical level, it's unimpressive." She stacked and unstacked the silver rings on her fingers, making a silvery clinking noise. Jordan Brewster had written a poem that the committee had voted on the week before. Tiny was pretty sure it had been about sex, but it was hard to tell. She'd used a lot of fruit metaphors, and on top of that, Tiny had never had sex, so she had nothing to compare it to.

Josh was scribbling something in a black moleskin notebook. He didn't look up when he said, "I dunno. I like it. It feels emotionally authentic."

"Well, should we vote on it?" Malin didn't so much suggest as command. Malin was in top form, presiding over the committee as she perched cross-legged on the table. She wore denim cut-off shorts over bee-yellow tights, black Converse high-tops, and a large, white, men's undershirt cinched at the waist with a black belt. Her multitonal hair (Tiny counted four but was sure there were more: auburn, honey, gold, strawberry-blond . . .) dangled defiantly in her face, perfectly contrasting with her dark brown skin.

There was a flourish of pencils, pens, and people ripping the corners off notebook pages. The results were never announced at the meeting—that would have been too humane. You had to wait agonizingly until the issue came out at the end of the year to see if your piece was accepted.

Malin collected the shreds of paper, marking cryptically in her notebook one tally mark for each vote. When all the votes were in, she looked up and smiled grimly.

"Next," she said . . .

Josh didn't look at Tiny once.

Maybe he *knew*, maybe he could just *tell*, because they shared some mind connection he hadn't even realized yet. If Tiny wished it hard enough, maybe she could make him notice her in the way she wanted to be noticed.

It's just that no one noticed her, not really. Not since that night three years ago.

There wasn't anything worth noticing, anyway.

Lu

The black lacquered door to Will's brownstone loomed before them like the gateway to Dante's Inferno. His family owned all three floors, and the whole school probably could have fit in there if they'd been stalking him on Facebook and knew about the party too. Or maybe they did. Lu had no idea how these things worked, and she didn't care.

"Are you sure we should be here?" Tiny's voice came out of the dark beside Lu. For a minute she'd forgotten Tiny was there.

"Of course," Lu said. She threw her shoulders back. Before Tiny could stop her, Lu reached over and readjusted the crop top, where Tiny had been tugging it down. "Look, it'll be fine—it's a party. Everyone will be drunk. You can talk to Josh."

"I'm not making any promises about that, by the way—"

"Yes, you are—"

"It's a fact-finding mission."

"No, it's not."

Lu didn't understand people like Tiny, who wanted things to

be different but refused to do anything about them. Lu was a doer. Sometimes she was impulsive and did things without thinking, but at least she did them at all. She didn't settle for the status quo. She changed things. She got her way.

"Do you think anyone will even be here? Maybe everyone's stayed home to study."

"Oh, seriously, fuck the SATs! I am so sick of that being all anyone can talk about!"

Lu had a mouth like a trucker. She cursed inappropriately *all the time.*

Lu, realizing she didn't have enough change for a soda from the vending machine: "Fuck!"

Lu, knocking over a canister of pens in the fifth-floor quiet study lounge: "Fuck!"

Lu, banging her funny bone on a bus full of old ladies: "Fucking shit!"

"Lu," Tiny said quietly. "Are you okay?"

"Fine," Lu snapped. "I'm fine." She hadn't told Tiny about Owen. There wasn't anything to tell. "Sorry." Lu sighed. "Look," she said, leaning against the front door and absently fiddling with the leaves on one of the cone-shaped shrubs. "I'm just trying to get you to live your life. It's for your own good. I mean, if I hadn't had the guts to approach Owen at his show this summer, we wouldn't have started hooking up in the first place."

"In secret."

"Not important," said Lu, waving her hand around dismissively. "The point is that you could absolutely kiss Josh tonight if you wanted to. You just have to"—here she put both hands on Tiny's shoulders and squeezed like those guys who stand behind boxers in boxing rings, coaches or whoever they were—"*believe. You. Can.*"

"Thank you, Luella."

"Don't call me that."

"'You're welcome' would be nice."

"You can mock me all you want," said Lu, "but I'm just looking out for you. Besides, I am impervious to mocking. Sticks and stones and all that crap."

That wasn't entirely true, and Lu knew it. Yesterday she had made the mistake of wearing her A WOMAN'S PLACE IS IN THE HOUSE . . . AND THE SENATE shirt to school. The soccer boys had had a field day.

Daybrook didn't have a football team. A lot of city schools didn't. So the soccer team was the catchall for every testosterone-addled brain in school. The soccer team at Daybrook wasn't like football teams at other schools or in the movies or whatever. For one thing, they weren't a bunch of dumb jocks or all, like, *Texas forever.* They were, for the most part, a special breed of boy Lu liked to call "smart rich assholes." They slunk around the school and down the street in a Harvard-bound pack, like they owned the island of Manhattan, money rolling off them in waves. For another thing, they sucked. They were the lowest ranked team in all five boroughs. Probably.

They surrounded her in the fifth-floor hallway, a bunch of hyenas circling a gazelle. Was Lu a feminist? Did she let her armpit hair grow wild under that T-shirt? Would she bake them a pie? Was she going to beat them up? Usually, when this happened (and Lu had a lot of cool shirts, so it happened more than she cared for), Will kept his mouth shut or pretended to check his cell phone or suddenly found the selection of lunch options fascinating. And Lu ignored him, and she ignored the rest of them. She couldn't let Will see her crack. Any of the others, maybe. But not Will. Never Will.

But yesterday Will had said, "Hey, Lu, I heard you burned all your bras. Good thing you don't need them." The guys had howled. And Lu couldn't keep her mouth shut. She wheeled on him.

"If feminists hadn't burned their bras in the 1970s," she said, "we would never have had advancements in women's rights. If we'd never had advancements in women's rights, the Supreme Court would never have tried a case like Roe V. Wade. If the Supreme Court had never tried Roe v. Wade, abortion would never have been legalized. If abortion hadn't been legalized, Rachel Keyes wouldn't have been able to get one last month. And if Rachel Keyes hadn't gotten that abortion last month, *you*"—she pointed her finger at Ben Sternberg—"would be a dad before graduating high school. So," she said, "what else did you have to say about feminism?"

No one else said anything.

"You guys shouldn't talk so loud in assembly," Lu said, and went to class.

She hated Will Kingfield. She hated Will Kingfield.

So why did she still think about him so much?

Lightning flashed above the rooftops.

Lu looked at Tiny and grinned.

"One Mississippi . . ."

Tiny grinned back. "Two Mississippi . . ."

"Three," they said together as thunder rumbled warningly on three. "Ooh, it's close!" Lu cried, clapping her hands. "Stormpocalypse, here we come!"

"Just ring the doorbell," Tiny said, looking dubiously up at the sky. "It's gonna pour, like, any second."

"You do it."

"Let's do it together."

"Fine."

And then they rang.

Will

Will pressed the heels of his palms into his eyes. When he pulled them away, black spots floated across his vision like morbid balloons.

Things had escalated pretty quickly. Now instead of five guys drinking Buds and playing virtual Golf in the den, there was something like fifty people at his house. They'd brought booze and mixers, like they always did. It was just another party at Will Kingfield's house.

Except to Will, this one felt different. More desperate somehow. He knew Jon was just kidding when he'd said it could be the end of the world, but something about this storm really did feel that way. Maybe it was because of the test the next day too.

Maybe he was just in bad shape today because he was still feeling guilty about what had happened with Luella. He knew he shouldn't have said anything. He should have just left her alone. But if anyone would appreciate the unlikely phenomenon of the exact right zinger flying out of your mouth at the exact right time, it was Lu. It must have been her influence on him. He hadn't even had a chance to think about it before he was saying it and then regretting it. The guilt was eating away at him, but that was nothing new.

A lot of things were eating away at him lately.

Sometimes, especially in moments like this when Will was standing in the middle of a party, people swarming around him, he would float out of his body for a second. And when he looked back down, he didn't recognize himself.

He would wake up in the middle of the night, gasping from some dream he couldn't remember. He would lay awake in bed for hours, trying to remember it, his brain churning. He would be exhausted the next day and fall asleep in class and fuck up in practice. He was fucking up more and more.

He had wanted this life. He wanted to be cool. And popular. And *known*. He wanted to be someone people would remember. Someone different than who he was. He had wanted protection from the fleetingness of the world and the stability of doing the same thing every day after school and hanging out with the same people on the weekends, people like Jon Heller who was the kind of guy everybody wanted to be. He didn't want the first thing people noticed about him to be that he was fat, and goofy to make up for it. So he got un-fat. He worked hard at it. He was strict about what he ate, and worked out obsessively, and weighed himself regularly. It changed his life. Now, he was all of those things he had wanted to be. He had everything he had wanted. He was someone different.

So why did he still feel like he was running away from something that would eventually catch up to him?

New Will was like a tidal wave he'd gotten caught in. He couldn't stop it and he couldn't swim against it. He just had to let the current take him where it wanted to go.

Swimming against the tide was how you drowned. Right?

Will could run however long or fast he wanted, do soccer drills till he was red-faced and panting and puking on the field; he could surround himself with people and parties and distractions and everything else that could drown out the noise. But he couldn't outrun that feeling of being stuck. Like so many things, it was an inevitability that was woven into the intricate parabolic equation of his life, drawing nearer and nearer to something he couldn't quite grasp and could never, ever quite reach.

He hadn't dated anyone in years. He hadn't even made out with anyone. On the outside, he was cool, he was unflappable, he was the star of the school, but on the inside he was so crowded with anxious dark thoughts that the truth was, there was no room for anyone else.

But like a spinning wheel of fortune, his heart seemed permanently stuck on the very last face it had beaten for, the last first thought he'd wake up to in the morning, and the last first face he'd think about as he slipped off into a doomed sleep. Someone he hadn't really spoken to since the night before freshman year of high school. A night he wished so hard that he could take back. Or do over. Or obliterate from existence. Or all of the above.

Luella Jane Austen. His first and last love.

And the one person in the world who hated his guts.

"Kingfield, you're up," Kenji said.

Will blinked. Everyone around the big kitchen table was staring at him, the beer pong game momentarily suspended as they waited for him to take his turn. He stepped up to the edge of the table and took the Ping-Pong ball from the cup of water on his right.

He took his shot. And in the moment of silence between when the small white ball left his fingers and when it dropped with a small plunk into a cup of beer not four feet away—

In that silence, the doorbell rang.

Nathaniel

The doorbell jolted Nathaniel out of his thoughts. He was standing in the corner, holding his beer, trying to figure out how to get himself out of the mess he'd gotten into. The beer was warm. The party was loud. Nathaniel was pissed off.

He told himself it was at Will, for luring him over with the promise of studying, then throwing a party instead. But really it was at himself, mostly:

For not having the guts to say no.

For not turning in his application on time.

For not trying to salvage his life by studying for the SATs like he knew he should.

But no time seemed like the right time to leave. And there was part of Nathaniel—a secret part that made him totally ashamed—that was having fun. And part of him that thought if he stayed, if he enjoyed his beer and forgot about the application and the test and had some fun, then maybe he and Will could be friends again. Real friends, not the kind of friends who ignored each other at school and then sometimes needed help studying when no one else was around to care.

Nathaniel had been studying for the SATs for months. He'd even gotten a tutor, paying for it with the bar mitzvah money he'd never spent and that had been languishing in some bond his grandfather had set up for him when he was thirteen. Tobias had gotten a perfect score. He'd won the Anders Almquist Scholarship. He'd gotten into MIT EAPS early admission. Nathaniel couldn't settle for anything less.

His brother had always been smarter. Cooler. And knew exactly what he wanted. Ever since Nathaniel was old enough to have memories, Tobias was the one calling the shots and Nathaniel followed along like some of his brother's magic might rub off on him.

Girls, especially, were really into him. One girl in particular. The only one who mattered.

Tobias's magic had never rubbed off on that particular area of Nathaniel's life.

Nathaniel wanted to be a geophysicist. He wanted to study energy and the way it moved through the earth. He wanted to one day stand at the tops of mountains, the sky expanding above him and the wind blowing through his hair, and conduct lightning through lightning rods and feel the phantom movement of ancient lava beneath his feet. He wanted to experience something bigger than himself. Energy was the biggest thing there was. Energy was everywhere.

But the Anders Almquist Earth Science Scholarship felt like a mountain he couldn't climb. And Daybrook had a reputation for producing winners, like his brother. He'd been working on his project for months, but even up until the night before it was due, something just didn't feel right. Something was missing. That magic zing. That spark. And he couldn't figure out how to fix it.

He wished he didn't care so much. Life would be easier if he didn't care about everything so intensely. If he could just be like Will, who didn't seem to care at all. Half the senior class was here now, and no one seemed to care about anything except getting drunk.

When they were little, he and Tiny and Will and Lu used to play Science Club together. They performed experiments with magnets and grew potatoes in soil and mixed solutions in beakers.

Sometimes Nathaniel still felt like a kid playing at science.

Tobias had made it look easy.

Then the doorbell snapped him out of it.

What was he doing here?

He had worked so hard. He couldn't just throw everything away now. Being at this party was not going to get him any closer to being the best he could be. He was only wasting time. He should leave.

Nathaniel put the beer down on a table and slung his backpack full of SAT workbooks over his shoulder. Will was taking his turn at beer pong; Nathaniel wouldn't even bother saying good-bye. He made his way through the crowd. He opened the door—

And came face-to-face with Tiny and Lu. His two childhood friends.

"Nathaniel," Tiny said, surprised.

"Uh, hi," Nathaniel said, the tips of his ears turning an involuntary shade of red.

"What are you doing here?" she asked, narrowing her eyes in suspicion.

What was he supposed to say? Will had asked if they could study together, then had thrown a party instead? How pathetic would that make him look?

"Um, what are *you* doing here?"

Maybe this, though—maybe it was a good thing. He had just been thinking about them, and there they were. His last link to the past. To that last summer he was really happy. His former fellow Science Club members. Right as he was about to leave.

Nathaniel didn't believe in signs. They weren't based in anything scientific. Signs had to do with faith and belief and the unknown. They weren't rooted in fact.

"See?" said Lu, turning to Tiny. "If this isn't a sign that we should be at this party, I don't know what is. Nathaniel." Lu grinned. "Lead us to the alcohol."

And so he put his backpack down. And he did.

Tiny

They followed Nathaniel inside, and the past came rushing back around Tiny as loud and vivid as the party itself.

The vaulted ceiling of the two-story main foyer towered above them. Tiny hadn't been there in a long time, not since the four of them used to hang out. The wall to her right was made of exposed brick, stretching so Everest-like above her head that there were, like, clouds obscuring the top. Right in the middle was a real working fireplace—a total rarity in a New York City apartment (Tiny's family kept stacks of books in their nonworking one)—and over the mantel hung a series of Picasso paintings that looked suspiciously like real paint—not like the framed prints her parents brought home from museum gift shops. Through the crowd, toward the back of the large open room, a wrought-iron spiral staircase curved seductively, like a beckoning finger, upstairs.

"It's like the fucking MoMA in here," Lu muttered under her breath.

To their left, the wall was made entirely of white custom bookcases, stacked with huge glossy art books and strategically placed decorative stoneware. In the center of the bookcases was a swinging door, and when someone barreled through it, Tiny could just make out a kitchen table cluttered with a rainbow of liquor bottles.

The giant foyer was packed with upperclassmen. It looked the way parties did in movies—except the music didn't stop abruptly, and it didn't feel like she and Lu were walking in slo-mo or anything. No one even noticed Tiny as she stood by the kitchen door, pulling at her crop top, staring nervously into the madness. A handwritten sign with the words IT'S THE END OF THE WORLD AS WE KNOW IT AND I FEEL FINE scrawled in red Sharpie was taped to the wall above the couch. A couple of kids were wearing pith helmets, and one had a parachute. Down the hall, someone was wearing a snorkel. Because a snorkel is the first thing you reach for in case of an emergency.

There was no sign of Josh.

"Lu . . . ," Tiny whispered.

"Don't worry," Lu said before she could even hear the rest. She linked a reassuring arm through Tiny's, and smiled grimly. "We'll be fine."

Outside the living room window, lightning flashed bright across the sky.

One Mississippi, two Mississippi, three—

Thunder rumbled ominously.

"Nathaniel!" Lu cried like a war general. "Onward to the drinks!"

"You're still very bossy," Nathaniel said. Tiny snorted. Lu frowned. Nathaniel pulled the sleeves of his sweater down over his hands. "They're in the kitchen," he said. Tiny noticed the tips of his ears were red. "This way."

Lu unlinked her arm from Tiny's and followed Nathaniel

through the swinging door, but Tiny paused. Her heartbeat sped up. She wanted to tell Lu to stop, that she just wanted to go home. She felt awkward in Lu's crop top and cut-offs, and what if she really did see Josh? It's not like she was actually going to talk to him. She was beginning to think this whole night was a terrible mistake. She should have just stayed home.

But she forced herself to push through the kitchen door behind them.

She hated herself for being so nervous, for losing herself so completely in the wanting that she wasn't even sure what it was she wanted.

Lu immediately marched up to the bar table and began pouring some kind of mixture of vodka and lemonade, while Nathaniel hovered by the wall between the door and the table. Tiny watched as people milled around the edges of the kitchen in small clusters, brushing up against the chrome refrigerator, the marble countertops, the shelves of expensive-looking copper pots and pans. It looked like the kind of kitchen that was more for show than for actually cooking in. All of the appliances looked spotless. Like a movie set.

She reminded herself that she wanted this. She had needed to go out tonight; she had agreed to it. If she'd stayed at home, she would have melted into that puddle of water on the floor, and no one would ever have seen her again.

"Here." Lu broke into her thoughts by shoving a red cup in her face. Tiny was still feeling woozy from the courage shots they took before they'd left her apartment, but when it came to Lu, she had to pick her battles.

So, she drank. She drank and drank because she didn't know what else she should do. Then she grabbed Lu's cup and drank that down too. She didn't taste a thing.

Lu's mouth hung open.

"Whoa," she said. "There was a lot of vodka in there." She eyed Tiny carefully. "Are you okay?"

"Fine," Tiny said, her smile bright and her speech only slightly slurred.

"Do you want some water?"

"Yes," Tiny said. "I love water."

"Ooookay."

The tap was running. A new red plastic cup was shoved into her hands. The water was cold and tasted slightly like lemonade.

"Sorry," said Lu. "There were no clean ones left."

Tiny shook her head. "It's okay. It's fine." The room tilted on its side, then righted itself. She blinked. She was going to be brave tonight. She was.

"Ready?" Without waiting for a response, Lu turned and pushed her way back through the swinging kitchen door.

Tiny sighed. She wondered where she would be without Lu and her *what ifs*, but sometimes that also came along with some impossible expectations.

She turned to follow—everything swaying sort of imperceptibly—but as she did, the swinging door smacked into her from the other side.

"Ow," said Tiny. "Hey!"

"Oh shit," a voice said at the same time. "I'm so sorry. I—"

Tiny looked up and then realized she was staring, her mouth open, at Josh. His black, black hair, his dark brown eyes. Those broody eyebrows. His mouth that turned up slightly on one side, maybe judging you, maybe smiling at some secret joke—it was impossible to say. It was the first time he had ever looked directly at her.

"Hey," she said. She was doing it! She was talking to him. It was like riding a bike for the first time without training wheels, exhilarating and terrifying and—

"Uh, hi." He scratched his stubble. He had *stubble.* "Are you okay? Did I hit you hard?"

"I'm okay," Tiny said, venturing a smile. "Possibly concussed, but . . ."

Josh frowned. "How many fingers?"

"Four."

"Nailed it. You're fine."

He patted her on the shoulder and then started to walk away.

"Oh, um!" Tiny basically shouted at him. "What did you think of lit mag today?"

Josh squinted at her. "You're in *Calamity*?"

"Uh," she said, waiting for him to recognize her. The pause grew unbearable. "Yeah."

"Yeah, well, listen, you should write something good for us. The quality of submissions is really going downhill lately. Today was brutal."

Tiny felt a jolt rip through her.

"I thought you liked today's poem? You said—you said it felt emotionally, um, authentic."

"Hm? Oh no. I just had to jump in with something otherwise Jordan Brewster would never have shut up." He looked right at her again, and smiled.

"What did you say your name was?"

"Tiny," Tiny said hoarsely.

"Right. Well, seriously, Tiny. Write something good. Save us all."

Just like that, he was gone, and Tiny was left standing there. It was like someone had ripped the beautiful hardwood floor right out from under her and she was falling through the gaping abyss, down, down, down, beneath the ground into the dark under-depths of the city.

Her one chance to finally get over her first kiss. Crushed.

There was a door on the other side of the kitchen. Leading away from Josh, away from Lu and Nathaniel, away from the rest of the party. She didn't care where it went. She just had to get out of there.

She pushed through it and took the stairs on the other side two at a time, her face burning.

Lu

"Tiny?" Lu turned around, but Tiny was gone. She lifted her eyes to scan the room, and her heart froze.

Standing directly across from her, separated by a sea of bodies, was Will. She knew he had seen her because he was frozen too. They locked eyes.

Immediately Lu spun around and began intently studying the framed photographs on the wall behind her. Just her luck, the first one she saw was of baby Will, splashing around in a kiddie pool. Naked.

"Fuck my life," she muttered under her breath.

"My parents put those up. Embarrassing, right?"

She didn't turn around.

"You really couldn't keep your clothes on as a kid, could you?" Lu tried to smirk, but it was as if she hadn't used her smirking muscles in a while and they kept twitching in the most uncool way.

"Nothing you haven't seen before," Will said automatically. Then, as Lu's shoulders tensed, he quickly added, "Sorry. I don't know why I said that. I shouldn't have—"

Lu was dying to see his face. Was he sorry? Curiosity got the better of her. Slowly, she turned around. He was just standing there, his hands in his pockets, and when she met his eyes, his cheeks turned pink, which was a weird look on him. Lu fought with every ounce of self-control she had not to let hers do the same.

Will cleared his throat. "So," he said, regaining some of his swagger. "You're at my party."

"It would seem that way, wouldn't it?" Lu replied, brushing her hair casually over her shoulder. Will raised an eyebrow.

"Why?"

"Why not?"

"I've never seen you at one of my parties before."

"You've never invited me."

"I didn't this time either."

Lu stared longingly back toward the kitchen, and Will followed her gaze, his expression bemused.

"Not that you're not welcome anytime," he kept going. "But here you are tonight, of all nights. It's the magic of Stormpocalypse. Where are all your theater friends? Couldn't make it?"

"You put a party invite up on Facebook. I wasn't the only one who wasn't in the mood to study tonight."

"Keebler," he said. "Come on."

"It's Lu now, thanks."

"Lu . . ." He trailed off, getting a look in his eye that Lu hadn't seen in years, and definitely had not thought she'd see ever again. Her stomach flopped over on itself like a humongous pancake.

"Will," she said, and by this time she was backing and twisting her way through the crowd—Will behind her every step—and into an empty little alcove behind the spiral staircase. "As hard as it may be for you to believe, I'm not actually here to see you." It was stupid of her to come, she realized for the first time. Impulsive. It was totally like her, to just do something like this without thinking it through first. What had she thought was going to happen? Had she been thinking at all, other than of a way to lure Tiny out on the night before the SATs with the promise of some fantasy moment with Josh that would never happen? She felt a pang of guilt, and fleetingly wondered where Tiny even was.

"So you say." Will seemed almost amused—delighted even—as he strode effortlessly to keep up with her. God, he had long legs. He had gotten really freaking tall.

His smirk had widened into this full-blown grin, and he had a bounce in his step she was sure she'd never seen at school. Totally weirded out, she ducked under his arm and made a beeline up the stairs.

"Why are you following me?"

"Why are you running away from me?"

"Don't you have more important things you could be doing? Where are all your groupies? Where's your precious *team*? Aren't you like *so embarrassed* to be seen with me?"

"Come on." He paused mid-staircase, serious. "Hey. Luella. Don't be like that."

"It's *Lu.* And I really don't have time for this. I have to go to Central Park to meet my boyfriend. He's a musician."

The words flew out of her mouth before she had a chance to think about them. As usual.

For a minute the look on Will's face betrayed his confidence.

"Who?"

"It's none of your business." She paused. "Owen Hoffman."

"That guy in that band? He's a pretentious dick," Will said with a snort.

"Your mom's a pretentious dick!" Lu snapped.

But Will was grinning, and Lu felt something drop to the pit of her stomach. It had been so many years. It felt like no time had passed at all.

"I can't do this," Lu whispered. And even through the noise of the party, she knew Will had heard her, because he didn't say anything to stop her.

She turned and ran the rest of the way up the stairs. She didn't even know where she was going, other than away from him. She'd come to the party, yeah. She'd accepted the dare he'd thrown out into the cosmos. Maybe some part of her knew if she came, something like this would happen. Maybe she'd wanted it to.

At the second-floor landing, Lu paused. She was slightly out of breath, and it wasn't from running as fast as she could up the stairs.

The hallway was deserted.

She was about to double back, when she heard a noise clattering up the back stairs at the opposite end of the hall, and seconds later Will came barreling through the door. She had forgotten there were stairs off the kitchen. The place was basically a palace.

They stood on opposite ends of the hall, facing each other.

"Luella."

"*Lu.*"

There was an awkward pause.

"I shouldn't have said the thing about the bras yesterday."

"You *think*?"

"Geez, don't get your panties in a bunch. I—" Then, off Lu's furious, blazing stare: "Okay, I shouldn't have put it that way. Come on. What are you, the language police? I—"

Lu had turned and was storming back down the hall in the direction she'd come from.

"Luella. Lu!" He sprinted after her, coming up around her other side and standing in her way.

"What do you want, Will?"

"I just . . ." He didn't actually look like he knew. "What *are* you doing here?"

Lu shrugged.

"That's not an answer. That's like five-year-olds who answer you with *because.*"

"It's Stormpocalypse." Lu looked away. "If the world's going to end tonight, you know, I thought I'd give you one last chance to apologize."

"*Me* apologize? I see you have lost none of your tactfulness in the years we haven't spoken," Will said.

"Oooh, sarcasm."

Lu looked at him. He looked right back.

"I'm *sorry.* About the bra thing. And . . . other things."

"*What* other things?"

"Uh-uh, Keebler," he said, wagging his finger. "That's all you're gonna get from me tonight."

"Typical."

"Well, what about you?"

"What *about* me?"

"How about you apologize to me?"

"*Me* apologize?" she said again.

"It only seems fair."

"Hardly," Lu snapped.

"Then I guess we"—he gestured between them—"are at an impasse."

Lu's breath hitched. She had never seen him look this way before. Like someone possessed. He didn't look like himself, not like the Will she used to know at all. But then, that was years ago. Before . . . everything.

"I hate you so, so much," Lu said.

Will sighed. "Wait—listen."

She felt tears spring to her eyes, and she forced them with all her might to stay deep down where they belonged. A deep rage began to bubble up inside her. At the tears, and at Will for making them come.

And then she was running past him, down the hall, to the stairs.

Will

Luella.

They didn't talk anymore, but that didn't mean Will didn't notice her. He'd seen every one of her plays, hunched in the back row to avoid someone seeing him and loudly calling his name. He laughed to himself sometimes, in the cafeteria, watching her fill her bowl with Rice Krispies and make a mess over by the cereal dispensers, earning her nickname all over again.

She was some figment of the past who lived in his memory and did dorky things that reminded him of a different time. But she wasn't, like, real. Sometimes he thought he had made her up to feel better about the asshole he'd become.

Then she just showed up at his party like . . . like all that hard work pretending didn't even matter. How could she do that? Get at the heart of it all, the truth of something, so quickly? So effortlessly?

She could find the old Will just by looking at him across a stupid crowded room. In his own goddamn house.

He'd fucked up again. Twice in two days. He was going for

a new record. Maybe before the end of the night, he'd be three for three.

He was suddenly dizzy. Luella was his last tie to his old self. If he snapped it for good, he'd be done for. He'd go floating off into the darkness of outer space, where he wouldn't know anyone, least of all himself.

And if he screamed for help, no one would hear him.

"Shit," said Will. Without Lu, he really did have nothing left to lose. She made him crazy. And now, she was gone. "Lu, wait!"

Gloriously crazy.

He ran down the hall after her.

All he could think about was finding Lu and making things right, and he had already forgotten about the insanity waiting for him downstairs, and Lu was running fast up the stairs that led to the top floor and he caught her arm and then they were standing there, facing each other in the narrow staircase. He could feel her pulse racing through her wrist.

"Just tell me this," Will said, quietly. "Why did you come to a party at my house if you never wanted to talk to me again?"

Lu fidgeted. "I was hoping to find a way to get back at you for yesterday. Maybe spike your beer with laxatives or something."

Will looked stricken.

"I *didn't*," Lu said. She looked him hard in the eyes.

Will sighed. "I'm . . . just so tired of everything." He rubbed his face and pressed his palms into his eyes.

"You made your own bed."

"You still care about me." He took his hands away and looked at her, a challenge. "Admit it."

"No."

"You made a mistake that night three years ago, Lu. You know you did."

"I did? *I* did? What about you? You just . . . you just . . . *let* me. You walked away." She looked away.

Will tried to get her to look at him again, but she wasn't having it. "And it was the biggest mistake of my life. I wish I could take it back. You have no idea how much I wish I could make things right. I think about it every day."

Lu crossed her arms and looked away. "You do?"

Will nodded.

"You want to be friends again? You want things to be okay between us?"

"Yes," Will said simply.

Lu looked up, looked him right in the eye.

"Then prove it."

Nathaniel

When they were kids, the only person who could cheer Tiny up was Tobias. He would sit with her, sometimes talking and sometimes in silence, until she was smiling again. She always did eventually. Nathaniel used to watch and wish it were him who could make Tiny smile again.

In the kitchen, he watched that stupid scruffy hipster guy leave Tiny standing there bewildered and sad. He felt the same familiar pull to make her smile. He hadn't felt it in so long—he'd pushed it away with everything else he'd felt that summer—but the muscle memory was there. It snapped right back into place.

Tiny ran through the door on the other side of the kitchen. And so Nathaniel followed her.

By the time he made it across the kitchen, winding his way between people, and through the door, he could see a red Converse sneaker turning left at the second-floor landing. And by the time he'd made it to the landing, a door was closing at the end of the hall. On the other side of *that* door was some kind of rec room–type lounge. Across the room, another door hadn't been closed all the way, and it was squeaking back and forth on its hinges in the wind, banging into something, so that the swath of moonlight splicing through the crack winked on and off, like disco lights. There was a couple making out on the couch, and a coffee table with a bong resting on it. A cool wind ruffled his hair. He walked toward the light, and pushed open the door.

Nathaniel blinked. He was standing on the roof, and beyond him, the expansive twinkling lights of the city breathed in and out like stars. The moon was huge and full and orange.

You had to be crazy to sit on a high open point like a roof in the middle of a lightning storm. You didn't have to be a geophysicist to know that. What was Tiny thinking? Nathaniel should have just gone back downstairs. Maybe even walked straight out the door and made his way back home.

But he couldn't do that. Now, if something happened to her, he'd blame himself.

So he stayed.

Tiny was sitting, her back against the side of the roof, her knees pulled up to her chest. Nathaniel took a step forward, but his sneaker hit something solid and he tripped and went sprawling. The door slammed shut behind him. Her head snapped up.

"Sorry!" Nathaniel shouted. "Uh, sorry."

"Are you okay?" said Tiny.

"Me? Oh yeah. Fine." He brushed himself off and grinned. "Ow, though."

She laughed, and he breathed out.

"Are, um. Are *you* okay?" He adjusted his wire-rimmed glasses. "Because you seem maybe"—he tried to think of the right word—"not."

She looked down, and a swath of brown hair fell across her face like a curtain. He felt a hiccup in his heart. She angrily wiped away a tear.

"I'm okay," she said.

"Do you want some company?" He took a step forward. "For old time's sake?"

Tiny didn't say anything. But she nodded. Nathaniel sat down next to her and crossed his legs.

"Hey," he said, nudging her a little with his elbow. "Want to know why the moon's like that?"

She looked at him like maybe he was a little crazy. But she said: "Yeah. Why?"

"It's the atmospheric pressure. From all the wind and the storm clouds."

"Cool," she said. She smiled, wiping away another tear. "Tell me more cool earth science facts."

"Really?" He sat up straighter. "You really want to know more weird arcana?"

She laughed. "Yes. I really want to know more weird arcana." She looked at him. "That is a total SAT word, by the way. You've been studying, too."

"Busted."

"Totally busted."

Nathaniel glanced over at her, but he didn't say anything.

Lightning flashed. One Mississippi . . .

Thunder rumbled.

"Whoa," she said. "It's getting *really* close."

"Well," Nathaniel said slowly. "Do you want to know why there's thunder and lightning but no rain?"

"I don't know," Tiny said. "Do I?"

"It's probably better that you know. In case it comes up on the test tomorrow, or something."

"Right," Tiny said. "I should be prepared."

"Yeah. You could use the extra studying, since you're at a party tonight and everything."

"Ugh, don't remind me."

"Sorry," said Nathaniel. "Well, it's a dry storm. They get them all the time out west, but they're really rare on the East Coast because of the climate. It's because we've been having an Indian summer."

"What's that?"

"An unseasonably hot, dry fall."

"Oh, Nathaniel." Tiny patted him on the knee. "You really did grow up to be a scientist."

He grinned and hoped she couldn't see the back of his neck turn pink in the dark. "We haven't had rain in months, right? It's why everyone's freaking out about all the rain we're supposed to get tonight." Nathaniel paused and tugged at his sweater sleeves. Was he rambling? Did he sound dumb? She wasn't telling him to stop. "That, and the lightning. There are some powerful electrical currents in the air tonight."

"Aren't the odds of getting struck by lightning really small, though?"

"Oh yeah," said Nathaniel. "They're, like, this big." He held up two fingers. "You have a greater chance of dying from getting hit in the head with a falling coconut."

Tiny laughed. "Is that a real statistic, Bill Nye?"

"Totally real. Besides, when lightning is grounding a foot in front of you, you run like hell or else—"

"You're forked?"

Nathaniel looked at her. She was smiling. Her cheeks were dry.

"Sitting on this roof probably isn't doing much to decrease our chances, though."

Another bolt of lightning zigzagged between the buildings. Nathaniel felt the muscles in his chest clench. He pushed away the memories; he was sure she was doing the same. He turned to her and grinned.

"One more?"

She nodded.

"Okay, this one's cool. Lightning follows the path of least resistance. It forks because it's finding its way through the spaces in the atmosphere that allow it to pass."

Tiny stared at the sky, so he looked up too, and together they watched as the beautiful bright forks found their way in the night.

"I know how that feels," she whispered. She shifted to face him. "So why are *you* at Will's party tonight, if the SATs are so important to you?"

"Will invited me over to study," Nathaniel said sheepishly. "So everything is really going according to plan."

"I didn't know you guys were still friends."

"We're not. Not really. What about you? What are you doing here?"

Tiny paused. "Lu made me come."

"I didn't know *you* guys were still friends."

"We're supposed to be. We say we are. But sometimes I think it's just something we say." She squeezed her knees in tighter. "I just didn't feel like being alone. I thought—there's this guy, and if I could get him to notice me . . ." She looked away.

Nathaniel looked down at his hands. "Is that why you're crying?"

"No." Tiny laughed. "He hit my head with the door and it really hurt! And it was just . . . embarrassing, I guess."

Nathaniel reached out to feel where she was pointing.

"There's a bump."

"I know!"

"I think you should have a really great night tonight, just to show him," Nathaniel said.

"I don't know," said Tiny. "The night's almost over. Something really good would have to happen to turn it all around."

"Well." Nathaniel grinned. "I wasn't going to show you these, but . . ." He pulled a stack of flash cards out of his jeans pocket and handed them to her. "Since you like arcana."

Tiny smiled without saying anything. She split the stack in half and handed one set to Nathaniel. She'd always had a really nice smile. It just sort of lit everything up.

"*Cacophony*," Tiny said.

"The sound of the party downstairs."

Tiny laughed. "Good one."

"Thanks. The definition of E equals MC squared," he said.

"Energy equals mass times the speed of light, squared. Einstein's theory of relativity."

"That one was easy."

"For you, maybe. Um." She rifled through her deck. "*Faith*," she said.

"*Faith*," Nathaniel recited, his eyes closed and one hand to his forehead like a tarot card reader. "The firm belief in something for which there is no proof." He opened his eyes. "In other words, the opposite of science. Did I get it right?"

"I'm not going to tell you," Tiny said, smiling. "You're just going to have to have faith."

He grinned and nudged her with his elbow. She nudged him back.

The sky flashed. A gust of wind came along and whipped the flash card right out of Tiny's hand.

"Oops," she said. They watched it spiral away into the night. She shivered.

"Are you cold?" he said. "Here."

He pulled his sweater off and handed it to her.

"Oh," she said, turning red. "You don't have to—"

"It's okay. I'm warm enough. This is actually a down T-shirt." He smiled, lopsided, and pushed his glasses farther up his nose with one hand while handing her the sweater with the other. "Superthin. Advanced technology."

She slipped it on and poked her finger through one of the holes. She smiled at him.

"Yeah," he said. "I know. My mom keeps trying to buy me new ones, but this is my favorite sweater. It has character."

"I remember this sweater."

"You do? Do you remember its name?"

"Of course!"

"Marcel," they said at the same time. They smiled in the darkness.

"Well, thank you for keeping us warm, Marcel."

The pause in conversation grew into a comfortable silence between them.

They stared at the sky.

"Oh man," said Nathaniel. "This storm is going to be crazy. You can just tell."

The door swung open with a bang.

"Luella, just listen!"

Lu came bursting onto the roof. "No!" she yelled as Will materialized behind her.

The door slammed shut behind both of them. Will spun around.

"Oh shit," he said. "No. No!"

"What's wrong?" said Lu. "What happened?"

"The door," Will said, his voice rising. "It locks from the inside. Where's the brick?"

"What brick?"

"The brick that's supposed to keep it open? Where is it? It's always right—"

"There," Nathaniel said, suddenly feeling sick. He pointed to the thing he'd tripped over. "That brick?"

The four of them looked where he was pointing.

"Shit," said Will. "Shit." He took out his phone and pressed something, holding it up to his ear. "Jon's not picking up. It's too loud down there for anyone to hear us. We're never going to get back inside! Now we're stuck out here right as it's about to storm." He kicked the brick and it went skidding across the roof.

Lu looked deflated. "Noooo. I have to get to Hurricane Fest! Or else—"

"Or else what?" said Will pointedly.

"None of your business." Lu crossed her arms.

"We can't just sit here; we have to find a way out," Nathaniel said, panic rising in his chest. "What about the SATs?" Now that he'd overslept and missed the scholarship deadline, that was all he had left. "My whole future depends on that test!"

A brilliant flash of lightning lit up the sky, followed immediately by a thunderclap so loud it shook the roof beneath them.

"I'm more worried about the lightning," Tiny said quietly.

Will yelled and hit the door with his palm. "We're going to get stuck out here and we're all going to die." He crouched by the door, his head in his hands. "This is bad. This is so bad."

The sky had grown dense with clouds, purple and angry.

Nathaniel couldn't see the moon anymore.

And the wind howled and the thunder clapped and the storm was coming. Nathaniel could feel it. They all could. The storm was coming, and it was coming for them.

There was another crack of thunder, and lightning coursed through the clouds, flashing bright like the middle of the day, and he could see Tiny and Lu and Will, all of them, their faces turned up toward the sky and the lightning that was crashing down on them, hard and loud and bright.

There was a jarring zappish noise, like when the power goes out.

But they were outside. And there was no power. Only the lightning. It snaked through them like blood, lighting up their bones, electrifying everything.

And then it was dark.

And then it was quiet.

THEN

The Last Day of Summer
Before High School
Three Years ago
Noon

The Collision of
Opposite Charges

Will

Black. White. Black. White. White.

Will watched with steely determination as the soccer ball careened in a near-graceful arc toward his head.

"Get it!" Nathaniel shouted from behind him. "Head the ball!"

As if in slow motion, Will aimed his head at the ball, thinking about how awesome he was going to be at soccer tryouts in the fall.

Then an image of Luella popped into his head, and instead of heading the ball with grace and athleticism, it smacked Will in the side of his head and he went down.

"Oh my god." Nathaniel came running over. "Dude. I'm so sorry. I thought you saw that! Are you okay?"

"Ow," Will mumbled.

"You have to stay focused, always watch the ball," Nathaniel said, kicking the ball up and bouncing it from knee to knee.

Will sat up and rubbed his head.

"You're really good. Remind me again why you're not going to try out with me?"

Nathaniel grinned. "No time. I'm creating my own independent study on geophysics. Plus, I had to beg *and* do an extra credit research paper to get into advanced earth science. I'm going to be superbusy." He dropped the ball and rested his foot on it. "Besides, I have a fundamental skepticism of the whole team mentality. I don't believe in organized religion or sports."

"Right. I bet that makes Bubbe Spencer thrilled."

Nathaniel's grandma was the daughter of a Holocaust survivor. Her dream in life was for Nathaniel to marry a nice Jewish girl and have Jewish babies and one day start an all-Jewish medical practice. Every time he went over for family dinners, Will had to watch Nathaniel explain to his Bubbe that just because he was into science, didn't mean he wanted to be *that* kind of doctor. He also wanted to be able to marry whoever he wanted. That last part always made Will laugh, because the thought of any girl getting over Nathaniel's awkwardness enough to marry him was absurd.

"Look, I'll drop it if you tell me to, but are you sure *you* want to be part of this whole team thing? Some of those guys on their own are nice and stuff, but when you get them all together in a pack, it's like—"

"A well-oiled machine?"

"I was going to say a bunch of hyenas, but okay. I just don't get why this is so important to you."

"One day, when you want to win a girl, Nathaniel, you'll understand." Will said this sagely, like someone who had won a lot of girls, when in fact he had won no girls and Nathaniel knew it.

Nathaniel threw the ball at him, and Will caught it with both hands.

"You sound like a giant douchebag," Nathaniel said.

"'Douchebags are hygienic products; I take that as a compliment. Thank you.'" He quoted *Wet Hot American Summer* and stuck his tongue out.

"Who is this girl you're trying to impress, anyway?"

"Anyone. *Any* girl, Nathaniel. I'm just tired of people looking at me, and my weight being the first thing they see." That was a lie. There was a girl, one girl, but Will wasn't ready to talk about her yet.

"No one sees that first but you."

Will threw the soccer ball back at Nathaniel, who kneed it gracefully and let it rest in the grass. "We've been indoor kids our whole lives. We're starting high school now! We have the chance to be completely different! Look. I'm a different person than I was in June. And I don't want to go back to the way things were. I have to keep moving forward."

"Okay."

"Like a shark cutting tirelessly through the dark waters of the ocean."

"I get it."

Will clapped a hand on Nathaniel's back. "It comes down to this. High school will be different than middle school. Do you want to go through the next four years being defined by the last four?"

"I guess not," Nathaniel said.

"I just want to be happy," said Will. "Can you let me do something I think will make me happy?"

Nathaniel kicked up the ball and headed it toward Will.

"As long as we'll still be friends when you're a hotshot soccer star," he said.

Will watched the ball sail over his head and roll through the grass a few feet away. Nathaniel groaned.

"I was distracted!" Will said. And he was. Because standing at the edge of the field, watching them and laughing, was Luella.

* * *

This was how the whole thing with Luella had started.

It was back at the beginning of the summer. The first day of his summer math enrichment program, which met on the Hunter College campus. Luella was the last person he had expected to see in the cafeteria. It looked like she had managed to make the cereal dispenser explode, and now she was wading in an ankle-deep sea of Rice Krispies.

"Crap, crap, crap, crap, *crap*," Luella muttered as she dropped quickly to the floor, trying to scoop as many handfuls of the tiny rice puffs as she could into her empty standard-issue, cafeteria-size bowl.

Will didn't know anyone else quite like Luella. She was a force of nature. Most girls were just confusing and scary and kind of foreign. They eyed him up and down, always making sure to linger on his extra chub and his glasses. They made him nervous.

But, man, not Luella, with her bangs and skinny elbows and chipped nail polish flailing all over the place. She was really something else. She had black hair and olive skin and green eyes and looked like a cat, like the kind of cat who might squirm around a bit but who'd snuggle up to you eventually, and not the kind that might maul you to death when you stopped paying attention (like Melissa Sissler, who had been in his class since second grade and who was definitely the secret-mauling type). Any other girl, and he wouldn't have cared so much if she embarrassed herself in the cafeteria. Besides, girls didn't ever really embarrass themselves anyway, right? They were, like, impervious to that kind of thing. They were all just so shiny and happy and giggly that they never seemed to care.

"Hey, Luella," he said, helping her up. "Are you okay? Have you drowned in the sea of Rice Krispies?"

"Nah, I'm wearing floaties." She looked up at him and cracked a sly smile, full of braces. She suddenly reminded Will of one of those little elves on the Rice Krispies box.

Will grinned. "I should call you Keebler from now on."

They were standing up now, and Will had already taken a clean bowl from the stack and traded it for the one with the floor-cereal. The line behind them was backing up.

"So," Will said. "What are you doing here? You're not doing nerd camp too, are you?"

"Nerd camp?" Luella looked dubious.

"Uh, yeah. Isn't that why you're here . . . ?"

"Oh, no," Luella said with a dismissive wave of her hand. "I'm taking acting classes this summer, and we use the Hunter theater." She grinned. "Nerd camp?"

"It's a summer math enrichment course," Will mumbled.

"Well, listen, I'm sure you have all kinds of exciting numbers to get back to." She grabbed an apple, tossed it coolly in the air, and then dropped it.

"You meant to do that?" said Will. "Is juggling part of your summer curriculum?"

"Shut up, math geek."

"See ya, Keebler."

"Yeah, see ya never." Luella picked up the apple, rubbed it on her shirt, and skipped off toward a group of kids wearing lots of black. "Also, wrong elves!" she called over her shoulder. "Those are the *cookie* elves! You mean Snap, Crackle, Pop."

"Too hard to say," Will called without missing a beat. "You're Keebler—deal with it."

After that, they hung out all the time. It was weird; usually they hung out in a group of the four of them—Will, Luella, Tiny, and Nathaniel—but this was the first time Will could remember when he and Luella had actually hung out alone.

One afternoon in particular, they had been standing outside the Hunter College theater. The parts had just been announced for Luella's theater program's production of *Cat on a Hot Tin Roof*.

"Yeeeeeeeeees!" she cried, pumping her fist in the air. "Maggie the Cat! Maggie the Cat!"

"Is this a good thing?" Will asked, dubious. "Are we happy about this? The cat sounds like a small part."

"The cat," Luella said breathlessly, "is the best"—breath—"part"—wheeze—"in"—cough—"the modern. Literature. Canon."

"Wow."

"Arguably."

"And you don't even have to memorize any lines. You just get to meow."

Luella smacked him on the arm. "Shut up. It's not a real cat." She jumped up and down and squealed. "I am *happy*!"

"Uh," said Will. "I bow out at squealing." He paused. "What are you doing?"

Luella's body was twitching and convulsing in the most ridiculous way. She dipped her hips to the right and then to the left, rotating her fists in a counterclockwise direction. The bottom half of her legs seemed disconnected from the top half.

"What," Will said as they began walking outside, "was that?"

"What?" Luella said.

"That thing you just did?"

"My happy dance?"

"Was that that thing with your hips and your knees?"

"My happy dance," Luella confirmed.

"Your what now?"

"Come on—don't you have one?" They turned a corner and walked out the door and into the daylight. Luella smiled wide, her braces glittering like small diamonds in the sunlight.

"Uh, no."

"That's so depressing. You have to have one! What do you do when you're happy?"

"Uh," Will said. "I smile? I laugh?"

"No, no, but what do you do when you're, like, so happy you're going to burst?"

"Umm . . ."

"I mean, *so* happy that all your happiness just has nowhere else to go?"

Will thought for a minute, chewing absently on the inside of his cheek.

"Yeah, I don't really get that way so much."

Luella flipped her hair over her shoulder. "What? You seem happy sometimes."

Will felt himself turning red. "Well, *now*, I guess. I mean, when we hang out."

She stopped dead in her tracks and turned to look at him. He took an involuntary step back. She cocked her head and looked him square in the eye. She looked like she was thinking really hard. Will felt like she was maybe trying to guess how many folds were in his temporal lobe.

He suddenly felt self-conscious. He shouldn't have said anything.

"We're really going to have to work on this," Luella said finally.

They flung themselves down on a shady patch of grass in the park. Luella stared at him.

"Now?" Will asked.

"Oh sorry, does now not work for you? Are you too busy whining about how depressed you are, like you're the star of some black-and-white French movie, to have time for trivial things like, I don't know, self-*expression*?"

"Fine, I—"

"Because I can take out my iCalendar and figure out a time that works for both of us. You know, maybe next Tuesday . . ."

"Okay, okay, shut up. Now is fine."

They got to work. Luella was a demanding coach.

"What's up with your arms there?" Luella was asking. "It doesn't look like you're happy; it looks like you broke your shoulder."

It was lunchtime, and while the rest of the kids in their respective programs were crowded around tables in the cafeteria, Will and Luella had fallen into the habit of bringing their lunch to the park. Secretly, Will was relieved to have a friend like Luella. He was glad to not have to sit with the guys in his program every day, listening to more jokes about his "wiggle in the middle." They thought it was hilarious. They had even made up this absurd dance about it. At first it was kind of funny, and Will joined in, humoring them, doing the dance with his arms up over his head just so he didn't have to ask them to stop. But soon the dance got old. It made him feel like he should lose weight or something. It was a relief to hang out with Luella, who didn't seem to notice. Or care.

"You said to get height," he said.

"Yeah, height as in the soaring heights of bliss, not popping your shoulder out of its socket." She made a sucking noise with her mouth. "It was a metaphor."

"If I popped my shoulder out of its socket, it'd be dislocated, not broken," Will shot back. "Plus, you have chocolate pudding stuck in your braces."

Luella made the sucking noise again. "Shut up."

"That doesn't sound like the attitude of someone who does happy dances on the reg."

"Look, I can't help it if my braces are like a magnetic strip for food and other things."

"Other things?" Will sat down, his legs splayed in the grass.

"Yeah, like toothpaste and stuff."

Luella sat down too.

"Toothpaste is a food." The corners of Will's mouth were telling themselves to behave, not to curve up too much.

"Uh, no. Do you eat toothpaste?"

"Well, no," Will started, "but—"

"Do you rely on it for vital nutrients?"

"I guess not, but—"

"Then it's not a food," Luella said, waving her hand dismissively.

A bird walked between them, beat its wings, and then flew a few feet away to where the remains of a cookie lay, unsuspecting. They looked at each other and grinned. Then stopped very suddenly, as if embarrassed that they both thought to do that at the exact same time.

"I gotta get back," Will said, standing up, his stomach sinking for reasons that were beyond him. "I have important numbers to crunch."

"Yeah, hop to it, math nerd!"

"Oh, I will, drama geek."

"Get your ass in shape, Kingfield," she said, standing up and brushing off her jeans. "You have to just let go, you know? Forget what other people think and just allow yourself to look a little dumb." She sucked on her braces again, and this time when she smiled at him, all the chocolate pudding had vanished. "You're too uptight, is what your problem is," she said. "You think too much."

"And you're a lunatic," Will shot back, annoyed.

"And you," Luella said, "are my favorite." She kissed him on the cheek and ran off ahead of him.

Will blinked away the memory. "Yo!" Luella was yelling now, laughing as she made her way across the field to where Will and Nathaniel were kicking the ball around. "Don't let me distract you!" Too late. Will knew for sure he was red. But somehow he didn't care.

Nathaniel

The three of them lay on the grass in Sheep Meadow, watching clouds roll across the hazy blue sky.

"Know what's cool about cumulous clouds?" Nathaniel said.

"*That* one looks like a unicorn eating an ice cream cone," Luella said, pointing.

"When they're greenish-blue, like that one over there that's rolling in, it means they're holding an extremely high amount of water."

"*That* one looks like a polar bear giving another polar bear a piggyback ride."

"Lightning originates in cumulonimbus clouds," Nathaniel said. "Warm air mixes with cold air and creates these atmospheric disturbances that are like collisions of opposite charges in the cloud. Then negatively charged electrons flow down to earth in this downward stroke called a stepped leader. But these positive charges called upward streamers are coming up from the ground at the same time, and when they collide, it causes this massive electrical discharge called a return stroke. What's interesting"—Luella coughed—"is that's the only part we see—the luminous flash. It's going back up, not down, like everyone thinks!"

"Nathaniel," Will said. "Why does everything have to have a reason? Why can't we just appreciate that cloud over there that looks like a T. rex throwing a baseball?"

"Oooh, good one," said Luella, laughing.

"Everything has a reason, Will. Everything in the known world is rooted in scientific fact."

"Want to know a fact?" Luella said, wiping sweat off the back of her neck. "It's hot as balls. I want an ice pop."

Nathaniel chose not to say it out loud, but it *was* too hot. The earth's atmosphere was breaking down. Tobias was working on a proposal for an interdisciplinary course for his freshman year at MIT EAPS, and had been talking about it a lot at family dinners. It was a further exploration of his Anders Almquist project, on the relationship between climate change and electrical storms, with a specific focus on the relationship between big cities, the atmosphere, and lightning.

"It's time for lunch," he said. "We have to go meet Tiny at the *Alice in Wonderland* statue."

They peeled themselves off the grass and started walking down the path.

Nathaniel couldn't wait to meet up with Tiny. She liked his weird science facts. Besides, Will was different when he was around Luella, especially lately. He made fun of Nathaniel a lot more. Nathaniel knew it was a loveable kind of making fun, but still. He wished they'd take him a little more seriously sometimes.

Nathaniel understood what Will was saying, about not wanting the next four years to be defined by the last four. Will might not think so, but he did.

There had been something he'd been wanting to say to Tiny, actually. Something that couldn't wait anymore.

Maybe he'd do it tonight, when they went with Tobias to track the lightning.

Tiny was waiting for them by the turnoff to the statue, bags of new school supplies at her feet. Nathaniel waved.

"Talulah!" Luella called. "You are prepared for the year ahead!"

Tiny grinned. "My mom kind of went overboard."

They got hot dogs and cold soda from a vendor, the cans dripping with melted ice. Then the four of them climbed up the statue and sat on the mushroom. The Cheshire Cat leered down at them.

"It like he knows school's about to start," Tiny said, grimacing. "Here, have a pencil." She extracted a brand-new, unsharpened pencil from one of her plastic shopping bags and stuck it behind his ear. "Good-bye, pencil."

"Good-bye, freedom," said Will.

"Good-bye, short shorts," Luella pouted.

"Good-bye, afternoons at the park," Nathaniel said.

"Guys," said Tiny, taking her phone out of her pocket. "Let's take a picture, to commemorate this momentous rite of passage. On this day in history, four friends said good-bye to their childhoods and embarked on the epic journey known as high school."

"There's a reason you're our spokesperson," said Luella. "You talk good."

"Come on—squeeze."

"Say E. coli poisoning!" Will said, holding up his hot dog and mugging for the camera.

"E. coli poisoning!" they said in unison.

"Let me see!" Luella leaned over and snatched the phone. "Nice. You have ketchup on your face, Will."

"Want to lick it off?" He moved toward Luella.

"Ew!" she squealed. "Get off!"

Nathaniel caught Tiny's eye, and she smiled.

He never got to say the thing he found the coolest about lightning. That the two necessary conditions were:

1) High electrical potential between two regions of space, and

2) High resistance standing in its way.

It made him think of high school, for some reason. He, Tiny, Will, and Luella were full of potential, creating all these atmospheric disturbances. And there was so much standing in their way.

It also made him think of Tiny.

Everything was changing. Part of him wished it could stay this way forever. The rest of him knew that was scientifically impossible.

NOW

10:00 P.M.

(10 Hours Left)

Energy Currents and Origin Stories

Tiny

Tiny opened her eyes. It was quiet, except for the wind, which still whipped her hair in all directions. It had been so bright, blindingly bright, just seconds ago. But now it took a few seconds of blinking to adjust to the darkness.

Her feet felt all tingly and weird. Quickly, she slipped off her sneakers. On the soles of each of her feet was a burn mark. A perfect charred circle where the lightning had entered her body. It shimmered a little in the dark. Whoa.

She had been struck by lightning!

She had felt it, felt the heat and the surge of electricity, the blinding brightness.

And she was alive.

"Guys?" she said tentatively. She still felt weird, light-headed. No one answered her. "Lu? Nathaniel?"

Moments ago the roof had been a wild, loud, *cacophonous* place. Now it was deserted. "Guys?" she said again.

No answer. Had they all left? No, the door to the roof was locked.

She squinted and looked around. On the other side of the roof, under a metal structure for an old water tower, was a lumpy silhouette. Tiny ran to it.

"Lu." She shook it. "Lu!"

Lu sat up groggily. "What? Is it time for the test already?"

"No. Lu, we're still at the party."

Lu rubbed her eyes. "We are? But I was having a really good dream." She blinked a few times and then looked up at Tiny. Her eyes went wide, and she jumped up. "Dude. What is going on?"

"We were struck by lightning," Tiny said breathlessly. "I felt it. And look." She showed Lu the bottom of her foot.

Lu studied her. Tiny couldn't help but notice the worry in her eyes.

"Tiny . . ."

"I know, I know, but—"

"You sound like one of the Spencer brothers."

"Lu," Tiny said quietly. "Just check your feet."

Reluctantly, Lu tore off her platform booties and inspected her feet. On the bottom of each were two black burn marks that shimmered in the faint ambient glow of the city lights.

"Oh my god," said Lu. "We got struck by lightning!"

Tiny could hardly believe the words. She hadn't even wanted to come out tonight. This was all Lu's fault. This never would have happened if she'd stayed home to study.

But she could never say that.

"This can't be happening." Lu's voice was high-pitched and breathy. "How are we alive?"

A shiver ran down Tiny's spine. "I don't know. We shouldn't be." Tiny looked around. "Where's Nathaniel? Where's Will?"

"Ugh, Will," Lu muttered. Tiny gave her a questioning look but didn't ask.

They put their shoes back on and split up. On the other side of the roof, Tiny saw something move in the shadows.

"Nathaniel!" She ran toward the shadow and knelt next to him. "Hey. Wake up."

Nathaniel's eyes were closed. He groaned and rolled over. Tiny breathed a sigh of relief. He was alive. He was breathing. He was groaning in his sleep. He wasn't dead.

"Nathaniel." Tiny shook him gently. "Are you okay? Wake up. I think—I think we all got struck by lightning." Nathaniel's eyes blinked open.

"Huh?"

"Can you sit up?" He did, leaning against the side of the entry. "Can you see me?"

Nathaniel looked at her. Recognition suddenly dawned on his face. "Tiny. I think—but you're all blurry. What happened?"

"Check your feet," Tiny answered. Nathaniel looked uncertain, but he unlaced his hiking boots and peeled off his socks.

"What are—" He looked up at her. "Those are burn marks." Tiny nodded. "It was really bright, and then"—his eyes got wide—"the lightning."

"Yeah."

He grabbed her arm. Something passed between them. A charge, a shock, something. Tiny pulled away in surprise. Her hands started to shake.

"Are Will and Lu okay?" he whispered.

"Well," Lu said, approaching them. She looked like she'd just seen a ghost. "*I'm* okay."

Someone else was with Lu. It should have been Will. It had only been the four of them up there on the roof. But it didn't look like Will. It looked, instead, like Jon Heller—Will's soccer co-captain, co-most popular boy in school, co-jerk.

"How did he get here?" Tiny said, pulling back a little. Jon always made her uncomfortable, like he had made up his mind ahead of time to make fun of whatever she was going to say. "Where's Will?"

"I'm Will," Jon said. He blinked at them. "Guys, it's me. What are you talking about?"

They stared at him.

"Jon," said Nathaniel. "Quit screwing around. Where's Will?"

Jon's eyes were getting wide. "Guys, this isn't funny. *I'm Will.*"

Lu looked around, her eyes landing on the polished steel door to the roof. She grabbed Jon's arm and dragged him toward it.

"There," she said, coming to a stop in front of the door. Jon stared at his reflection in the shiny metal.

"What the hell is happening?" he whispered.

"You're pulling a prank," Lu said, her eyebrow raised. "An elaborate one. What, is this some kind of joke, making fun of us because we don't belong here? Did you two plan this out in advance?"

"It's not a prank, Lu," Jon said. "I promise. I'm—I'm not Jon. I'm Will. I just . . . *look* like Jon."

"Right." She crossed her arms. "Okay. Tell me something only Will would know."

"God, Keebler, why don't you just believe me?"

Lu turned pale.

"Keebler?" said Tiny. "Nice try, but no one calls Lu that."

"Actually," said Lu. "One person does." She cleared her throat. "Or did."

"I'm so confused," Nathaniel said. "What are you trying to say, that you look like Jon Heller on the outside, but you're Will on the inside?"

Will/Jon nodded vigorously. "Yes! That's exactly what I'm trying to say."

"Well, I'm just going to say it," said Lu. "What the hell is going on? You can't change everything about yourself in ten minutes!"

"It would be nice if you could, though," Tiny said.

"Trust me, I know," said Will, or Jon. "This is messed up."

"Maybe it was magic lightning." Lu tightened her ponytail. "I wished something bad would happen to you, and it did!" She looked up at the sky. "I'd also like the SATs to be canceled!" Will/Jon gave her a withering look. "What? What's *your* explanation?"

Nathaniel stood and looked around.

"There!" He walked to the center of the roof, and Tiny followed him, because listening to Lu and Will—Jon—whatever—was weirding her out. The four of them stood there, looking down at a giant, charred mark on the tin floor of the roof. It looked almost like a four-pointed star. "It struck the roof," he said, "and then"—he made a zigzag motion with his hands between the four of them—"the current traveled through anything touching it. That's why we have burn marks on our feet. That's where the lightning entered us."

"Entered us," Tiny repeated, shivering. "That is so. Creepy."

"Does that mean it's still *in* us?" said Lu, sounding kind of manic.

"Maybe," said Nathaniel, thinking.

"Maybe?" Will/Jon was yelling now. "Did the lightning really do this? Did the lightning make me look like Jon Heller?"

Nathaniel looked thoughtful. "It could have. A major change in energy currents *could* create a corresponding change in a person's cellular make up. Like how superheroes get their powers in all those origin stories. But real, I guess."

"So, what? Like Spider-Man? Or the Flash? You're saying I'm like a superhero? And my power is that I can make myself look like my soccer co-captain?"

"I don't know why it would make you look like Jon, specifically." Nathaniel paused, running a hand through his curly brown hair. "Only you could really know the answer. Maybe it has some sort of personal significance?"

"Hm." Will/Jon scratched his chin. "I don't know. I mean, it was his idea to have the party tonight. And I just couldn't really say no—"

"Guys," Lu said, "are you listening to yourselves? We are in the real world, not a comic book. We just got hit by lightning and you're discussing the nuances of superhero powers?"

Nathaniel and Will blinked. "Right," Nathaniel said. "We should worry about getting off this roof first. Then we should tell someone. This is really dangerous. I mean, Lu's right. The current could still be inside us. If we touch something with this amount of electric current running through us, it could . . ." He made an explosion noise.

"Good," said Will. "This night needed to get worse."

Tiny had been watching all of this quietly. She said: "We should go to the hospital. All of us. Together. This is serious. We can't just figure this out on our own."

"No!" Everyone turned on her.

"Why not?" she said, shrinking back. It felt wrong, but part of her was excited that Science Club was all back together again. She missed this. She missed them.

"Well, okay, for starters, they'll want to know why we were on the roof during a hurricane," said Will. "And then we'll have to say that we were having a party. And then they'll call my parents in Majorca. And then when they come home, I'll be grounded for the rest of my life. That is, if they even recognize me." Will's face—Jon's face—whatever, was growing panicked. "Which they won't. They'll send me to live with Jon Heller's parents. But no, wait"—more panicked—"Jon will already be there. Everyone will be terrified. I'll be labeled a freak of nature and sent to Arkham Asylum."

"That's a fictional place. Besides, you should have thought of that before you threw a party," Nathaniel mumbled.

"Sorry, what was that? Did you not come over and drink my beer?"

"I came because I thought we were going to study!"

"Well, I'm definitely not going to the hospital," said Lu. "I hate hospitals."

Tiny only knew bits and pieces of the reason Lu hated hospitals, because for a person who loved to talk about herself, Lu didn't really like to feel vulnerable. Tiny had figured out, through occasional comments and jokes, that Lu's dad had been in the hospital for a while with early stage prostate cancer. He'd had chemo and everything, and had gone into remission. Not even a month after he came home and life got back to normal, he'd left Lu and her mom for his nurse at the hospital. Tiny thought this was probably a big part of the reason why she didn't trust people a whole lot. Case in point: They were supposedly best friends, but Lu had never even told her this story outright.

"Look, we can't go to a hospital, and we can't stay here!" said Lu. "We could get struck again!"

"Well, how do you suggest we get off the roof, Luella? The door's locked." Will pointed. They all turned suddenly to the door.

Nathaniel scratched his head and pushed his wire-rimmed glasses up his nose. Then he walked over to the door and jiggled the handle. "See?" Will said. Nathaniel pulled on it harder. "It won't—"

The heavy metal fire door came flying off. Like, literally, flying off in his hand. Tiny ducked. Nathaniel looked shocked as he chucked this big and heavy and solid piece of metal across the roof as if it weighed nothing more than a feather.

"Whoa," said Nathaniel, pushing up his glasses.

"What the hell?" said Will. "How did you do that?"

Nathaniel blinked in shock. "I have no idea."

"You just threw that thing away like the Hulk!"

"It wasn't that heavy," Nathaniel said. "I just kind of tugged it a little, and it came off."

Tiny glanced at Lu, who was rubbing her arms as if she were cold.

"Hey," she whispered. "Are you okay?"

"Yeah," said Lu. "I just—I can't feel anything."

"What?" Tiny asked.

"I feel . . . I feel kind of . . . numb."

"Maybe you're just cold?"

"I think it's the lightning," Lu said darkly. "It's still inside me. I can tell."

Tiny felt overwhelmed. She felt small. Mostly, she felt relieved that the lightning hadn't seemed to affect her in the same bad way it had the other three. The shiny metal door lay at her feet. It sure looked heavy. She bent down to try to lift it herself.

But when she saw her own reflection in the polished metal, her stomach jolted.

Her image, pale as it was, especially now, was more than that—

more than just pale, more than just easy to overlook. More than just another anonymous girl floating through the halls of school. No—this was something else. It flickered in and out, once, twice, like a winking flame. It didn't look like she was really there. It didn't look like she was *solid.*

There was a distant rumble of thunder and a restless flash of lightning right above her, like someone was taking a picture. The sky flickered, the light casting shadows on her skin, playing tricks on her eyes in the middle of the night. Tiny stood up quickly, watching the light dance across her arm.

No, she realized with a start. She watched it dance *through* her arm.

It was like looking down at your body in a dark room. Like just being able to make out the faintish glow of skin. A rogue finger. The bony curve of an elbow. Everything just shy of translucent.

That was what her hand looked like. Just shy of translucent. She could see *through* it. Right through her skin and bones to the roof below. For just a minute her hand looked like heat coming off the sidewalk in the dead of August.

She looked almost—but no, it was too crazy to even think. She looked almost like she was turning *invisible.*

This couldn't have been happening. Just because Tiny felt invisible, didn't mean she actually *was.* It had to be a trick of the light. She was just freaked out. That was it.

She breathed in and out, trying to steady herself. It was nothing. It was just the wind and the lightning flashing steadily from beyond the clouds, and the contagious fear that something terrible had happened to them. It was just the light and her mind. Just her own mind.

Could it be possible that somehow she was really, truly, in real life, turning invisible? That everything she had always secretly wanted and yet been so afraid of was coming true?

"Well," said Nathaniel. "Door's open. I guess we have a way off the roof now."

"So, where do we go?" Will asked. "What do we do now?"

"What? Why do *I* have to come up with a solution?" Nathaniel took his glasses off and wiped them nervously on his T-shirt.

"Because you're the smart one," Will said.

"Because you always used to," said Lu.

"No, I didn't," said Nathaniel. "It was my brother. He always knew what to do. I just followed along."

Tiny's chest tightened.

"But we can't ask Tobias," she said. She put a hand on his back. Nathaniel looked up at her. His Adam's apple moved up and down, like he was swallowing hard. "I wish we could. So can we ask you?" Nathaniel looked down at his hands, fidgeting. "Will you help us?"

"I don't know," said Nathaniel. "Why me? What makes you think I'll know the right thing to do?"

Tiny chewed her lower lip.

"What about Tobias's paper?" she said. "The one he wrote for that scholarship?"

"The Anders scholarship?" Nathaniel asked.

"Yeah. Could we get that? It might have answers."

"Where would it be?" Lu asked.

Nathaniel paused. "School," he said. "It's bound and published in the school academic archives." Something sparked in his eyes. "Actually, yeah, this could work. Tobias was storm chasing, kind of. His paper was on the relationship between climate change and electrical storms, specifically on the question of whether the atmosphere of big cities is more conducive to lightning. If we can get down there and find it, we may be able to figure out what to do without having to go to a hospital or tell our parents."

"Uh, what?" Will looked disgusted. "It's a Friday night, and you want us to go back to *school*?"

"You don't have to come with us," said Lu. "You can just stay that way forever." She turned back to Nathaniel. "Okay, so it's settled. We're going to school to find the answers in your brother's paper."

Tiny closed her eyes just as another flash of lightning lit up the sky behind the clouds. The storm seemed to be hovering right above her. For one brief, eerie moment, Tiny had the feeling that it was waiting for her to decide what to do.

She could walk through that roof door and go home. Take off this stupid outfit and put on her oversize T-shirt dress. Crawl under the covers and wait, against all odds, to reappear.

The SATs were tomorrow. Only the single most defining moment of her high school life.

But it was hard to care about a stupid test when you were kind of disappearing.

"Let's go," she said. "If we hurry, we can beat the rain."

Lu

She wasn't cold.

It wasn't even that cold out. And yet Lu could hardly feel her fingers. The skin on her arms felt numb, like her mouth felt that time she'd had a cavity filled.

Would they think she was crazy if she said something? Wasn't lightning supposed to hurt? Was it possible that it had made her numb instead? Or was she imagining it? It's not like there was something outwardly wrong with her, like Will. Or that she'd done something totally crazy, pulling a door off its hinges like Nathaniel. She just felt kind of weird.

Or actually, she didn't feel anything at all.

But they were already making their way through the door Nathaniel had muscled open, and Lu felt like the time for saying something had passed. Maybe it was better to just get downtown to school, find Tobias's paper in the archives, and get the answers they needed as soon as possible. Maybe if she were lucky, the numbness would wear off by then and she wouldn't have to say anything at all.

It was just as dark inside as it was outside.

The power was out.

The couple was still making out on the couch as if nothing had happened. The four of them kept going, back through the upstairs hall, the many rooms, down the stairs, through the party. What a fucking castle.

Inside, the place was in total chaos, and people were squealing and huddled together in clusters across the vast foyer. Every few seconds a lighter flicked open or a flashlight turned on, throwing pinpricks of light across the apartment like stars at a planetarium. Lu grinned at how fucking poetic she was sometimes.

When they passed through the living room, Will/Jon muttered, "Crap. I hope it's dark enough that no one goes mistaking me for the real Jon."

Lu shot a sidelong look at Will, and felt a twinge of satisfaction. Will got everything he wanted. So let him struggle for once.

Except Will wasn't exactly struggling. It wasn't *that* dark, and people were definitely mistaking him for the real Jon Heller. As in, full-on moving out of his way to let him pass. There was some Red Sea–level parting going on. Lu gawked. Was this what life was like for Will, too? No wonder he'd wanted to be cool.

As he squeezed between two brunette sophomores to get to the front door, one of them turned and put a hand on her hip, all like, *Ex*-cuse *me*. When Will moved out of a shadow, she instantly flashed him a smile. "Oh, hey, Jon!"

Will looked freaked. "Uh, hey," said Will. "Sorry, who are you?"

The girl burst out laughing. "You are so *funny*!" she said, and turned back to her friends.

Lu caught Will's—or Jon's—eye.

"Shut up, Luella," he said.

Lu grinned. "I didn't say a word!"

They made their way through the party, past the leering IT'S THE END OF THE WORLD AS WE KNOW IT sign and the guy wearing the snorkel, laughing a sinister, horrible laugh, and out the front door, where Lu paused to take a giant breath. She made up a mantra that she repeated over and over in her head.

I can breathe.

I am not anesthetized.

I am a renowned warrior.

The four of them stood on the stoop for a second. Lu looked at the others.

Flash—

Tiny, her best friend, flickering in and out like she was some kind of hologram.

Flash—

Will, her onetime friend and maybe more, who had changed so much since the years in between, had completely transformed again into a totally different person.

Flash—

Nathaniel, the brains behind the operation, who had disappeared off the face of the planet or at least the high school social scene, and thrown himself into his work, was now, kind of, bizarrely, superhuman.

And then there was Lu, cut off from everything, numb to the heat, the cold, the wind, and anything else that might come her way.

They had been struck by lightning, all right. But the bigger question on Lu's mind was: What the hell had the lightning done to them?

The sidewalk was dark, but it hadn't started raining yet. The clouds rumbled discontentedly, and she knew that it would rain soon. The sky was black, and the clouds were heavy, and she couldn't see the stars. The storm wasn't over.

It was only just beginning.

Will

They walked to the subway, hoping it hadn't been shut down yet.

On the way, Will thought about fear. He mentally cataloged all the things he'd been afraid of since high school started.

Making the soccer team.

Not making the soccer team.

Lu loving him back.

Lu *not* loving him back.

Staying the same.

Not staying the same.

All his fears came in twos.

Then Will thought about the thing that plagued him the most:

Turning into someone he didn't recognize anymore.

He'd wanted to be someone different. Well, here he was. It's like the lightning *knew.*

Will flinched. He thought about how hard he'd worked the past three years to turn into the person he'd become. The crazy diets, the compulsive workout routines, waking up at five a.m. to run every day just to feel like he deserved his spot on the soccer team. Going along with the team groupthink mentality, letting the guys decide what he did and where he went and who he talked to. Lately the anxiety spirals, the nightmares. Pretending to be someone he wasn't. No, not pretending. Believing.

He turned to Nathaniel.

"Hey, dude?"

"Yeah," Nathaniel said.

"Even if we did go to a hospital, I don't think . . ." He paused to think about how to phrase this. "I don't think they'll be able to fix the kind of problems we have."

Nathaniel's expression darkened. But maybe it was just that they were passing between two streetlamps and a shadow had fallen over them.

"I was thinking that too."

"Do you really think your brother's paper will have the, um, answers?"

"I don't know," Nathaniel said. "But right now I don't have any other ideas." He paused. "If anyone has answers, it's Tobias."

If Tobias had the answers, then Will could get back to his normal self. Everything would be fine. He could return to the party, take the SATs, and then life would go back to the way it always was. Or at least, had been lately.

He glanced at Luella. But then she might not ever speak to him again. She was barely speaking to him *now.* She was the last person he expected to show up at his party. But she was the one he was happiest to see.

She had said to *prove it.*

But what did that even mean?

Girls were so confusing.

The green light of the subway glowed brightly ahead of them. Will felt the ground rumble beneath his feet. He looked up at Lu, Nathaniel, and Tiny. His old childhood friends. The three people who used to know him better than anyone else in the world.

"Is that thunder?" he said. Nathaniel's pupils dilated and his ears almost visibly perked. He looked like a wise owl.

"No," he said, breaking into a run toward the subway entrance. "A downtown train!"

The four of them ran down the steps. The train was just pulling into the station. He reached for his MetroCard, but—

"No!" Will slapped his forehead. "I left it at home!"

"Just jump!" Nathaniel yelled. And then, as Will watched, his mouth gaping open, Nathaniel launched himself like a pole jumper over the turnstile without paying. Actually, launching himself wasn't really the right word for it. It was more like leaped. Floated. *Flew.* "Whoa," he said when he landed.

"Dude," said Will.

Lu grinned. She ducked under and scooted her way through. Lu was always one devious suggestion away from being a criminal.

"Hurry!" Nathaniel yelled.

Tiny followed Lu, swiping her MetroCard.

The conductor was announcing the next stop.

"Will!" called Lu.

Will tried to squeeze under the turnstile, but he didn't fit. The train doors were closing. Nathaniel held them open with both hands.

"How is he doing that?" Lu asked.

"I don't know, but it won't matter if Will can't get through!" Tiny said.

Then Will tried to jump, but it wasn't as easy as Nathaniel had made it look.

Finally Nathaniel let go of the doors and ran back to Will. He pulled the turnstile clean off the hinges. Will burst through just as the train was pulling away.

"Come on!"

He stepped back, cursing under his breath.

"It's okay," said Tiny. "We'll wait for the next one."

Will stole a glance at Nathaniel. He hadn't even broken a sweat.

The seconds ticked by. Then minutes. He fidgeted and paced. *"Attention."* A tinny voice crackled over the speaker system. *"Due to inclement weather, for the safety of our passengers, subway service is being preemptively suspended until further notice. . . ."*

They all groaned. Will balled his hands into fists.

The four of them turned back toward the stairs. It was going to be a long night. But Will would sooner drown than give up.

Nathaniel

"Okay, it's okay. It's just a minor setback." Nathaniel paced. They were on the street again, in the dark. "We'll figure something out."

They'd only been underground for five or ten minutes, but somehow the street seemed even more deserted now than it had before. All the sane people were looking for shelter. They were going home, and the four of them were getting farther and farther away from it.

Nathaniel took out his phone to find the screen was full of alerts.

SUBWAY SERVICE: SUSPENDED.

BUS SERVICE: SUSPENDED.

METRO-NORTH AND LONG ISLAND RAILROAD SERVICE: CANCELED.

ALL FLIGHTS IN AND OUT OF JFK, LAGUARDIA, NEWARK: CANCELED.

REDUCED TAXI SERVICE.

TRAFFIC BAN: STAY OFF THE ROADS!

HURRICANE WARNING: IN EFFECT FOR THE TRI-STATE AREA.

FLOOD WARNING: IN EFFECT FOR NEW YORK CITY.

"Shit," Nathaniel said. "These alerts all came in the last hour. The weather reports must be getting worse."

"I knew I should have listened to the news," Tiny muttered.

The others crowded around his phone as Nathaniel pulled up Weather.com.

"The rain is supposed to start tonight and continue through Sunday evening. It's no longer being considered a hurricane. It's now being called a *superstorm*."

"Jeez. I was just kidding about the whole Stormpocalypse thing," said Will.

"Superstorm Eileen," Lu said. "Who comes up with these names? Sandy? Gloria? Iris? They all sound like grandmas."

Nathaniel groaned. "They just need a Superstorm Bubbe, and my grandma will be happy."

"Should we go home?" said Tiny. "Maybe we should all go home. We'll be safe there, and maybe by the morning these weird side effects will have gone away. We can all FaceTime and check in."

"I don't know," said Will. He still looked like Jon Heller, complete with the purposefully messy prep school hair and the perpetually squinty, kind of stoned look that girls were always saying made him look like James Franco. "The party's still going on. What if I run into the real Jon? Or someone else mistakes me for him?"

"Yeah," said Lu. "Plus, it's just really creepy."

"And I want to get to the bottom of this," Nathaniel said. "Figure out what's going on." What he didn't say was: it's what Tobias would have done. Tobias wouldn't have run home. He would have led the four of them downtown and he would have done the math and made it right. He would have used his superbrain to figure out how to fix things.

Nathaniel turned to face the empty street. No subway. No buses. No cabs.

"Should we hitchhike?"

"No way, dude. I may be big, but that's how people get straight-up murdered."

"Uh, guys," Tiny said. "Where's Lu?"

Lu wasn't standing with them. She wasn't down the block, in one direction or the other. Lu was gone.

Will looked stricken. "Where did she go?" He turned to Nathaniel and grabbed the neck of his T-shirt so tightly in his fist that he lifted Nathaniel off the ground. "Nathaniel! What should we do?"

Nathaniel had no idea what to do, to be honest. He wasn't a leader, deep down. He couldn't even wake up in time to turn in his scholarship application. Everyone was suddenly turning to him because he was the smart one, because tonight he had some kind of weird superpowers, and he felt like he had to live up to them. What they didn't know was that he didn't feel worthy of having them.

One minute he'd been getting ready to take the most important test of his life, and he got suckered into being at this party because he didn't have the guts to say no.

And then the next minute there he was on the roof, wanting so badly to make someone smile. Hoping for something. It was something he hadn't felt in so long.

The feeling of wanting to be a hero.

Because when the lightning had lit up the night so brightly like that, all of them, faces upturned, and he had looked over at Tiny—who had been just standing there, her eyes closed, all bathed in light—he'd thought for a moment that it was the most beautiful thing he'd ever seen in his life. It was like he'd never really seen her before, not ever, and then all of a sudden there she was, like the lightning had cut a path through the darkness on the roof right to her, and he could see her so clearly, it was like her insides were lit up and there were her kidneys and her lungs and esophagus and liver and heart beating wildly like she was an X-ray that had been electrified.

She'd seemed so lonely up there on that roof, so tired of being invisible. And he suddenly had the weird feeling, small but persistent, pushing its way to the surface of his mind, that he needed her to understand she wasn't alone. And maybe he needed to know for sure he wasn't alone, either.

Where could Lu have gone? He felt responsible now, for the group. He had to lead them to the answer. Even if it took all night. And tomorrow. And the next day. They would make it through the storm, and they would come out the other side.

It was what Tobias would have done.

11:00 P.M.

(9 Hours Left)

ATMOSPHERIC DISTURBANCE

Tiny

The wind was starting to sound operatic.

"Where could she be?" Will was frantic. "She's all alone out there in the storm!"

"She can handle it," Tiny said. "If anyone can, it's Lu. She's scrappy."

Will considered this. "That's true."

"She's tough. She'll be okay. And she'd be super pissed if she knew you were talking about her like she's some princess who needs to be rescued."

Will/Jon's face turned pale, probably at the thought of Lu being super pissed at him again.

"Besides," said Tiny. "I know where she is."

Will and Nathaniel turned to her. "You do?" they said in unison.

Tiny nodded. They weren't as close as they used to be, but Tiny knew Lu almost as well as she knew herself.

"She went back to Central Park. To Hurricane Fest."

She had gone to find Owen.

They took off in the direction of the park. Lu hadn't been missing for that long, so she couldn't have gotten too far. Tiny watched her reflection in the windows of stores and apartment buildings as they ran, flickering in the dark between each brightly lit streetlamp.

She felt a weird mix of fear and elation. She was disappearing. She definitely was.

At the entrance to the park, they stopped. "Which direction is Hurricane Fest?" Tiny muttered.

"You got me," Will said. "Weren't you and Lu going to go there anyway?"

"Lu was the one who knew where we were going—not me."

And that's when Tiny realized something.

Going out tonight, it had never been about her and Josh.

Lu's plan was always to go find Owen. Tiny had just been her excuse.

The boys were watching her. She couldn't even meet their eyes.

She wondered: If she stopped holding on to this friendship, would Lu miss her? It was the last connection she had to her old life, before the night Tobias—

A pair of figures emerged from the dark.

"What the hell is that?" Will whispered. "We probably shouldn't just stand around here so late at night."

"Don't make eye contact," Tiny whispered back.

"Good thing Nathaniel is strong as fuck."

"Just because I can tear a door off its hinges doesn't mean I can take on two guys who are fighting back," Nathaniel said.

As the figures drew closer, Tiny realized it wasn't two big guys. It was a guy and a girl, maybe a few years older than they were. The guy was short, with a jet-black asymmetrical haircut, and a beard.

The girl was ethereal and flowy, her long, shocking red hair swirling in the wind. They half danced, half slunk toward them. It was hard not to notice them—they looked like they were in a movie, floating dreamily along the path between the streetlights and weaving between the trees.

They were like an indie prince and princess.

"Hey," Tiny said. "I recognize them."

"Those kids went to Daybrook?" Will made a face. "I've never seen them before."

"Yeah," Tiny said. "They graduated last year."

"They don't look familiar."

"They did theater," Tiny explained. "And since I'm sure you wouldn't dare step foot in the theater for any reason other than assembly . . ."

Will glowered. "I've seen school plays."

The princess skipped past, unknowingly knocking Tiny backward as she found a lamp pole to lean against, sighing.

It felt stupid to have been brushed aside by such an incredibly beautiful person. Tiny wondered if the princess had even seen her. She pulled back and looked down at herself. Tiny looked like someone had tried to erase her with a not-very-good eraser. Still there, but just a little bit less there than she'd been before the girl had pushed her out of the way.

The guy shouted: "Ladies and gentlemen!"

Tiny looked around. It was just the three of them.

"If the world ends tonight, let it to go out in a blaze of art and beauty! Let the last thing you remember be Shakespeare! On this dark and stormy Friday night, we are proud and honored to present to you: Shakespeare in the Park!"

"I've always wanted to see Shakespeare in the Park!" Tiny said.

"More like Shakespeare at the Park Entrance," muttered Will.

"Hey," the girl said, opening her eyes. "This is no amateur performance. We go to Tisch School of the Arts. Can we continue?"

The guy got down on one knee and put a hand over his heart. Will snorted.

"But, soft!" Romeo stage-whispered. "What light through yonder window breaks? It is the east, and Juliet is the sun."

Juliet sighed and twirled around a lamppost like a hipster Elizabethan stripper. Tiny half expected her to pirouette away on a breeze.

"O, Romeo, Romeo, wherefore art thou, *Romeo*?"

"Shall I hear more, or shall I speak at this?"

"Speak at this!" Will shouted.

Tiny gave him a look, but she wasn't sure he could see it.

Inside, she couldn't help resenting them, though. Just a little bit. Sure, they looked all romantic and cool, and everyone was smiling like Romeo and Juliet weren't going to have a tragic miscommunication and kill themselves in a few acts. But there was no such thing as a happy ending. That kind of stuff didn't happen in real life. Star-crossed lovers weren't meant to be together—that was why they were *star-crossed* and not just *regular* lovers.

Tiny knew this better than anyone. She knew it in her heart and lungs and on the underside of her skin—places it was hard to get it out.

"Oh, come on," she snapped. "Romeo and Juliet die at the end." She didn't realize she'd even opened her mouth until she looked up and saw that the actors had paused between lines. Her voice echoed in the awkward silence.

"Hey!" Juliet shouted, one hand on her hip.

"Do you mind?" Romeo said angrily.

"I mean, seriously?" Juliet flipped her hair over her shoulder. "I think everyone knows that already."

"What the hell?" Will said, throwing up his hands. "I didn't!"

Nathaniel rolled his eyes. "Dude, really? We read it in freshman English."

"No," said Will. "*You* read it in freshman English."

"Whatever," Romeo added. "There are, like, a million movie versions. There's really no excuse."

"Well, sorr-ee for having a social life and not spending all my free time with my nose in a book, like some people." Will jutted his chin at Nathaniel.

"Listen," Nathaniel shot back. "It's because I spend all my time studying that I might be able to help us get out of this nightmare."

Tiny let them argue. She turned back to Romeo and Juliet.

"Sorry," she said. "We're having a bad night."

"It's okay," said Romeo. He looked closer and squinted. "Whoa," he said. "You're transparent."

"Yeah." Tiny shrugged, like, *What can ya do?*

"What happened?" Juliet asked, wide-eyed.

"I got struck by lightning."

Juliet grabbed Romeo's hand and gasped.

"That is literally the most dramatic thing I've ever heard," she said.

Tiny didn't know how to respond to that.

Juliet took a step back and appraised her. "Hmm," she said. "I might be able to help." She reached into her purse and extracted a makeup bag. "May I?" Tiny opened her mouth to say no. Then she closed it. Then she opened it again.

"Okay. Why not try it?" Juliet got to work. She dusted some

powder over Tiny's face and brushed a rosy shimmery blush onto her cheeks. There was a zing of eyeliner and a whoosh of mascara and a slick of berry gloss across her lips.

"Pucker."

Tiny puckered.

"Look."

Tiny looked at her reflection in the little compact mirror. In the movies, putting makeup on the invisible girl always seemed to make people notice her. So was it helping? Was the girl who looked back at her more beautiful than she had been before? Was she someone worth noticing, now that her eyes were lined and her lips were glossed? Her heart lifted at the thought. But then Tiny saw herself fade just a little bit more, behind the blush and mascara, like a waning lunar eclipse. And her heart fell again.

"Feel any different?" Juliet asked hopefully.

"No," Tiny said. "I'm sorry. But thanks anyway."

"Man," said Juliet. "I really thought that would work."

Tiny thought of something. "Actually, maybe you can help. We're looking for Hurricane Fest. Do you know where it is?"

Juliet beamed. "Yes! We just performed there."

"You could hardly hear us over the music," said Romeo. "I can't believe it hasn't been broken up yet."

"But the music is good," Juliet added. "If you go now, you'll probably make it in time to hear Unsexy Gum. They're great."

Unsexy Gum. That was Owen's band!

"It's just down that path and under the footbridge. You definitely can't miss it."

"Thanks," said Tiny, grabbing Nathaniel and Will by the sleeves. "We owe you one!"

"Good luck!" Juliet called. "You were our most enthusiastic audience all night! Except for you." She frowned at Will. "I don't know who you think you are, but if you keep making fun of things, you'll miss out on everything."

"On what?" Will asked.

"On all this." Juliet spread her arms and twirled. The wind caught her dress and swept her hair up like a Disney character. Tiny thought she might be about to break into song. "Anyway, see ya," she said. And they started walking down the path out of the park.

"Godspeed!" Romeo waved. "'Our doubts are traitors, and make us lose the good we oft might win, by fearing to attempt!'"

"Whatever that means," Will muttered. "Whatever any of that means."

The night air was heavy, and the wind was still blowing like mad. Juliet's perfect twirly beauty still taunted her. Despite the makeup, she felt even more invisible. Tiny wondered if, when Juliet saw Romeo at that party, all the decisions were suddenly easy for her. She wondered if Juliet ever really stopped to wonder, wait a minute, if I let this guy into my life, will I end up dead in some mausoleum in Verona somewhere? Probably not. Because there's no way to know how things will end up until they end up there.

Tiny wondered where she would end up.

The truth was, she didn't fit in anywhere, and if she could choose one group to fit into, she didn't even know which one it would be.

It was why she was always grateful to be friends with Lu. She admired Lu, she really did. Lu didn't want to fit into any of the groups. Lu said "fuck you" to groups. Except that meant if she didn't have Lu, she had no one left.

"You're, like, the only person I can be strange with," Lu told her on the last day of sixth grade. They had been sitting outside the Guggenheim Museum and gulping down ice cream and the promise of summer. Ahead of them stretched infinity more warm breezy start-of-summer days like this. Even then Tiny knew exactly what Lu meant, because she felt it too.

In *The Great Gatsby*, which was fast becoming her favorite book, Nick Carraway says this thing: *The rock of the world was founded securely on a fairy's wing.*

When Tiny read it, her heart stumbled a little. It made her think of how a person's whole life could be anchored to something so intangible. A crush. A grade. A college. An image of yourself you have in your head. A best friend.

I have to find Lu.

Tiny blinked, standing in the middle of Central Park. She looked down at herself under the orange glow of a streetlamp. Her skin flickered in and out. She hesitated.

She realized in that moment that she had a choice.

If she fled the park and ran for home, she would only continue to fade into nothingness. She would dry up and float away with nothing more than a little pop. She'd fizzle out like a lightbulb in a power outage.

Or she could smack her berry-glossed lips, stand a little straighter, and keep going down the path ahead. She might have been fading away, but she hadn't lost sight of herself just yet.

The risk in the decision lay, not in making the right choice, but just in taking the leap to choose. In the act of choosing itself.

She didn't know what would happen at Hurricane Fest, or the rest of the night, but she knew something would. As Lu would say, *What if?*

And for once in her life, she wanted to find out badly enough to risk choosing.

Lu

Hurricane Fest was festive.

A hidden corner of Central Park was transformed into a strange nighttime urban park wonderland. Strings of white twinkle lights and colorful paper lanterns were woven through the trees, and someone had strewn oriental rugs across the grass so it felt like they were in an elaborate outdoor bohemian living room. Lu was impressed that the cops hadn't discovered it yet. It was for sure not sanctioned by the parks department.

Everyone was dancing. A pile of wooden pallets formed a makeshift stage on one side, and the band was rocking out. A huge generator buzzed in the corner, powering the whole operation. It was almost possible to forget when and where you were. It could have easily slipped her mind that Superstorm Eileen was bearing down on them, and that the SATs were less than nine hours away.

Lu tilted her head back and looked up: the clouds still churned, dark gray against the dark black sky, no moon, no stars, just the rumble of thunder and the currents of lightning. It didn't look like they were touching the ground right now, just shooting out horizontally, suspending between the clouds themselves like ionic spider webs.

No one cared about the storm. They just wanted to dance, and party, and ignore things like safety and not dying. That was the weird thing about New York. There were all those buildings, all those places for people to hide. When the streets were empty, all those eight million people had to be *some*where. And it looked like a lot of them were here. This was a pocket of the city that existed in an alternate dimension.

Lu felt her way in the twinkle-lit park, through the crowd. The thunder was so loud that she should have been able to feel the vibrations running through the ground, through the rugs beneath her feet. But she didn't. She couldn't feel anything at all.

She stood on her tiptoes and tried to see through the ridiculous crowd. She thought she saw the familiar-looking back of his head up by the stage. So she barreled through. She wanted to make a scene, but she kept it in and tried to be cool. People shoved her and elbowed her and stepped on her with pointy-toed shoes. But Lu couldn't feel any of it. She was numb.

She was *invincible.*

She grinned.

But when she pushed through the crowd, there he was—with his arm around another girl.

Earlier, in the subway, Lu had seen through the windows of the subway cars as they'd passed her and the others by. Their best chance at getting downtown, hurtling away from them into the dark underground tunnels of Manhattan. But she'd gotten a glimpse. She'd seen what life *could* have been.

Everyone else on the train seemed like they were in full-on storm-panic mode. Everyone was wearing some kind of raincoat or carrying an umbrella or had bags of groceries because they had thought ahead and were now on their way home to hunker down and wait out the storm.

Everyone had looked *prepared*.

It only made the strange numbness surrounding Lu feel worse. It had started in her fingers and toes, coating the skin on her arms. But now she couldn't feel her face, her feet, her legs, the tips of her ears. It was seeping in under her skin, too. What if it reached her lungs? What if she stopped breathing? What if it reached her heart? What if it stopped beating?

So when Tiny, Will, and Nathaniel weren't looking, she had turned on her platform heels and run like the wind currently howling between the trees of Central Park.

Lu's usual MO when faced with feeling (any kind of feeling) was to run. And now was no exception.

The sky was black and blue and so was her heart, but she couldn't feel the bruise.

She pictured a forcefield around her, a bubble of energy no one could fight their way through.

On her way to the park she passed Hunter College. Where she first became close with Will, three years ago. Where she took her very first acting class.

It had come in pretty handy all this time.

"Owen?" Lu tapped him on the back.

He turned around.

"Lu!" he said. "You came!"

"Uh, you asked me to." Lu glanced at the girl behind him. She had a blond pixie cut and was giving Lu the side eye. "What's going on?" Lu said.

Owen glanced at Pixie Girl. "I'll be right back, Jess." He touched Lu's elbow. "Come on," he said. "Let's find somewhere quieter." She used to love it when he touched her elbow like that. It was calm, reassuring, like he knew where he was going. Now she couldn't feel a thing. Except, well, kind of embarrassed.

They found a spot near a tree farther back from the stage. Lu pushed her black bangs out of her eyes and looked up at him. They stood there on one of those stupid Persian rugs in the middle of the park, some stupid orchestral indie band playing in the background like they were in some movie, and all the while thunder was rumbling closer and closer. For a second Lu let herself wonder if he was going to apologize, to tell her she misunderstood the whole thing.

"Hey," she said.

"Lu," Owen said now, on this night, on this rug, in the middle of this park. "Hey. I'm glad you came." Then he hugged her.

She couldn't feel his arms around her. She couldn't feel the warmth of his neck against her cheek.

She pulled away.

"What are you doing?" she said.

"What?" he said, grinning his stupid crooked grin. "I can't hug you?"

Lu pushed herself away. "No. I got your texts."

"Yeah," he said, "listen—"

"I think we should end this." Lu cut in early, before he could say anything else.

"You do?" he said, surprised.

"Yeah, I do. And you're clearly busy, so I'll let you get back to Pixie, or whoever—"

"Who, Jess? That's my friend from band camp."

"Band camp?"

"Uh-huh, she came to the show. But listen, don't end this. We were having fun, right?"

"Yeah," Lu said, narrowing her eyes. "Fun. In secret."

"Come on, Lu. It's us! We don't need all those labels and restrictions. Those are for boring uptight people."

Lu hesitated. She paused to consider what she felt. Right now it was hard to feel much of anything. And maybe it was because of that that she wasn't afraid when she said:

"What if I said I do want those things?"

Owen furrowed his eyebrows. He put his hand on her shoulder.

"You're great," he said. "But I can't have a girlfriend right now. Things are really taking off with the band, and, like—that's where all my energy needs to be." He squeezed her shoulder. "Can't we just keep hanging out like this?"

"So wait," she said. "You're not breaking up with me?"

Owen laughed. "Of course not! You're the coolest!"

"But you don't want to be my boyfriend."

"Right," said Owen. "Got it."

"So what did you mean when you said you wanted to talk?"

"Oh," said Owen. "I just wanted to make sure it was all good. Because I'm kind of hanging out with Jess, too, and—"

"What?" Lu took a step back.

"Are you upset? I thought we were cool."

Lu thought for a minute. Maybe she should pretend that it was. But then, suddenly, she thought of Will. And she surprised herself.

"No," she said. "It's not cool. Nothing about this is cool."

Lu realized something: She might have been invincible on the outside, but it still hurt on the inside.

"Aw, Lu." The wind was whipping his floppy hair around, and he had this weird look on his face, like when someone else has this horrible accident you are in no way part of and you feel helpless and small and sorry and wish you could help, but the truth is there's nothing you can do. "Friends though, right?"

She opened her mouth and closed it again.

Nothing hurts you.

You are an impenetrable fortress.

You are a renowned goddamn warrior.

"Friends?" Lu said. "I don't want to be your—"

"Fuck you!" someone shouted. "You're not Lu's friend!"

Lu's head snapped up just in time to see a fist connect with Owen's face.

And he fell down.

Will

No one had ever prepared him for the feeling of his fist connecting with someone's jaw.

"Ow!" Will shook his hand. He wasn't sure he liked it.

But holy shit. He'd punched someone!

"Take that!" Will crowed over the sound of the electric cello in the background. "You can't treat Lu that way!" Tiny and Nathaniel were cheering behind him.

"Will!" Lu shoved him. As much as it hurt, he was glad she realized it was him and not Jon Heller randomly coming to her rescue. "What the hell are you doing? I can take care of myself!" Then her eyes grew wide. "Wait." Her head whipped back to Owen, lying on the fancy patterned rug, groaning, and then back to him. "Will?"

Will puffed up his chest. "Yep. You said to prove it so—"

"First of all, I don't need *saving*." Lu rolled her eyes. "I'm not some dumb damsel in distress."

"Told you," said Tiny.

"Are you kidding? I can't believe you like that guy. Is that the kind of guy you want to be with, Lu? Really?"

"If you think he's so lame, why did you turn into him?"

"I—what?"

"You did it again. You turned into Owen."

"I *what*?"

"Does anyone have a mirror?" Lu yelled into the crowd. A girl who was standing nearby, filming the whole thing on her phone, pressed a button that made the screen go shiny and reflective. She offered it to Lu, and Lu shoved it in Will's face.

Will's jaw dropped.

He didn't look like Jon Heller anymore. He didn't look like himself, either. His cheeks had sunken in, and his cheekbones were sharp, and his hair had grown long and shaggy and swept across his eyes. He pushed it away and saw the face looking back at him clearly.

"You transformed into *Owen*?" Lu was pointing between them. She turned her face upward and shouted at the sky: "What the hell, lightning? I don't get you!"

At the sound of his name, Owen groaned loudly and sat up. "Hey, what's going on? Some asshole punched me!"

"Don't talk to him that way!" Lu yelled. She punched Owen too, and he fell back down.

Will beamed at her.

"Look at you!" Will said. "Defending my honor."

"Shut up." Lu pushed him.

"You shut up!" He pushed her back.

"Ugh, I can't believe you turned into *Owen*," she groaned. "Of all people. Seriously, Will!"

"It's not like I can *control* it! It just . . . happens!"

That was only partly true, Will was starting to realize. He wasn't able to control when and where he changed—*that* part was true. But both times he had been thinking about that very person before he morphed into them. On the roof, he had been thinking about how much like Jon Heller he was becoming. And here, in the park, he had been wondering what Lu—his Lu—could see in a guy like Owen. Would Lu like him better if he were more like this band hipster? Was that more her type, or whatever?

Would he be happier that way?

And then boom. He *was* that band hipster.

It was a very weird feeling.

Tiny came bounding up and threw her arms around Lu. "You totally showed him! I'm so proud of you, Loozles!"

"Yeah, well . . ." Lu turned red, but she was kind of smiling. Will loved to see her smile like that. It was a rare, unguarded moment. She turned to him. "Did you come all the way here just to do that?" She nodded her chin at Owen, still lying unconscious on the rug.

"Well," said Will. "I mean, yeah."

Lu's smile deepened into something more than a smile. Something Will couldn't describe.

"Thanks," she said. This time he was the one who turned red.

It had been a long time since he had felt this way. But being here with her tonight calmed the inner voices telling him he was the worst, that he was doomed, that he wasn't the same person he used to be. The voices that told him he'd turned everything in his life into a big worthless mess. And that he was one too. Lu made him feel like a better person somehow.

He looked around him for the first time. He was surrounded by lights and music, and kids dancing and laughing and having *fun*. No one was overthinking things or paralyzed by fear. No one thought they might get struck by lightning or drown in the rain that was supposed to come pouring down at any minute. They were just living. Will was living too. He hated the way Lu and Owen looked together. He hated imagining her with anyone else but him. He'd been feeling this way for three years, and just kept pretending it away. But tonight he was having a hard time pretending.

Maybe tonight was a night for second chances. Maybe it was a way of reclaiming who he used to be.

Maybe the lightning had been a *good* thing.

"What?" he said. Nathaniel was saying something.

"I said, we actually came here to get Lu so we could make it down to school and figure out whatever it is the lightning did to us," he said. "But if you want to stay here and be a hero . . ."

Will stopped listening. He grabbed Lu's hand. "Hey," she said, squirming away. "What are you doing?"

"Come on," he said. "Let's dance!"

"Owen! I mean, Will!" She looked at him. "Are you insane?"

"Maybe," said Will. "Maybe I am."

"Everything is so easy for you," Lu said, looking up into his new, weird face.

He couldn't get used to this different facial architecture. He couldn't make the same expressions he used to. He didn't feel like himself. Whoever that was. Maybe that was the point. *That* was what the lightning was trying to tell him.

Will shook his head. Talking like the lightning really was magic. He was starting to sound like Luella.

"You have no idea," said Will, "how very untrue that is."

And then there was a flash that lit up the sky above the trees. It turned the inky sky to day.

And then thunder. A booming so loud that it shook the concrete.

And then the snapping of a tree trunk. Will looked up. They were standing under a massive towering oak strung with lights and paper lanterns that had caught fire in the lightning and was beginning to burn.

It took a second for him to realize that the burning tree was falling. It was falling toward them.

Nathaniel

No one wakes up in the morning expecting to be a hero that day.

In fact, the more Nathaniel read about heroism, the more he began to think that people who did heroic things were wired that way. Like, they didn't think about it; it wasn't a conscious decision they made ahead of time. They just acted on instinct and a sense of right, and then later history and context framed them as heroes.

Nathaniel wondered how history would frame him now. He was standing in the middle of Central Park, surrounded by the chaos of a major atmospheric disturbance, holding an oak tree above his head with his two not particularly muscly arms.

Will, Tiny, and Lu were staring at him, incredulous.

"Dude!" yelled Will. "You saved us!"

Nathaniel grinned. Because here was what had happened:

1) He felt a deep rumbling coming up from the core of the earth and through the soles of his sneakers

2) He sensed a change in the electrical charges that were colliding and zapping around like supercharged bees in the cloud above him

3) He heard the crack and saw the lightning in slow-motion, watching in awe as it descended in jagged steps from the sky

4) He knew exactly which tree it was going to strike

5) Before he knew what had happened, he'd beaten the lightning to the tree.

The whole thing took less than a second.

He wasn't just a hero; he knew that now. The lightning had turned him into a *super*hero.

Thinking about it in a glass-half-full kind of way, getting struck by lightning and turning into a superhero was sort of the culmination of all his comic-book-reading childhood dreams. He must have experienced some kind of kinetic absorption, pulling energy from the lightning and converting it into a kind of power he'd never felt before: physical strength, sharper senses, a keener mind, superhuman instinct. He could do anything he wanted. He could *be* anything he put his mind to.

He could have a cool nickname, like Lightning Man or The Zag.

But if he looked at his situation in a glass-half-empty kind of way, that presented a problem. In the years since he'd been a child, he'd grown up into someone who didn't want to be a hero. He didn't want to be responsible for having that kind of power over someone else's life. That was something he'd learned the hard way. Nathaniel had spent the past three years working toward someone else's dream. Trying to fill someone else's shoes. He'd let Tobias be the one to lead, the one to shine. And Nathaniel had followed. He had never felt worthy of finding his own thing to shine at. He had never thought he could.

Now that he could—he didn't know how.

Before he could think about it too much, he sensed another bolt of lightning brewing in the sky above. In a flash that was all but invisible to the naked eye, he caught another tree in his hands and tossed it to the side. Zipping to the other side of the stage, he pushed a group of kids out of the way of a jagged flash of white.

But he couldn't be in two places at once. There was a limit to his powers.

And across the clearing, another tree fell on the generator, exploding in a shower of sparks. The power cut out and plunged the park into darkness, except for the orange glow of the makeshift wooden stage smoldering and bursting into flame. Kids around them were screaming, pushing into one another to try to get out of the way. He had to get back to Tiny, Will, and Lu.

His ears perked up.

It was like his brain was picking up radio waves on a superhigh frequency.

Across the field, he could actually hear someone knock into Will, who knocked into Lu, and now they were bickering.

His eyesight sharpened.

It was like his eyes had a super high-tech autofocus zoom function.

And he saw Tiny standing there, the action swirling around her. She was trying to help. But no one seemed to see her trying or helping.

The hair on his arms stood on end. He could feel it. The collision of opposite charges in the clouds above them. Crackling with energy. Ready to strike.

He was off and running before the lightning zapped, before it even hit the tree towering over her. He came crashing into her, pushing her out of the way.

The two of them went flying, knocking over Lu and Will and

rolling 55 feet, 7 inches, and 2.25 centimeters (superbrain!) before landing in a heap on the grass.

"Oof," said Tiny. She actually said the word *oof.*

Nathaniel's senses were in overdrive. He was picking up so many things.

Lu's voice complaining loudly.

Tiny breathing.

The gritty sting of branches and dead autumn grass scraping along his arms and legs. The adrenaline pulsing through his head and the crashing of atoms in the air all around him.

He opened his eyes. Tiny was lying under him, staring back.

"Uh, hi," Nathaniel said. He was lying on top of her, arms on either side of her head.

"Hi," said Tiny.

"I'm trying not to crush you."

"Better you than the tree."

Nathaniel smiled. "Just trying to keep things in perspective." The two of them struggled to stand up. "Um," Nathaniel said, looking at her, all concerned. "Are you okay? Are you hurt?"

"I don't think so. Just some scrapes." She squinted and frowned. "Did you hit your head?"

"I don't know. Maybe?"

"You're bleeding."

"I am?"

"Right there," Tiny said, pointing.

Nathaniel brought a hand up to his forehead, just above his right eyebrow. A trickle of blood made its way down his cheek. "Oh man. I guess I did."

Tiny smiled. "You saved us. That was . . . brave. It reminds me of . . ." Then suddenly the smile faded from her face.

She didn't have to finish. Nathaniel knew what she was going to say.

Something suddenly looked different about Tiny. It could have been the glow of the fire crackling around the stage, but her face seemed to flicker, just for a moment. He thought he saw the grass through her skin.

"Are you okay?" he asked.

She looked up at him. "I don't think so. I'm worried I—"

"Dude!" Will barreled into him, still looking like Owen. "You have a head trauma!"

Nathaniel coughed and changed the subject. "Do you think I need stitches?"

"I *said* no way," Lu said, hobbling over. "No hospitals."

"Yeah," said Will. "We agreed. Besides, that'll heal up overnight. Don't worry—I get hit in the head all the time." Lu looked at him. "What?"

A siren blared. Blue and red police lights cast their faces in blue, then red, then blue again. "Break it up!" Kids scattered everywhere. "Anyone without ID is going to jail. Move it!" A couple more cop cars were pulling up, as well as a few ambulances.

"Run!" said Will.

"This way!" said Nathaniel, leading them in the direction of the park entrance, toward the street.

They were a bleeding, possibly concussed mess. Where did they go from here? It crossed Nathaniel's mind that they could go home; they *should* go home. Home was safe and dry. Home had Band-Aids and late-night snacks and parents who knew everything, or thought they did. But what else waited for them there? More of the same?

Not tonight. Tonight there was no going home.

What made him think that the solution to their problems would be at home within the safe walls of their apartments, other than instinct and a sense that that was where the solution had always been?

At home there were Band-Aids, yeah. And study aids. And a warm dry bed safe from the rain that was supposed to begin before morning. Home was where trustworthy newscasters advised them to be, and the walls of their concrete buildings would protect them from the lightning that seemed to be tracking them like they were some kind of prey on the nature channel.

But there was an emptiness at home too. And out here in the city streets there was thunder and lightning and music. Here, in the middle of the city, where he should have felt like a speck of dust floating in the cosmos, here—surrounded by Tiny, Lu, and Will—for the first time in three years he wasn't lonely.

Nathaniel didn't know how to see the future—that wasn't one of his superpowers, at least as far as he could tell—but he knew they couldn't go home yet. They had to stay together. They had to fix this, whatever it was, together.

They ran down the street, in and out of the shadows of streetlamps, as more cop cars descended on the park.

The music had stopped when they weren't paying attention.

THEN

The Last Day of Summer
Before High School
Three Years ago
3:00 p.m.

The Downward Stroke

Nathaniel

He and Tiny walked across the park to the West Side.

They walked quietly, not saying much, just coexisting in comfortable silence. It was always comfortable with Tiny.

Nathaniel didn't feel like going home. Tobias had been packing for college all week, and the apartment was covered with suitcases, clothes, books, and all kinds of gadgets. There was no room for Nathaniel. Every time he was there, he felt like he was in the way or in the process of being crowded out.

He was happy for his brother, in theory. Tobias was smart and worked hard. It was just that he kind of got everything he wanted. He nailed every conceivable academic achievement. His parents worshipped everything he said and did. It was a little hard to compete. He felt like a carbon copy of his older brother—almost the same, but not quite as good.

He wondered what life would be like when Tobias was at college. Would he have to work twice as hard for their attention? He couldn't help but be afraid that unless he was Tobias, they just wouldn't care that Nathaniel was still right there.

It wasn't just his parents who he was worried about. He stole a glance at Tiny, walking next to him.

Things were changing, whether he wanted them to or not. He felt . . . things.

It was just . . . he didn't know. He wasn't sure how.

But he thought about how Tobias always said that sometimes you have to take a risk, even if the odds are stacked against you. If you don't experiment, the answer will always be no.

The day was hot and humid, and he wiped sweat from his brow with the back of his arm. He was sweating for other reasons too.

"Hey," he said.

"Hey, yourself," said Tiny.

"So there's this natural disaster movie film fest at IFC next weekend."

"Cool," said Tiny. "Are they showing *Twister*? Nothing is as good as *Twister*."

"They are, indeed, showing *Twister*!" Nathaniel's heart had migrated up behind his eyeballs, and he became momentarily blind from nerves. "Want to go?"

"Uh, yeah," said Tiny. "Obviously. What else are they playing?" Nathaniel's heart now popped happily in his brain. "Luella is going to be so excited. Are they playing *Armageddon*? That's her favorite."

The pieces of Nathaniel's deflated heart sunk back down to his chest.

"*Armageddon* is not even a disaster movie," he said. "It's a space movie."

"It is so a disaster movie. Are you kidding?"

"Well, they're not playing it. Sorry."

"Fine," Tiny said. "Jeez. Why are you being weird?"

But while she was talking, a new fear was blooming in Nathaniel's brain. Suddenly he wasn't as scared of asking Tiny out. Suddenly he was more worried that once high school started, they wouldn't stay friends at all.

"Because I am weird," Nathaniel said. "This is how I am. I'm just being me."

Heat lightning simmered in the distance.

"I don't know. Maybe if you think I'm so weird, we shouldn't even be friends anymore."

"Stop," Tiny said. "That's not what I meant." She exhaled loudly. "Besides, it's not like I'm so normal, or whatever."

But she was. At least, compared to him. And now the seed was planted in his head. Was he weird? Was it normal to be so obsessed with facts and hard science?

He thought about those charges colliding up in the sky, the necessary conditions for lightning. He realized it was true: nothing can stay the same; it went against every law of physics. Things were already in motion. And an object in motion stays in motion. It was just the way the world worked. It was just science.

Tiny

The comfortable silence wasn't so comfortable anymore.

Tiny walked away, a strange feeling in the pit of her stomach. Nathaniel was being so weird lately.

Like, the other day.

She had been over at his apartment, hanging out. It was a hot, humid afternoon, and the only sane place to exist was somewhere with AC. Nathaniel, Will, and Luella had gone out to get snacks, and it was Tiny's job to find a good movie on Netflix. She had volunteered, because Tobias was home.

Tiny went right to the eighties movies and started scrolling. Tobias strolled in like he was just on a casual walk around the apartment and happened to pass the den. He plopped down next to her, kicked off his hiking boots, and put his feet in her lap.

"Gross!" said Tiny. "Get your sweaty feet off of me."

"What?" Tobias wiggled his toes. "These feet?"

"Um, yes, why are you even wearing socks in summer?"

"Because I was wearing shoes," Tobias said, like it should have been obvious.

Tiny refocused on the TV. "*Sixteen Candles*!"

Tobias groaned. "No."

"Why not?"

"Quirky high school girl has a crush from afar on an older, unattainable guy, but through a series of hilarious yet heartfelt misunderstandings, they end up together? Please. No. Barf."

"It could happen," Tiny said.

"Not likely. Keep scrolling."

"*St. Elmo's Fire*. Eighties-era Rob Lowe!"

"No," said Tobias. "Only girls like that movie. Next."

"Are you even watching this movie with us? Who gave you veto power?"

"No one. I don't wait around for people to give me things. I carpe them."

"Okay, well carpe this: *The Big Chill*!"

"Depressed grown-ups having affairs. Pass."

"*Pretty in Pink*?"

"She should have ended up with Spader. No."

"Ugh, you're the worst! Here." She handed him the remote. "You pick."

He scrolled. "*Weird Science*," they said at the same time, as Tobias pressed select.

"I should have guessed," said Tiny.

Tobias grinned. "Two boys scientifically engineer the girl of their dreams? Classic."

When Tobias said "girl of their dreams," Tiny blushed for no reason. Or maybe there was a reason. Maybe her brain had turned it all around and thought he was talking about her.

Being around him made her skin instantly warmer, like she was a kettle that had just been put on a burner. All she wanted was to lean in and put her head on his shoulder. To feel his breath rising and falling under her. She didn't even want it in a conscious way, the way you want an A on a term paper or a bagel sandwich for lunch. It was like her body had a mind of its own. She couldn't stop staring at his lips, especially when he took his glasses off to wipe them on his T-shirt, and she knew he couldn't see. When he put his glasses back on and smiled, she fought a full-body urge to run her fingers through his curly hair. She wanted to feel his arms around her. To know what it felt like to be held tight by someone other than her mom, or Luella.

She thought about him when she closed her eyes at night, and in the morning when she opened them.

Tiny was half afraid that any minute now she'd lose control entirely, forget all basic sense of human decency, and lean right in and kiss him.

"Are you hot?" Tobias said.

"What?" Tiny blinked.

"It's too hot in here. Let's go lie on the kitchen floor."

The kitchen floor was widely known as the coolest place in the house, especially in summer when the tile was nice and cold from the air conditioner.

Tiny's arms were stretched all the way above her head, and she had been trying for at least a minute or two to get herself as straight as humanly possible, straight as a board. It was an impossible feat, and one of those things you do for long spaces of time without really thinking about it; though she was concentrating hard, she wasn't really there at all. Her mind was floating upward, like a balloon, like the heat. Lying next to Tobias was making her giddy. Their arms were both extended over their heads, and their fingertips were barely touching. The Spencers' dog, Isaac Newton, kept nosing Tiny's armpit, and she desperately wanted to snap her arms down and push him away, but she didn't want to disrupt the moment with Tobias. Isaac Newton couldn't get enough of people's armpits.

"Are you all packed?" Tiny asked.

"No."

Tiny kicked Tobias's socked foot with hers. "Why do you wear hiking boots all the time?"

"I don't know. Because it reminds me that if I keep hiking, eventually I'll get where I'm going."

"I'm so jealous," Tiny said. "You're doing, like, real things. You wrote a paper that's been published." She rolled over onto her stomach and rested on her elbows. "I'd give anything to be published."

"You will be. You'll be a famous author one day, and I'll come to your book signings. What are you working on now?"

"A short story about a boy and a girl who meet on the moon."

"How are they on the moon? Do they work for NASA?"

"It's the future. She's in one of the last colonizing missions from Earth, and he was born on the moon and grew up there. He can breathe in the moon's atmosphere and she can't, so she has to keep her helmet on all the time. They hold hands in zero gravity, and they can only communicate through a sign language that they made up."

Tobias shifted over to his side. "So what happens? In the story?"

"Eventually she wants to kiss him so badly the girl takes off her helmet and dies. It's very tragic."

"A tale of star-crossed love," Tobias mused.

"Yes." Tiny smiled. "Literally. Because of—"

"The stars. In space. I get it. You," he said, laughing, "are a singularity."

"Is that a good thing?"

"Yeah." He propped himself up on his elbow and looked at her. "It's a good thing."

Goose bumps exploded across her skin like fireworks. She coughed to break the silence. "Well. What are *you* reading?"

"Right now I'm reading a book about the discovery of gravity," he said. "So, you know, star-crossed love. Tragic ending. Same sort of thing."

"Sounds like a real page-turner."

"Actually, it is. I love gravity. It's my favorite of all the fundamental forces."

"You have a favorite *force*?"

"What, don't you? To me, the coolest thing about gravity is a constant. That once things are on a certain trajectory, it's almost impossible to change them."

"Momentum." Tiny nodded like she knew what she was talking about.

"Exactly."

"Does it ever make you think about the big things?"

"Big things?"

"Yeah, like fate and stuff. How, if we're on a path, it's hard to change the path. Like how some things are inevitable. Like they're meant to happen."

"That's a pretty loose interpretation of science."

"Okay. What about this? If things with a lot of mass have their own force of gravity, and love is like this all-consuming massive thing. I mean, doesn't it make you wonder if it has its own gravity? Like maybe there's a scientific reason why star-crossed love is destined to crash and burn."

Tobias grinned. "Maybe."

"Or how there's like, a scientific reason why two"—she almost said *people*—"um, objects are drawn to each other. Come on, think about it!"

"I think about it a lot, actually."

He was looking at her again with this hard to understand look on his face. Isaac Newton came over and nosed his way between them, getting all licky.

"Ah!" Tiny pulled away and wiped her mouth. "Isaac Newton kissed me!"

"Isaac Newton!" said Tobias. "You beat me to it!"

Tiny couldn't bring herself to look at him. Was he serious? Her heart was pounding.

The door in the hall opened and then closed, and the sounds of Will and Luella arguing about which Doritos flavor was better, Cool Ranch or Nacho Cheese, filled the apartment. Suddenly Nathaniel was standing in the kitchen doorway. Tobias and Tiny stood up quickly at the same time. It felt weird, like they'd been caught doing something they shouldn't. Even though, really, there was no reason to feel that way. Maybe it was the look on Nathaniel's face, which was hard to read, but felt mad at them somehow. She looked over at Tobias. And she knew they both felt it standing between them.

"We got snacks!" Luella announced, barreling into the room.

"You can be the judge of which Doritos flavor is better, Tiny," Will said.

"Nacho Cheese," Tiny said without hesitating.

"Yes!" Luella said at the same time that Will said, "Oh, come on!"

Tobias stuck his hands in the pockets of his cargo shorts and shuffled his feet awkwardly. "I guess I should go study."

"It's summer vacation, man," said Will.

Tobias shrugged. "Not according to my summer reading list." Tiny thought he looked a little sad.

"Oookay," said Will.

Nathaniel was quiet throughout all of this. Tiny watched him carefully.

"Hey," Tobias said. "The world spins. That's a fact. But you better spin with it if you don't want gravity to hold you down or throw you off. You know?"

"That doesn't even make sense, scientifically," Nathaniel mumbled. Tiny was the only one who heard him. Will and Luella were watching Tobias leave. They glanced at each other, then quickly looked away.

They were all quiet for the rest of the afternoon, even during the funny parts of the movie.

NOW

MIDNIGHT
(8 HOURS LEFT)

BODIES IN SPACE

Tiny

They ran until the park receded behind them and the sirens were swallowed up by the howling wind. She felt like they were emerging from a dark forest into another world. Fifth Avenue stretched out before them again, the tall buildings looming over them, silently watching.

Nathaniel wasn't being himself tonight. He was acting like . . . well. That moment where he'd pushed her out of the way of the tree. It was just like a different moment three years ago.

An off-duty cab swished past down the deserted street.

Tiny shivered. She walked to the curb. In the window of a parked car, her reflection was hard to see.

Another off-duty cab swished past.

"Crap," said Will. "The traffic ban. I bet they're all off duty and heading back to wherever cabs go when they're off duty."

Tiny had to keep reminding herself it was Will. He still looked like Owen, and it was getting confusing.

"You know," Will said, "sometimes I'm jealous of kids in the suburbs who can just get in their cars and drive wherever they want. Put on the radio. Hit the open road. Think of the freedom."

"Not me," said Lu. "I don't want to worry about taking care of it." She began to tick items off on her fingers. "I don't want to pay for gas, I don't want to feel like I have to give rides to people just cause they asked, and I don't want to have to worry about driving drunk." She paused to breathe. "Give me the subway any day."

"Agh, guys!" Nathaniel grabbed at his curly hair. "You are literally driving me crazy! Do you not understand what a big deal this is? If we don't get help soon, we could die!"

"Die?" Lu's hands fell to her sides.

"Yes, die! It can't be good to have all this electricity pumping through us. It's like a state of perpetual electrocution!"

Tiny wondered what would be worse. Dying from perpetual electrocution—or fading away into invisibility, forever.

She could feel them all falling back into those same familiar roles. Nathaniel was the smart one. Will was the funny one. Lu was the dramatic one. And what was Tiny? The shy one? The one they all took for granted?

Lu and Will turned to Nathaniel and crossed their arms.

"What?"

"We're waiting for you to suggest something." Lu raised one eyebrow, which was a disconcerting thing Lu knew how to do. And did a lot.

"I don't have *all* the answers."

"Yes, you do, buddy," Will said, slapping Nathaniel on the back. "You can't fool us after that stunt back there in the park. You're our superleader. Guide us."

Nathaniel ran his hands through his hair.

"Well. Okay."

In the distance, Tiny saw the far-off light of an empty taxi.

"There!" she cried, and her heart swelled with hope. "Look!"

"Yes!" Will pumped his fist. "Victory!"

Tiny ran out into the middle of the street. She waved her arms up and down.

But the cab didn't stop. It didn't show any sign of slowing down. It didn't even see her.

"Stop!" Tiny yelled. It was getting closer.

"Get out of the way!" Lu called. But no. She wouldn't. She would *make* it see her. She jumped up and down and waved her arms frantically. She closed her eyes and screamed, "Stop!"

Something heavy collided with her. But it wasn't metal and rubber and glass. It was flesh and bone and smelled like boy. The taxi screeched to a stop as Nathaniel pushed her out of the way.

The wind had been knocked out of her. She struggled to stand.

"It didn't see you," Nathaniel said. Like it was just dawning on him. "The people in the park didn't see you. *I'm* having a hard time seeing you. Tiny, are you—did the lightning—is that why—?"

"Guys!" Will shouted out the window of the cab. "Move it! The meter's running!"

"Come on," Tiny said, grabbing his hand. "There's no time." They piled into the back with Will and Lu.

Nathaniel and Will and Lu—did they not *notice* what was happening to her? Did they not even know she was disappearing? Tiny balled her hands into fists at her sides.

"Whoa," said the driver. He was an elderly little guy, with a balding head and a graying beard. "Where are you going? I was just about to go off duty for the night."

"Chambers Street," said Nathaniel. "Chambers and West Broadway."

The cab driver shook his head.

"No. No way. Too far. I'm heading back to Queens; it's the opposite direction for me."

Tiny leaned forward. "Please," she said. The driver squinted at her.

"Are you okay?" he said. "Your skin . . . I know it's dark back there, but . . ." He shook his head. "I must need glasses."

"We really need to go to Chambers Street," she said, avoiding the question. "It's life-and-death."

"You teenagers and your drama," he said. But when he saw the look on Tiny's face, his eyes softened. "Fine. But you better give me a *big* tip."

They all nodded vigorously. "Yes! Thank you. Seriously, thank you."

But the front passenger-side door was slamming shut too, and a girl turned around to face them.

"I'm not letting you steal my cab," she said, breathing hard. "I was waiting forever out there."

"No *way*," said Lu. "We *need* this."

"So do I!"

"Not as much as we do!"

"It's mine," they both said at the same time. "No, it isn't. Yes, it is."

The cab driver turned around. "As long as I'm taking you, I can take you both," he said. "There're no cabs out there. There's nothing. Because of the storm."

"It's not even raining yet." The girl pouted, looking at Lu like that was her fault.

The driver pulled away from the curb and took off.

"I'm only going to Sixty-First and Park," she said.

"What!" said Will, wheeling on her. "You were going to steal our cab to go ten blocks?"

The girl scoffed. "I can't *walk* in these!" She nodded at her heels, which Tiny had to admit were unreasonably high.

"I know you," said Will. "You're the girl from my party. The *excuse me* girl."

"*Your* party? That's a bit narcissistic, don't you think?"

Of course she wouldn't recognize him. He still looked like a completely different person.

Will grunted but said nothing.

Tiny leaned back and looked out the window, watching the buildings tick by along Fifth Avenue. The streets were deserted, and there were hardly any cars on the road with them. She felt a little better now that they were heading toward school. Tobias might have been a lot of things to her, to all of them, but without question, he was really smart. Tiny knew the answer would be in his paper. She had no doubt that even though he wasn't right there in that cab with them, wedged between Tiny and Nathaniel, her arm touching his, he would be able to save them all.

The girl in the front seat turned around again. "Don't you guys think it's weird that Will Kingfield threw a party and then, like, disappeared?"

With great effort, Will turned from the window to look at her. "What are you talking about?"

"Everyone was talking about it. No one knew where he was. It's like he left his own party. *Super* weird, right?"

Will bristled. "Maybe he was sick of his house being full of people he doesn't know. Maybe he didn't even want to throw a stupid party in the first place."

"Right." The girl snorted. "You're an expert."

Will smiled at this. "How do you know I'm not?"

"Because," she said. "No one's an expert on Will Kingfield. He's the hottest guy in the senior class, but he's such a *mystery.*"

"Oh *god,*" Lu groaned.

"He is?" Will blinked.

"Yeah," she said, her voice growing dreamy. "Who *is* Will Kingfield?"

"Yeah," said Lu. "Who *is* Will Kingfield? Enlighten us."

Will stared at her. "I . . . I guess I don't even know."

The girl turned to him, excited. Clearly, this was a topic on which she was prepared to expound.

"Okay," she said, "here's what we know. He's co-captain of the soccer team. He is mega-smart." She was ticking items off on her fingers. "He has the sickest abs—"

"How do you know that?" Will interrupted.

"Amelia felt them." Her eyes glittered. "At the homecoming dance. They danced next to each other for half of a song, and she totally touched his abs. She said it was like touching a brick wall."

"Who's Amelia?" Will said, mostly to himself.

"Uh, Amelia?" she said. "You know, *Amelia*? Anyway, he had this whole meteoric rise to popularity and stuff, right? But nobody's that perfect. Where did he come from? What does he think about before he falls asleep at night? Who *is* he?"

"Whoa," said Nathaniel, who had been quiet until now. "You've thought about this a lot."

The girl leaned back in the front seat and sighed. "I would give anything to make out with him for, like, five minutes."

Will considered this. "What if you guys have nothing in common?"

"Uh, who cares?" She looked at him like this was the stupidest question. "I'm not really interested in doing much talking, if you know what I mean."

"I thought you were so interested in knowing the real him?"

"To a point," she said. "Mostly I just want to lick his face."

"Ew," said Will.

"Ew," said Lu.

"Hey!" The girl turned around and gave them a look.

"Sorry, I didn't mean to say that out loud. Look, you seem nice, kind of, but I don't really think you're his type."

"How could you possibly know that?" asked the girl.

"I think I can make a pretty educated guess on this one."

"Well," she said, "you never know, right?"

"Well," said Will. "Okay. What are your thoughts on Ibsen? Have you ever read *Hedda Gabler*?"

Tiny noticed Lu suddenly got quiet.

The girl scrunched up her nose. "No," she said. "Who's Ibsen?"

"Just one of the most radical feminist playwrights of his time. He talks a lot about people being boxed in by society and labels and striving for beauty and greatness and a life bigger than ourselves."

"Oh," the girl said, raising her eyebrows as the cab pulled to a stop outside a big apartment building. "We're here." She handed the driver a couple of dollars and jumped out of the car.

"Too bad you'll never make out with Will Kingfield!" Will called out the window.

The girl threw up her middle finger before disappearing into the lobby.

The driver glanced in the rearview mirror, and turned up the radio.

"What people have begun calling Stormpocalypse has now been classified as a superstorm. The Northeast has yet to see any rain, but with areas of the south already flooded, this promises to be the worst storm to hit the eastern seaboard in decades. . . . Rain is predicted to begin anytime between now and seven a.m. this morning. . . . Emergency procedures are already being put into place. . . . We advise you to stay off the roads. . . . If you can, stay home *. . . for the safety of yourself and others. . . ."*

"Still want me to take you to Chambers Street?" the driver asked.

"Yeah," they all said at the same time. They looked at one another.

"I guess we still have to try," Tiny said. If anything, it made her want to try harder.

The cab skirted through the park and down Columbus Avenue.

The driver eyed them in the rearview mirror. "Supposed to be one hell of a storm," he said. "Where are you kids headed in this crazy weather?"

Tiny looked at Nathanial. He shrugged. "School," he said.

"School!" The driver laughed. "You're serious? So studious and focused on your futures. You're not afraid of getting struck by lightning?"

"We were," said Tiny. "Now we're afraid of something else."

"See," said the cab driver, whose name, Tiny noticed on his cab driver's license, was Gus. "To me, there're two kinds of fear. You got good fear, and you got bad fear." Gus adjusted the rearview mirror so he could see them. Columbus Avenue became Ninth Avenue.

"Good fear protects you from getting hurt. Don't put your hand on a hot stove. Avoid dark alleys. Stay away from high, open places and trees during a lightning storm!" He chuckled to himself. "Bad fear, though. It makes you think twice about taking the kind of risk that might turn out to be good for you. Applying for a job. Telling someone you love them. Writing the great American novel. Bad fear protects you from life. Keeps you from really living!" He threw a fist up in the air, and the car swerved a little. "You listen to the bad fear, you may as well just disappear." He turned around and met Tiny's gaze over his shoulder. The car swerved again. "You see what I mean?"

Tiny felt goose bumps on her arms.

They slowed down as they neared Thirty-Fourth Street. There was some kind of commotion up ahead.

"What's going on?" Lu stuck her head out the window. "What fresh hell is this?" The cab came to a full-on stop. A stream of people marched past the window. "Are they holding *signs*?" Before anyone could stop her, the door had opened and closed and Lu had gotten out.

"Not again," said Tiny, getting out after her. Nathaniel and Will followed.

The cabbie stuck his head out the window. "Hey, kids! I took you all this way! You gonna pay me?" Lu was disappearing into the crowd. She couldn't let Lu disappear on them again. If she did, if they couldn't find her, she could die.

"Tiny!" Will called, running ahead. "Come on! We're going to lose her!"

Tiny was worried that if she didn't stay close to them, she'd lose them too. She'd disappear in the crowd—literally, disappear—and that would be the last time anyone saw her. She had to follow them.

"I'm sorry!" Tiny shouted. "Listen, what's your phone number? I promise, when this is all over, I'll make sure you get your money."

Gus frowned. "And a big tip."

"And a big tip. Promise."

He cursed, and then his eyes softened again. "I like you, kid. I don't know why, but I do." He tilted his head. "I feel like I've met you before. But." He threw up his hands. "In a city of eight million people, everyone looks a little familiar." Tiny was half paying attention, already running backward. Gus shouted his phone number after them. Tiny keyed it into her phone and pressed save. "I promise!" she called. "Thank you!"

"Good luck out there!" Gus called, and drove off in the opposite direction.

Lu

The crowd was a moving, living, breathing thing, and it swept her right up.

Even if Lu wanted to swim against the current back to her friends, she wasn't strong enough to do it. Lu dove right into the throng. Lu dove headfirst into most things.

The mass of people was moving east, toward Broadway. Lu moved with them.

"Guys!" she yelled. "I'm stuck!"

"We're right behind you!" Will's voice echoed from somewhere nearby.

The streets were packed with people.

"So this is where everyone in Manhattan is," Lu heard Will shout.

"People are even stupider than I thought!" That voice belonged to Nathaniel. "An End of the World rally? Really? Why does everyone think the world is going to end tonight? There is no scientific proof! None at all! It's just speculation! It's just—"

"A feeling!" Tiny shouted.

Someone on a bullhorn shouted something, and the crowd roared, surging forward.

"Hey!" cried Lu. "Someone stepped on my foot! Hard!" It was weird, though. She sensed the pressure on her foot, but she couldn't feel the pain. At all.

She looked up at the signs paraded above her head.

THE END IS HERE.

LET THEM TAKE US.

WHAT HAPPENS NEXT?

"Uh," said Lu. "Well, this is terrifying."

The crowd was so loud, she could hardly hear Will shouting as he pushed his way toward her, or Nathaniel and Tiny, who were yelling and pointing behind her. The bullhorn-shouter yelled about something being nigh, or pie, or something.

Lu spun around. A wild-looking woman was coming at her with a kitchen knife. Lu's first thought was that it was to cut the pie. But she looked way too angry for that. "Sinner!" the woman yelled. *"Sinner!"* Lu stood there in her PROSE BEFORE HOES T-shirt and eyeliner and platforms. She knew she should run. She knew this woman was going to stab her with that kitchen knife. She wouldn't feel it, but she would bleed, and she would die.

She would never be able to tell her mom she loved her.

She would never be able to say sorry to Will.

The crowd was closing in on her, and she knew she should move, but she didn't know what direction to move in. Everywhere she looked, there were people. In the great debate between fight or flight, Lu felt nothing. She stood there, paralyzed.

Then, someone picked her up from behind and flung her over their shoulder.

"Hey!" she screamed. "Put me down! Will! Will! *Where are you?*" She wasn't sure what she was thinking, though. Now that Will was basically Owen, he didn't have a lot of muscle. Lu wasn't fully confident he'd be able to fight his way through the crowd to get to her. For the first time all night, Lu felt panicked. She felt alone.

It was a feeling she didn't like.

This lightning power was turning out to be more of a curse. She would so much rather be numb on the inside than numb on the outside.

"Okay, Lu! It's just me!" Nathaniel shouted over the din. He carried her as if she weighed no more than a feather, and was sprinting through the crowd, knocking people over with just a touch. "We're getting out of here!"

He pushed his way through the mess of people.

"Nathaniel!" Lu shouted down at him. "Are you actually getting *stronger*?"

"Yes!" he yelled, excited. "It's like I'm accelerating—each thing I do makes me more super! Like a video game character collecting power-ups!"

"You're such a nerd!" Will yelled from behind them, where he and Tiny were running to catch up.

"Like you don't know what that means!" Nathaniel shot back.

Lu helped them through the crowd by wildly swinging her weaponlike heels every time someone crazy-looking got too close. They made it to the sidewalk, and barreled through the sliding electronic doors of a nearby store. The doors closed behind them. Lu's ears rang in the sudden quiet.

The white, white light, buzzing and fluorescent, was jarring after the darkness outside. Aisles stretched out uniformly before them in perfect endless rows.

"Where are we?" Lu asked.

"Kmart," said Tiny. "I think."

"That was wild," Nathaniel said, looking out the glass doors. "People are taking this Stormpocalypse thing really literally."

"Much. Too. Literally." Lu slid down the wall, gasping. She couldn't feel the blood pumping through her veins. She couldn't feel how hard her own heart was beating. But she knew she could have died back there, and she had too much unfinished business to do to die tonight.

"Is everyone okay?" said Tiny. Will—still Owen—was leaning with both hands against a checkout counter, wheezing.

"Can. We. Please. Stop. All. This. Running? Owen is not in good shape." He coughed. "I think he's a smoker."

Lu remembered how kissing him always tasted like cigarettes and cheap whiskey. Or cigarettes and beer. Or cigarettes and Oreos, that one time.

"He is," she said.

Two bored and tired-looking cashiers were standing there, shooting suspicious glances their way.

"We're closing in ten," one of them said, nodding to a sign near the door.

STORM HOURS
OPEN 'TIL MIDNITE
GET YOUR EMERGENCY SUPPLIES HERE!!!
2-FOR-1 BATTERIES
*****STORM SPECIAL!!!*****

"We'll just be a second," Nathaniel said, flashing them a *can you believe this weather?* smile and shrug that looked psychotic, given the circumstances. "Whew, it's crazy out there!" He motioned for Tiny, Will, and Lu to follow him away from the checkout area. Kmart was totally deserted. They were the only freaks who were out for some light shopping during Superstorm Eileen. Everyone else had prepared hours ago—or was beyond saving.

Lu hoped the four of them didn't fall into that latter category.

Then she heard a familiar zap.

Once again they found themselves suspended in darkness.

"The power's out," Nathaniel said. Then, "The doors are powered by electricity. We're trapped in here until it comes back on."

"Not again," Lu groaned. "Can't you, like, break down the door or something?"

"The horde is still out there," Nathaniel said, peering through the glass. "I don't want to draw attention to ourselves." He paused. "Or spook them."

"They're not zombies," Lu muttered. She grabbed Tiny's hand for reassurance. She actually had to grab it twice because it was so hard to see. "Hey, Tine," Lu said. "I can hardly see you in the dark."

"I know," said Tiny. "It's because—"

"Shit!" Lu interrupted, looking at her arm. "I'm bleeding. I didn't even know I got cut back there!" Lu shivered. It was weird not to feel pain. That crazy lady with the knife had sliced her arm, and she hadn't even felt it. "Come on. As long as we're stuck in here, let's go find some Band-Aids. I don't want to bleed on my favorite shirt." She paused. "What were you saying?"

"Nothing," said Tiny. "Never mind."

"Oookay," said Lu. She hated to admit it, but she was relieved. There had been more than enough talking about feelings already tonight.

"We'll stay here and look for a way out," Nathaniel called after them.

Faint light filtered in through the glass sliding doors, growing dimmer and dimmer the farther they ventured into the store. In the first aid section, Lu squinted in the dark as she tried to make out the different kinds of Band-Aids.

"Oooh, look how awesome these are!" Lu said with delight. "Disney Princess Band-Aids! If I were a Disney character, I think I'd be a cross between Jasmine and Iago the parrot." Tiny snorted with laughter. Lu grinned. "Right?"

"So right. Who am I?"

"Oh, Tiny. You're like a cross between Ariel and Mrs. Potts."

"Mrs. Potts?"

"Don't look so pissed. That's a good thing. Mrs. Potts is a caretaker."

"Mrs. Potts is a teapot."

"Tea is very nourishing."

There was a pause. "You think I'm a caretaker?" Tiny said quietly.

"Of course," said Lu. "You take care of me."

Tiny smiled. Lu actually felt nice for the first time all night. It was rare that she said something that made someone else feel good.

"Yeah," she continued. "You're always concerned about my feelings and not wanting me to make mistakes or take risks or do anything that we don't know the outcome to." Tiny's smile faded, but Lu wasn't sure why.

Was it the darkness playing tricks on her, or was Tiny *especially* hard to see? She looked like a Polaroid developing in reverse.

She wanted to ask Tiny if she was okay, but she hadn't in so long that it felt weird to do it now. So she kept quiet and just refocused her attention on the Band-Aids.

"Lu," Tiny said. "Are you worried? I mean, about all this?"

Lu picked up a box of Band-Aids. "Hm. I don't know. Kind of. Hey, it gets us out of studying!"

"But . . . you could be in real trouble. We all could."

"Tiny," Lu said to her. "Lightning can strike you when you're standing on a roof. A tree can fall on you when you're dancing in a park. You can get broken up with out of the blue, and chased by a crazy Rapture nut down a street, and locked in a Kmart with the power out. But all those things have already happened to us tonight. So how could things possibly get any worse? I'm not going to worry, because there's no point. And you shouldn't either. We're together. Best friends. The dynamic duo. Talulah. Tlu! We can do anything." Lu wasn't sure if she was trying to convince Tiny or herself.

Tiny picked up a box of Band-Aids and examined the back.

"Lu," Tiny said.

"What?"

"Do you notice anything different about me?" Lu squinted at her in the dark. It was hard to see Tiny. But then, it was hard to see anything. Was it the lightning? Was it making Tiny disappear?

Even worse, was it possible she hadn't even noticed until now?

Lu knew she should say something. But maybe it was the numbness or something. She was tired. She was sick of talking about how terrible everything was, and how they were all going to die. She was exhausted from just having so many feelings about it all. And she wanted to make Tiny say it out loud. She wanted her damn friend to stand up for herself, for once. Why did Lu always have to do it for her? Why was she always the one pushing Tiny to take the risks?

"Nope," said Lu. She was being a jerk, but she didn't care. "Kinda hard to see anything in here though."

Tiny put the box back onto the shelf and turned to face her. "Is there something going on between you and Will?" she blurted.

Lu threw a hard look in her general direction.

"No," she said. "Nothing."

"It seems like there is."

"Well, there isn't," Lu snapped. She would talk about it when she was ready. Which was probably going to be never.

There were lots of times she could have told Tiny about Will and what had happened between the two of them the summer before freshman year. But she didn't. She had never told anyone. She couldn't bring herself to say it out loud. And then after the summer, when she was ready to talk about it, there were too many other things to deal with. The last thing Tiny probably wanted to hear about was some stupid boy drama. Tiny had real problems to think about; they all did.

"Just drop it, Tiny. Please. You don't have to fix everything. You don't have to fix *me*." She couldn't see Tiny's face, but in the dark silence, she knew she'd hit a nerve. "Don't take the Mrs. Potts thing literally."

So maybe she was still in a bad mood about Owen.

"I'm not trying to fix you," Tiny said. Lu had never heard her voice like that before—low but strong. "I just wish you'd tell me the truth for once."

And just like that, Lu felt shitty again. She really was becoming a fortress of solitude. If she didn't do something to stop it, soon she wouldn't feel anything at all, no matter who she hurt in the process.

“I’m going to find a flashlight,” Tiny said. Did her voice sound hurt? Lu couldn’t tell. “You can pick out your own Band-Aids.”

“Fine.” Lu picked up a pack of neon-yellow Band-Aids and stalked off toward the bathroom to dress her wounds.

And to protect herself from any more.

Will

"You know," Will said. He was sitting against the wall by the check-out counters while Nathaniel was inspecting the mechanism on the electric doors, looking for a way to pry them open manually. "Some deep subconscious part of me must have wanted to be Owen. But I don't think I really do."

"You don't?" It was still pretty dark, but the light from outside was shining in through the glass, so they could kind of see. The cashiers were complaining loudly that it had been more than ten minutes and they just wanted to close up and go home. "There has to be a way to override this thing manually," Nathaniel muttered.

"Nah," Will said. "He takes himself too seriously. Plus"—he sniffed his T-shirt and made a face—"I think I'm allergic to cigarette smoke. My throat feels all itchy."

Nathaniel pushed a button, but nothing happened.

"Lu would have broken up with him eventually. He just got to it first. I don't see her with someone like that."

"Really." Nathaniel stopped what he was doing and looked up. "Who do you see her with?"

"I don't know," said Will. "Someone different."

"Elaborate, please."

"Someone who would be willing to chase after her. Stand up for her. Fight for her."

"Uh-huh."

"Someone like . . ."

"You?" Nathaniel said.

"Me?" said Will. He flipped Owen's hair casually out of his eyes. "Oh, I don't know."

"Please." Nathaniel walked over and sat down next to him. They leaned against the wall. "I never noticed it, until tonight. I guess because we haven't all been together since . . ." He didn't finish. "How long have you two been . . . you know?"

"Dude," Will said. "Are you trying to have a heart-to-heart with me?"

"A what?"

"A heart-to-heart. It's what my mom used to call it when we had, you know, like, an important chat about feelings."

"Okay," said Nathaniel. "Yeah. I guess we're having a heart-to-heart. We're stuck in here until the power comes back on, so we might as well." He paused. "I mean. We haven't had one in a long time, so."

Will looked down at his hands.

"Yeah," he said. "It's about time, right?"

"So. What's going on?"

"It started that last summer before high school. We were both doing summer classes at Hunter, and we started hanging out a lot just the two of us."

"And?"

"And now I'm pretty sure she hates me."

"How come you never told me?"

"Well, there was a lot going on that summer and fall. I didn't want to bother you with it."

"Okay." Nathaniel fidgeted with the laces of his hiking boots.

"Why are you even wearing hiking boots?" Will said. "There is literally, like, nowhere to hike within a hundred-mile radius."

"They're comfortable," Nathaniel said. "They have good traction. And . . ."

"And what?"

"No, it's dumb. Never mind."

"It's okay. I'm not gonna make fun of you if that's what you're afraid of."

Nathaniel untied and retied his laces. "They remind me that if I keep trekking forward, I'll get where I want to go, eventually."

Will didn't say anything. That was a nice thing to think.

"It's stupid," Nathaniel muttered. "It something Tobias used to say when he was in high school."

"I like it."

"Will," said Nathaniel. "Are you okay? You're acting really weird. I know we haven't really hung out in a while, but you don't seem like yourself."

"The thing is," Will said slowly, "I don't even think I know who *myself* is." He sighed. "I'm just freaked out by all this. The storm and the lightning and everything." But that wasn't true. It was more than that, and he'd known it for a while now.

"We need to regroup," Nathaniel said. "We need a game plan for getting downtown to school. That will make all of us feel better.

If we figure out what's going on, then maybe we'll be able to fix it."

"Yeah." Will laughed. "See? You're good at leading us."

"I don't know."

"Stop being humble. You totally are." Nathaniel's stomach rumbled, loudly.

"I'm hungry. I haven't eaten since the Cheez-Its earlier."

"I *knew* you were eating Cheez-Its!"

"It's my study snack."

"I know! I remember!"

"Want to go find some food?"

"What is there to even eat in here?"

"Let's go raid the snack aisle." Nathaniel grinned. "There has to be at least one perk to getting stuck in a Kmart. Unlimited free snacks."

Will nodded, even though Nathaniel couldn't see.

"We'll figure it out," Nathaniel said. "I really think we will."

"You don't know that. There is no factual evidence to support that theory."

Nathaniel looked surprised.

"That's true," he said. "Huh."

Will knew he was talking about figuring out the weird lightning powers, but he hoped Nathaniel also meant everything else. He'd forgotten what it was like to have a friend who cared how you felt, and if you were okay. It was something he didn't want to let go of anytime soon.

"Come on," he said. "I'm hungry too."

They walked down the aisles, which grew darker the farther away they got from the light streaming in through the front doors.

"This is going to sound crazy," Nathaniel said. "But hear me out.

What if we got a frozen pizza from the freezer aisle and heated it up in one of the display microwaves in the electronics aisle?" He raised his eyebrows. "Amazing, right? I would kill for a pizza right now."

"I thought you were supposed to be the science expert," Will said. "Don't we need electricity to run a microwave?" He gestured at the darkness. "If we had that, we could get out of here."

"Oh," Nathaniel said. "That's embarrassing. You're right."

"I can't tell if you're more upset about being wrong or not getting to eat pizza."

"Both, I think. Pizza is my all-time favorite food. If I could eat one food for the rest of my life, it would be pizza."

"Even microwave pizza?"

"Oh my god, yes, especially microwave pizza. There's some preservative in the sauce that I swear is like crack."

Will laughed. "I haven't had pizza in three long years," he said. "It's basically empty calories. Like, a lump of carbs and dairy and sugar. Nothing about pizza is good for you. I never let myself eat it."

Nathaniel stared at Will in the dark. "I literally cannot compute anything you're saying right now. It's like words are coming out, but you're speaking a foreign robot language."

"That's not funny."

"Beep, boop, boop, beep."

"I had to give up a lot of things I love to stay in shape, Nathaniel. You think I could have gotten to where I am now by eating pizza?"

"I knew Soccer Star Will was in there somewhere. You're not so different, even though you look it."

"Soccer Star Will wouldn't be Soccer Star Will if he didn't work hard at it." He paused. "I used to love pizza though."

"What about beer? You drink that, and that's just empty calories."

"That's different," said Will. "Beer is social currency. Pizza is just delicious for no reason."

"What's the point of giving up something you love to be someone you maybe kind of hate?"

They had found the snack aisle. As their eyes adjusted further to the dark, the various bags and labels came into focus.

Nathaniel tossed a bag of Doritos to Will.

Will felt the familiar weight of the bag. He opened it, and the smell of nacho cheese wafted over them.

"Life's too short," Nathaniel said. Even though he vastly preferred Cool Ranch, Will was starting to agree.

Nathaniel

"Hey," a voice said in the dark.

A girl-size shape materialized next to him, and Nathaniel realized it was Tiny. But the shape never fully came into focus. He could just make out the blurred edges of her face, enough to see the scared look in her eyes. "Want to come find a flashlight with me?" she said.

Nathaniel looked at Will. "You okay to stay here and wait for Lu?"

"It's my lot in life, Nathaniel."

"What?"

"Nothing. Yeah, I'll wait for her."

"Keep checking for a way out."

Nathaniel followed Tiny deeper into the dark store, away from the light filtering in through the glass doors. He could just make out her faint silhouette ahead of him. His heart pounded at being so close to her, this girl he used to think about so much, in the dark. He hadn't felt this way in so long. He hadn't felt not alone in forever.

Eventually they found the camping aisle. Nathaniel's eyes had almost fully adjusted to the darkness now, and he could see tents and backpacks and camping stoves and Frisbees and coolers all around them. There was a whole section of flashlights. Tiny took one off the wall.

"Do you think with everything going on, they'd mind if we opened this and used it before paying?" Tiny looked legitimately concerned, and Nathaniel laughed.

"I would literally be shocked if those cashiers were even there when we get back. There's going to be, like, a cashier-size hole in the glass doors, and we'll be able to climb right through it. I think you're fine." Tiny fumbled in the dark; he heard the sound of tearing plastic and then something clicking into place. Then the space between them was flooded with light.

He could see her a little better now.

"You can see it," she whispered. "Can't you?" Nathaniel swallowed hard, and nodded.

"You're disappearing," he said.

Tiny slid to the floor, and the circle of light descended with her.

"No one has seemed to notice tonight. Lu and Will are too wrapped up in their own problems." She clicked the flashlight off and on again, fidgeting. "I always felt like I could talk to you, Nathaniel. I wish we were still friends."

"We can still talk," Nathaniel said, sitting next to her. The light enveloped him again. "We're talking now."

"I don't want to disappear," she said. "This the first time I've ever said that out loud."

"What do you mean? Not just tonight?"

"No. I used to want to. I just wanted to be invisible. I actually tried to be. After that summer, I just felt so . . . like I didn't want anyone to see me or talk to me. Like I didn't deserve to be loud or myself or alive. Like who I was wasn't good enough somehow. And now . . ."

Nathaniel looked down. The flashlight illuminated a circle of soft light around the two of them. He knew what she meant. He had spent his whole life trying to be a certain way, and it wasn't enough. He always kept trying, though. He always had to try.

But tonight it was easy. He was everything he had always wanted to be.

He was like his brother. Larger than life. He wished Tobias could see him right now.

"This storm makes me think of him," Nathaniel said. "He should be out there in it, tracking lightning, collecting data, talking about the electromagnetic forces at work in the sky, not even caring that he might get hit. He should be out there. The least I can do is be out there too."

"Me too," said Tiny.

"I should have been there that night. I think about it every day. I stayed home for such a stupid reason."

"It wouldn't have changed anything," Tiny said. "Besides, you couldn't have known. Everything seems easier in hindsight. But nothing really is."

Somewhere on the other side of the store, they could hear Lu and Will yelling. Tiny shone the flashlight straight ahead. It cut through the darkness like a knife.

"I guess we should find them," she said. They stood up.

"This Kmart seems ill-equipped for emergency situations," Nathaniel remarked. "You'd think they'd have a backup generator or floodlights or something."

Tiny pointed the flashlight toward the sound of their friends. In the dark, she fumbled for his hand.

"Come on," she said. "All we can do is keep going forward and take it one step at a time." He might have been imagining it, but he thought he saw her smile. "At least we have each other."

Nathaniel was grateful for the dark, because there was no question he was blushing. "Well," he said. "This is better."

They half stumbled, half flash-lit their way through the aisles, two bodies in space. For now, all they could do was follow the voices in the darkness.

Tiny

The four of them sat in the snack aisle. They were stuck. The cashiers had vanished into the darkness, not even leaving cashier-shaped holes in the glass doors for them to escape through. They couldn't leave until the power came back on. But sitting here, in the dark, made the lost time all she could think about.

"It's weird," Tiny said, to distract herself. "Being back together again. The founding members of Science Club. Did you guys ever think this would happen?"

"Ha," said Lu. "No."

"Me neither," said Nathaniel.

"If the soccer guys could see me now," Will said. "Hipster hair and skinny jeans and hanging out with a bunch of misfits in a Kmart in the middle of the night."

"Is that how you think of us, Will?" Lu asked. "Just a bunch of misfits? Is that why you abandoned us?"

"I abandoned you?" Will looked genuinely shocked. "I abandoned *you*?"

Lu just looked at him pointedly.

"You're the one who's gotten all judgy," he said.

"Judgy!"

"Yeah, with your weird slogan T-shirts and big boots and eyeliner and crazy theater friends. Dating a delinquent musician who probably broke a hundred laws tonight by putting on that show. Do you think he had a permit for those generators? No. And do you think those fires would have started without the generators? *No!*"

"What about that makes me judgy? If anyone's being judgy here, Will, it's you."

"This is ridiculous," Nathaniel said. "I know why we grew apart. It's because we're all too self-absorbed to see what anyone else is going through. No one's even asked me how I'm doing. Do you think it's been easy for me tonight? After everything that happened with my brother, and now having some kind of weird superpower that's basically turning me into him? Do you guys even know what kind of pressure I'm under? You think my parents will expect anything less than perfection after raising a son like Tobias first?" He paused. "Do you think *I'll* expect anything less?"

"Nathaniel," Will said. But he left the word hanging there without finishing the sentence.

"Right. You were too busy thinking about pizza and soccer and Lu and your hair."

"Lu?" said Lu.

"You say you're not happy with who you are. You say you want to be someone different. But who you look like is only a start; you have to change on the inside, too, Will."

"Lu?" Lu said again. "You were thinking about me?"

"So not the time, Lu," said Will.

Tiny realized she was guilty of it too. They all were. She let how other people saw her rule her life. First Tobias. Now Josh. The lit mag committee. Her parents and Lu and her teachers. All the things people said to her every day that made her feel not good enough or special enough or pretty enough or talented enough. It wore you down after a while.

You started to believe them.

"Wow," Lu was saying. "I feel like I'm learning a lot about boy friendships tonight."

"That's not funny," said Will.

"We don't make fun of *your* friendships," Nathaniel said.

"That's because our friendship is perfect," said Lu.

Before tonight Tiny would never have said anything. But now—

"Stop," she said. "Just stop."

Lu spun around.

"Sorry, what?"

Tiny turned red. "Lu. Our friendship is *not* perfect. We aren't best friends. We're just two people who coexist near each other more often than other people."

"What are you talking about?"

"Best friends actually *talk* about things! Real things! They tell each other the truth!"

Lu's mouth fell open.

"And, Will, no one cares about your hair or your skinny jeans. In fact, no one cares what you look like at all."

"Hey!" Will sat up straighter.

"Nathaniel," Tiny said. "If you don't want to be like your brother, don't be like your brother. And if you do, then do it, and be even better than he was. It's up to you."

"Wow," said Nathaniel. "Don't sugarcoat it."

Tiny felt a weird, familiar feeling. Energy buzzing around inside her, needing to burst out. Her hands started to shake, and she balled them into fists at her sides.

"And I never stand up for myself. I never say what I really think or feel. I'm afraid to be myself. So now I'm going to be myself. And maybe if I do, I'll stop disappearing."

She started off down the aisle.

The floor began to hum, and then the walls began to vibrate, and then the lights zapped back on throughout the store. She squinted against the harsh fluorescence.

It was like the lightning knew. Like it could hear her.

"Whoa," Lu said, running after her. "What just happened?"

"Did she make the power turn back on?" Nathaniel was running after them too.

"Guys," said Will. "Where are you going? The door is that way. We can leave now!"

But Tiny was already walking away.

1:00 A.M.

(7 Hours Left)

The Kinetic Energy of Grand Gestures

Tiny

It was time for her to take this night and her fate into her own hands.

She walked down the brightly lit aisles until she saw the sign for school supplies. She found a pad of lined paper and a black Magic Marker. Then she sat down on the floor, and in big bold swipes she wrote her poem from memory—the one Josh Herrera had totally panned at the party earlier. Whatever. Fuck him. She wrote her name at the top. Her real name.

She sat back and looked at her work.

It was a good poem. She thought it was good. That was all that mattered. What was Josh's problem?

He's a pretentious jerk, Tiny's brain answered. She couldn't believe she'd never seen it before. She'd spent so many years believing the illusion, she didn't even realize there was a real person behind it. She'd gotten caught up in the hype.

But she guessed that maybe everyone was guilty of that.

Tiny stood and walked with great purpose to the copy center. She put a few coins in the Xerox machine and then punched in

100. She watched it pump out copy after copy of her awesome poem.

Nathaniel, Lu, and Will were watching her like they were on a safari and she was a wild animal they didn't want to spook. They didn't know what she was going to do next. But they didn't try to stop her.

"Okay," she said, holding the stack of poems. "Now we can leave."

No one argued with her.

Outside on the street, the Rapture rally had moved on, leaving Herald Square eerily empty. The wind was blowing even harder now than it had been earlier, sweeping bits of litter up into the air in a cyclone of garbage.

"I guess it was more of a Rapture parade," Lu said, holding up her arms as a plastic bag flew past her face. "I wonder where they marched off to."

"Maybe the Rapture came early," said Will.

"Tiny," Nathaniel said. "Can we find a way back to school now?"

"No," Tiny said, gripping her stack of poems tight to her chest so they didn't blow away. "Not yet. I'm not finished."

"What are you talking about?"

"I'm talking about a grand gesture. I'm talking about facing my fears."

"But we have to get to school," said Will. "So we're not stuck this way forever. I thought that's what we agreed."

"School can wait a little while longer. Science or no science, there's something I have to do first. Something I have to do for myself. It's about time."

"Tiny, this is crazy!" Lu was next to her in a flash. "You sound legitimately bonkers!"

Tiny looked around at the three of them. "Yeah, well, you all got to be crazy for a little bit tonight. I never get to be crazy. Not ever. I'm the careful one. The cautious one. The one nobody notices. So now it's my turn."

"Okay," Lu said slowly, backing away. "Well, you know I never turn down an adventure. Where are we going?"

Tiny turned uptown—it was the opposite direction from the one they needed to go in. She knew that. But right now she didn't feel like being logical.

"This way," she said, and started walking against the wind, shielding her face. After a second, the others followed.

In a few blocks, a fancy-looking couple emerged from a dark side street. The woman wore a sidewalk-sweeping black gown that fishtailed out at the bottom in a swirl of sequins. The man wore a tailored tuxedo. A gust of wind blew the bottom of her dress up in a sequin tornado.

It was an odd thing to see two people dressed up for a black-tie gala in the middle of a superstorm. It was odder, still, that they both wore elaborate masks, festooned in feathers and fur.

"What . . . ?" Nathaniel said. "Did they not get the memo that this entire city is shutting down?"

"Did we?" said Will.

"Where do you think they're going?" Lu whisper-yelled above the wind.

The couple stayed a good half a block ahead of them for a few minutes. Wherever they turned, Tiny turned.

"Are you following them?" Lu asked, clearly losing her mind with excitement over the idea.

"No," said Tiny. "But I have a weird feeling we're going to the same place."

"Hurry!" The woman laughed, clutching the man's arm. Her voice echoed across the empty street as they clattered uptown. "Star light, star bright. The first star I see tonight."

"Come on," Tiny said, taking off even faster.

She followed the couple down Thirty-Sixth Street and then turned onto Fifth Avenue.

"Where do you think they're going?" Lu asked, catching up.

"The question is more like, where are *we* going?" Nathaniel said.

"Do we have to be dressed up for this?" Will asked, making a face. "I left my formalwear at home."

"Shhh," whispered Tiny. "Don't draw attention to us."

"Hey," said Lu. "So what'd you write on that stack of paper you're holding?"

"You'll see when we get there."

Ahead of them, the couple stopped in front of the Empire State Building. A tired-looking doorman stepped out to greet them.

"I wish I may?" he asked.

"Have the wish," the man said, and handed him a feather. The doorman stepped aside, and the couple swished into the lobby.

"Come on," Tiny said. The four of them approached the lobby entrance. The doorman stepped up to greet them.

"The first star?" he asked.

The four of them glanced at one another. Tiny shrugged.

"I see tonight," she said and handed him one of her poems. The doorman looked at it, surprised. He looked at her, and then looked closer.

"Looks like you could use a wish," he said. "Take the elevator to the top."

"I can't believe that worked!" Lu crowed as they ran across the gleaming art deco lobby to the elevator. "Is that one of your poems? Please, can I read it? Pretty please?"

"Yeah, can we read it?" Nathaniel was peeking over her shoulder.

"No! No one can read it. Not yet."

"Good," said Will. "I don't get poetry."

Lu shoved him. "Shut up. Hey," she turned to Tiny. "What are you going to do with all of those?" Lu was bouncing up and down on her heels. "This is so exciting!"

The elevator dinged, and the huge brass doors opened. They got on.

On the way up to the top, they made funny faces at the security camera.

"Smile," sang Lu, holding up her camera to take a picture of the four of them. "That's a good one," Lu said. "We don't even need a filter. These elevator lights are incredible! I wish we had them at school." Tiny could hardly even see herself in the picture. No one mentioned it.

Then the doors were opening and they tumbled out onto the observation deck.

They found themselves in some kind of twenties-era speakeasy masquerade party. The wind was blowing wildly this high up, and men and women milled around in sequined formalwear, clutching the feathers in their hair and the masks on their faces to keep from flying away. Tiny, Lu, Nathaniel, and Will were the only ones not hiding their true identity.

There was a bar set up on one side, with old-fashioned barkeeps in suspenders and newsboy hats mixing up fancy cocktails that they served up very carefully to avoid spilling into the wind. Off to the right, a brass band played boisterous jazz, and under a canopy of tiny light bulbs that swayed back and forth, people danced on a polished wood dance floor.

A gilded sign on the side of the building read: URBAN EXPLORERS CLUB.

Tiny grinned. Every time she thought her world was small and sheltered, she was reminded that the city—and the world around it—was so much bigger than she ever imagined.

There was magic everywhere in this city. You just had to know where to look.

Beyond the storm of sequins and feathers and flying vodka gimlets, there, in front of them, was the most famous view in all of New York. The buildings glittered beneath the storm clouds. Tiny stared in awe.

Whoa. She looked out at the magical view. She'd seen it in so many movies and so many TV shows, and read it described in so many books. But she'd never seen it like this, all lit up in the middle of the night, like it was just for her. She was suddenly glad she had left home tonight. Sometimes you had to step outside in the middle of a storm and get struck by lightning to see everything you could have missed. The stars peaking through the clouds in the sky mirrored the glittering streets below. For a minute, even with the lights and music and members of the Urban Explorers Club dancing and laughing around them, it felt like their own private city. She spun in the other direction. She could see the Hudson River now, and beyond it, New Jersey. A helicopter flew past them, bright against the darkness like a ghostly whale floating above them in the deep sea.

"This is so cool," Nathaniel said under his breath.

"Watch," said Tiny. She walked to the edge of the observation deck, closed her eyes, and made a wish. "Star light, star bright. The first star I see tonight."

Lu smiled. "I wish I may."

"I wish I might," Nathaniel jumped in.

"Have the wish I wish tonight," they all finished together.

Then Tiny blew out hard. Across the city, a window in Midtown went dark.

"Cool!" cried Lu. "You blew out that window! How did you do that?"

"Magic." Tiny grinned. Actually, she'd read about it on some blog. There was a statistic where every five seconds a window light goes off or on in New York City. While that may not have been 100 percent statistically accurate, the odds were pretty good of lining up.

"I want to try!" Lu stepped to the edge of the deck.

"Don't forget to make a wish, Luella," said Will.

"I *wish* you'd stop calling me Luella." Lu brushed past him and paused, closing her eyes. Then she blew, and a light went out in the Freedom Tower.

"That better have been a good wish," said Will.

Lu grinned. "Oh, it was."

Nathaniel met Tiny's eyes. "Do you have a wish?" she asked him. He didn't say anything, and just nodded. Then he closed his eyes and blew out the light in a window on the other side of town.

"So," Nathaniel said. "What did you wish for?"

"That I'd have the guts to do this." She held up the stack of Xeroxed poems with a flourish. "But I need some help reaching over the glass partition." Nathaniel, Will, and Lu hoisted her up. "Okay," she said. Her heart was beating super fast. "Here goes nothing." She released her fingers.

The wind caught the stack of papers as they fell, scattering them away into the night.

"Gravity," she whispered, as she watched them fall.

She was a little bit in shock. She couldn't believe she had done it. Her words were scattering all across the city.

Lu helped her down. "That was really brave, Talulah."

They turned around. Nathaniel was peeling one of the Xeroxes off his face, where the wind had blown it.

"Oh," Tiny said. "Sorry, I—"

"Shhh." He finished reading. "You wrote that?" She blushed and nodded, though he probably couldn't see it. "I don't know what to say."

Tiny had never wanted Nathaniel to read her poems. They were her way of working through what had happened three years ago. This one was about that night with Tobias.

"I'm sorry," she whispered.

"Are you kidding?" said Nathaniel. "Don't apologize. Not for this. This is really good. *You* are really good."

Tiny smiled, a real smile. "Thanks. I hope everyone down there agrees." She smiled wider. "But that's not really the point anymore."

"I'm glad you've stopped hiding."

"This is only the beginning."

She looked down at herself—she could hardly see her body in the dark. The light from the paper lanterns and twinkle lights shone through it like glass, as if her skin were the memory of a song, and the lights were trying to remember exactly how it went.

"I hope."

"Don't hope," Lu said. "*Know.*"

Thunder shook the roof, and lightning flashed above them. The lights on the Empire State Building went off. They found themselves, once again, in the dark. The music stopped playing abruptly. Everyone cheered.

Everyone except Tiny, Nathaniel, Lu, and Will.

"Oh shit," said Will. "Is that the power again, or are they closing?"

"Why does that keep *happening*?" Lu moaned.

"The lightning is following us!" Nathaniel cried.

"Let's get out of here!" Tiny yelled over the wind. They made their way through the crowded roof, back toward the elevators. "Come on. Now we can keep on going to school."

"Hey! Disappearing girl!" Someone was calling her name above the wind, in the dark. Tiny spun around, flabbergasted that anyone else at this party knew her.

It was the unfairly beautiful hipster Juliet, standing by herself on the edge of the dance floor. She rushed over to them, the wind twirling the hem of her skirt.

"I thought that was you! I'm so glad to see you here. You haven't seen Jasper, have you?"

"Who?"

"Oh." Juliet slapped her forehead. "Sorry. Romeo. Jasper's his real name. I'm Cleo."

"I'm Tiny," Tiny said. "I haven't seen him since the park. What happened?"

"We were on our way to this party and got separated in that Rapture rally. I kept going, hoping we'd just meet here. But I can't find him!"

"Actually, it was a parade," Lu said.

"What?"

"Nothing," said Tiny. "Ignore her. Do you know where he could be?"

"No! I'm so worried. Will you help me look for him? Please? I'm scared to go alone." Tiny looked back at the others. Nathaniel scratched his neck nervously. They had taken this detour—it was Tiny's fault. But now they had to get to school. Wishing on stars and throwing poems and caution to the wind could only get them so far. Eventually they had to look to science for the answers.

"We'll help you." It was Will who spoke. Everyone turned around. "What?" He shrugged. "Guys, her *true love* is somewhere out there, and we have to help her find him!"

Lu narrowed her eyes in his direction.

Tiny looked up at the sky. It was almost two in the morning. They didn't have much time left. But Juliet had helped her when she needed to find Lu. They couldn't leave her alone out there in the storm.

"We'll have to hurry," Nathaniel said.

The elevator was still working. They hurtled back down to earth.

2:00 A.M.

(6 Hours Left)

Weather Balloons

Lu

Of all the crazy things that had happened so far, the craziest was that Will Kingfield suddenly believed in love.

(But she would just go along with the plan and see if it was true.)

Will

Lu had told him to prove it. Well, game on.

Besides, Tiny was right. He had been focusing on the wrong things. He had been focusing too much on himself. Now was his chance to think about someone else for a change.

It had been all about looks and image and what other people thought of him. But Will was good on the inside, too. He knew he was. He just had to find his way back to himself, again.

They stood on the street in front of the Empire State Building. The wind was howling around them, and they had to shout to be heard.

"Okay," Will said. "Any ideas where he might be?"

"Well." Cleo fidgeted with the twirly hem of her dress. "There were three parties we'd planned to perform at tonight. The Urban Explorers Club speakeasy, a sweet sixteen at the Plaza, and a wedding at the Museum of Natural History. As we were getting pushed in opposite directions by the crowd at the Rapture rally, all I heard him say was, 'Meet me at the party!' But he didn't say which one!"

Nathaniel's face fell in dismay. "But all those places are in the opposite direction of school!" Will shot him a look.

"Are you really going to stand between two star-crossed lovers?"

"Yeah, Nathaniel, don't be the reason they get *crossed* in the first place," Lu added.

"I mean, okay." Nathaniel shook his head like he had no idea what was going on anymore. "You'd think I was trying to help or something."

"It's okay," Tiny said to him. "It's just like Romeo says in the play: 'I am fortune's fool.' We have to do this now, even if it makes us fortune's fools. Don't worry—we'll get to school. I have faith."

"Faith." Nathaniel took a deep breath. "The firm belief in something for which there is no proof."

"See? You'll be fine tomorrow."

"If we make it to tomorrow," Nathaniel grumbled.

"We will."

"You know this goes against everything I believe in. No facts. No logical explanation. Just a feeling."

"God, Nathaniel, you need to loosen up," said Will.

"We'll hurry," Cleo said. "I have a car. I guess I could do this myself. I just hate the idea of getting stuck out there alone in the middle of the storm. You guys have no idea how good it felt to see some friendly faces."

Cleo's car was a 1992 Jeep Grand Wagoneer that looked like it had belonged to her grandfather. It was plastered with indie band stickers and underground theater posters.

"That one's vintage, from when my grandpa toured with Phish," Cleo said, proudly pointing to a faded neon fish. "Jasper and I can't afford much right now, car-wise, so we have to use my grandpa's old wagon. We're trying to save money to put up this modernized adaptation of *Macbeth* that we're working on. It's, like, this psychological thriller set on Wall Street. We're going for this kind of *Gone Girl* vibe. We already found this abandoned warehouse we can use for free, and Jasper's roommate goes to fashion school and is doing all our costumes. So really, we just have to pay for publicity."

"This thing looks like it's about to fall the fuck apart," Lu said.

"Isn't it so cool? It runs on veggie oil."

"Do you always leave it unlocked?" Nathaniel asked, dubiously trying the handle.

"No one's ever tried to steal it," Juliet said proudly. "But you can see why I didn't want to drive it alone in a storm."

"I can't imagine it holding up in a light breeze," Will said.

Lu's eyes lit up. "Hey! An Unsexy Gum sticker!"

"They're my favorite band." Juliet smiled. Will glowered. "You know," she said to him. "You look a *lot* like the lead singer. Are you two related?"

"No," said Will, and crossed his arms. "I hate that guy."

The five of them crammed in. "Roomy," Will said. He sat in front next to Cleo. Lu, Nathaniel, and Tiny squeezed in the back. Cleo adjusted the rearview mirror, snapped in her seat belt, and slid on a pair of mirrored Ray-Ban aviators. "Whoa, whoa, whoa," Will said. "Lose the shades. It's dark enough out there, and the last thing we need tonight is to get into an accident."

She rolled her eyes, like Will was the biggest tool. "These are *prescription.*"

Cleo pulled out of the narrow spot and down the dark street. She turned onto Fifth Avenue and floored it.

"Whoa," Will said again, grabbing his seat. "Hang on!"

As they drove (and Will held on for dear life), Will wondered what kind of guy a girl would travel across the city in the middle of the night during a superstorm to find. Maybe he had been thinking about this in a narrow-minded way. Going after Lu. Proving things to Lu. He knew why none of it was working. He could suddenly see why it was only making her more pissed off.

None of it was real.

He was too in his head about it. It was all for show. Maybe he needed to work on himself more, figure out who he really was. Maybe he needed to be happy in his own skin before he could expect Lu to care about him as much as he still cared about her. And once he did, he needed to have confidence that the kind of guy he wanted to be was the kind of guy Lu thought was worth fighting for.

He glanced over at Cleo to make sure her hands were at ten and two.

"Chill," she said, taking her eyes off the road and turning to him. "I got this." Will stopped abruptly when he saw his reflection in her aviators. He did a double take, and swiveled the rearview mirror back around to face him. His mouth dropped open.

"Hey!" Cleo shouted, swerving to the right so that the car drove up onto the sidewalk. "Lay off, dude! Don't touch my mirror! I thought you were the one who was all for automotive safety." But when she straightened the wheel and came to an abrupt stop, she looked at Will and her jaw dropped too.

Suddenly they were *all* staring at him. With trembling hands, Cleo took off her aviators. Will's chest felt tight.

"What is going *on*?" Cleo's voice was shaking. "I thought maybe disappearing girl was, like, a trick of the light or something. But this is fucking, like, *what*?"

Will caught his reflection in the rearview mirror. His hair was suddenly coal black, buzzed short on the sides with a kind of asymmetrical faux-hawk thing going on up top. He had a beard, too. He scratched it. It was itchy, and it made his face hot.

"How did you do that? Is this some kind of performance art piece?" She looked around the deserted street, panicked. "Get out. Get out of the car. Now!"

"Listen," said Will. "I know this looks—uh—weird. I couldn't explain it even if I wanted to. But you have to believe it when I say that we're risking our lives to help you right now, so I'm begging you, please, just go with it and try not to ask too many questions."

Cleo's face scrunched up like she was weighing her options.

"No one's ever risked his life for me before," she said, thinking it over. "Okay, I won't kick you out. But I can't promise I won't ask questions." She started the car again. Every few seconds she looked over at Will and shook her head.

"Eyes on the road!" Will cried. His new asymmetrical haircut was blowing everywhere in the wind that was coming in through a crack in the ancient window.

Fifth was almost deserted. The car sped whip-fast up the avenue, a straight shot.

Lu leaned over and stuck her head between the front seats. "So, you're a professional actress, huh? That's cool. It's kind of, like, my dream."

"Really?" Cleo smiled in that weird fake way girls do when they feel like they're being threatened. "What have you done?"

"Not to brag, but I've done a lot. Lady MacB, Nora Helmer, Heidi Holland. I played Maggie the Cat before I even got to high school."

"Nice," said Cleo. "I did Gertrude in summer stock last year. Have you ever been to Williamstown? That's where everyone gets their start. You have to go next summer."

"Cool," said Lu. "I keep telling these suckers it's a good thing I don't have to worry about the SATs tomorrow, amiright?"

Cleo's mirrored shades locked with Lu's eyes in the rearview. "I aced my SATs," she said. "Tisch won't even look at an applicant with subpar scores. Most acting conservatories won't either. Unless that's not the kind of actress you want to be." She laughed to herself. "I mean, if you're not serious about your craft, you can always do toothpaste commercials!"

Lu sat back in her seat, hard. "Oh," she mumbled. "The guidance counselor said that too. I thought she was just trying to trick me into taking them." Will tried to pat her knee in a comforting way from the front seat, but Lu swatted his hand away.

They parked across the street from the Plaza and ran up the steps.

"Uh, excuse me." A white-gloved doorman stood in their path. He eyed Cleo's metallic legwarmers and Will's new edgy Jasper haircut. "Are you guests of the hotel?"

They all looked at one another.

"No," Nathaniel said. Lu elbowed him.

"We could have lied," she said through her teeth.

"I'm afraid I can't let you in. Due to the storm conditions, we're restricting access to the main lobby for the safety of our guests. Please find somewhere else to . . . carouse."

"No, no, she's a performer," Will said. "She's performing here tonight." Cleo's face grew red. She coughed.

"We weren't actually, like, *hired* to perform," she said. "Technically. This is more of a guerilla theater experience."

"So how are we going to find Jasper?"

"Please," Cleo said to the doorman. "My Romeo is in there."

The doorman shook his head. "All the girls say that. What is it about a storm that makes people so dramatic? Listen, miss, it's for the safety of the guests."

Cleo's shoulders slumped. A single tear slid down her cheek. "But what if I never find him?"

The doorman's face softened just a little. "There, there. He's out there, princess. You know what they say. You'll meet him when you least expect it."

"I've just"—her lower lip trembled—"been searching all night."

While this was happening, Will turned oh-so-casually around. He looked at Lu. Lu looked at Nathaniel. Nathaniel looked at Tiny. Maybe they could use what was happening to her to their advantage. Tiny looked a little like a TV ghost, pale and see-through.

He looked meaningfully at the front doors, then back to her. Tiny nodded.

She took off through the revolving doors, spinning around and around.

"What the?" The doorman jumped back.

"It's the wind!" Nathaniel shouted.

"It's a ghost!" Lu said, pointing.

"It's a security hazard, is what it is!" he shouted. A luggage cart from inside came rolling through the door, and the doorman took off after it. Nathaniel, Will, Lu, and Cleo hurried through the door when the doorman wasn't looking. On the other side of the lobby, Tiny jumped out from behind a potted palm.

"Boo!" she said.

"Nice work," said Will. "To you and Cleo."

"Why, thank you," Cleo said, bowing deeply. "Do you even know how long it took me to learn how to cry on cue? I use it every chance I get. It comes in *so* handy."

Inside the lobby of the Plaza was as grand as the movies made it seem. The old-fashioned lamps and plush red fancy carpets felt cozy and warm in the middle of the wild storm. Huge green palm fronds cast tropical shadows across their faces.

"That's the Palm Court," Lu said. "I recognize it from *Eloise*."

"I'm going to look for him," Cleo said. "I'll meet you guys back here."

Will heard thumping bass coming from the Palm Court. "Do you hear that?" A smile spread across his face. "Come on."

The enormous room was lined with arched windows, and above them was this cool geometric glass ceiling. True to its name, the Palm Court was studded with palm trees. Round dinner tables were set up across the room for guests, and on the dance floor in the middle of the tables, a group of younger kids were dancing to some hip-hop song from a couple of years ago. A spangly banner read HAPPY SWEET SIXTEEN!

"Uh, Will?" Lu said.

"Yeah?" He looked down. A group of younger girls were standing in front of him, giggling.

"Are you the guy who does Shakespeare on the street?" one of them asked. "I recognize you from Instagram."

"Me?" Will almost laughed at the thought. Then he remembered he now looked like Jasper. "Er. Yeah. I guess I am."

"Will you perform for us?" The girl batted her eyelashes.

"Oh no, not tonight. I—"

"Please! It's my birthday!"

"And a very happy birthday to you," Will said, "but I don't know any—"

The girl crossed her arms over her chest. The girls behind her did the same. All of Will's old girls-are-scary instincts kicked in. They were wearing a lot of makeup and short dresses. These were definitely the kind of girls who would maul you in your sleep.

"Okay, okay," said Will. "Shhh." He cleared his throat.

"You have to stand at the front of the room."

"Um—I—okay." The girl was already pulling him to the front of the dance floor by the arm. Will stood there awkwardly and looked out at the crowd, which had fallen to a hush. "Okay." He didn't even know that Romeo and Juliet died at the end—how was he supposed to recite an entire monologue? "Uh, but soft, er, what light, um, is shining through that broken window . . . ?" The girls were looking at him dubiously. And then he caught sight of Lu watching him. There was a smile on her face. Not a teasing smile, but a real one. Suddenly the right words began to pop into his head, falling into place like dominoes. He got down on one knee. "It is my lady, O, it is my love! O, that she knew she were!"

When he looked up, he met Lu's eye. Her cheeks were red.

"Ay, me," Lu said, her breath catching in her throat. She coughed to try to cover it up.

"She speaks! O, speak again, bright angel."

"'Tis but thy name that is my enemy," Lu whispered. Her eyes flickered in the strobe light still flashing on the dance floor. Will put his hand on his heart.

They recited the rest of the balcony scene, right there as if they were the only two people in the Palm Court at the Plaza Hotel. The room was silent. The world had fallen away around them, and it was just him and Lu. Staring at each other.

The girls burst into applause. "Oh my god," the birthday girl gushed, clutching her chest. "Did you guys feel that? Look—I have goose bumps." She held out her arm. "You must have practiced that, like, a hundred times for it to be so good."

"Yeah," Will said, still looking at Lu. "We've had some practice."

The hip-hop music came blasting back on.

"Ladieeeees, and gentlemen, let's get Romeo and Juliet and their friends up here on the dance flooooor!"

"Oh no, thanks," Will said. He and Lu, Tiny and Nathaniel began to back out of the room. But the birthday girl and her friends were already grabbing their arms and pulling them back. The music pumped through the speakers.

"Dance! Dance! Dance!" the girls chanted. Will and Lu looked at each other. Will took a step toward her.

"Guys!" They turned around. Cleo stood in the doorway, waving and shaking her head. "He's not here!"

"Gotta go!" Will shouted, smiling and waving. "Thanks for letting us perform. Good night!" He bolted for the door, Lu, Nathaniel, and Tiny behind him.

"I don't see him," Cleo said sadly when they reached her.

"We'll find him," said Tiny. "Don't worry."

"I don't think this was the right party after all."

"Then we'll go to the museum," said Will, with a glance in Lu's direction.

He was determined now to reunite them.

He owed her that.

"We won't give up."

He shot a side-glance at Lu. She was watching him thoughtfully.

Nathaniel

Outside, the wind was howling. Just blowing everywhere. It was blowing the flaps of the great awning this way and that. It was blowing the horses and carriages lined up alongside the park, making the horses whinny and jump. It almost blew over Lu, who lost her balance in her platform booties, but Nathaniel used his newfound strength to stop her from falling into the street.

They all piled back into the aging Jeep Wagoneer. Cleo was behind the wheel, Tiny next to her this time. Will and Lu shared the backseat, Nathaniel sandwiched between them. They kept looking at each other over his head. He was not pleased.

"I'm so curious," he said to Cleo, to distract himself. "How do you get this car to run on vegetable oil? It's a great alternative fuel source."

"Well," Cleo said, turning the key in the ignition. The engine roared, then sputtered, then squeaked out. She tried again, but it didn't even squeak this time. Just wheezed. "That may be true, but it's not the most reliable."

"Well, what do we do now?" Lu crossed her arms.

"I have an idea," Nathaniel said. (Thanks, superbrain.) "They were lining up the horse-drawn carriages on the side of the building, probably to keep them safe or to lead them back home for the night. We can take one! We're not that far from the museum; the carriage could get us there pretty fast."

"Nathaniel," Tiny said. "Do you know how to drive a horse-drawn carriage?"

"No," he answered. "But how hard could it be?" He could use his intuitive new brain to figure it out. Secretly, though, Nathaniel was worried. So far tonight, he'd been all show—pushing people out of the way of cars and stopping falling trees. But he hadn't done anything to fix their problems. He didn't even know where to begin. He was still relying on his brother for the things that mattered.

They approached the line of carriages on the other side of the street, and stopped in front of the first one. The horse was one of those massive Clydesdales, with a glistening chestnut coat and white legs that flared out in furry bell-bottoms. A plaque on the side of the carriage said, WILD BLUE YONDER.

"I bet that's her name," Nathaniel said, reaching out to pet the horse's soft white muzzle. The horse bucked and kicked her hooves up. She flicked her thick white tail and stomped her hind legs. Nathaniel suspected that animals were particularly susceptible to electric currents. The horse had probably felt a shock when he'd touched her.

"Whoa," Nathaniel said, knowing, somehow, not to make eye contact. He held out his hand for her to smell and then stroked her muzzle gently. "Good girl. You're okay. We're your friends. We just want to take you for a quick ride. Is that okay?"

The horse looked skeptical. Nathaniel could tell; horses were very intelligent.

They climbed aboard.

"Come on, Wild Blue Yonder!" Nathaniel said, somehow knowing exactly how to gently guide the horse across Fifty-Ninth Street to the West Side.

They trotted along briskly. Nathaniel, as he'd predicted, was easily able to figure out how to steer the horse, who soon seemed to grow a liking to him. Nathaniel even thought he could see her smiling.

"You guys," he called back. "I think she likes me!"

"Cool!" Lu called from the carriage, where she, Will, Tiny, and Cleo were snuggled under a furry throw blanket. "The previous passengers left champagne back here!" Nathaniel couldn't turn around, but he could hear the sound of popping and fizzing behind him. He couldn't ask for a sip; he was the designated horse driver, after all.

Still, he wished he could have one.

Nathaniel always felt a little left out of things, a little bit on the outside. At first, after that summer had ended and high school had begun, he was always turning down plans to hang out with Will or Lu or Tiny so that he could stay in and study. And eventually he wasn't turning anything down, because the invitations stopped. He always had to remind himself why he was working so hard.

It wasn't easy. There were moments when he lost his conviction and wondered if he should give the whole thing up. His parents would understand. They knew they couldn't expect to have two geniuses in the family. His bubbe would understand. She always said Nathaniel needed to have more fun.

The one person who wouldn't, who couldn't understand, was

Nathaniel. He felt responsible. He'd kind of started the whole thing. He owed it to everyone to finish it. He owed it to Tobias most of all.

Tonight he was finally proving to himself and to everyone else that he could be just as good as his big brother. Even—he dared to hope—better.

Still, was it so bad that he was jealous of everyone drinking champagne in the backseat? Maybe he didn't want to be super, really. Maybe he just wanted to be himself—whoever that was.

The dark shadow of the park flew by on their right side, the glittering hotels along Central Park South on their left. The stalwart horse pushed bravely against the wind. At Columbus Circle, she veered right, and the carriage sped right up Central Park West. They passed the Dakota, the famous building where John Lennon was shot. They passed the place where Drunk Santa fell out of his sleigh in the original *Miracle on 34th Street*. Driving up this part of the Upper West Side reminded Nathaniel of the old Woody Allen and Nora Ephron movies his parents used to make him watch with them on weekend nights when everyone else was out having fun. People in those movies were always falling in and out of love and having miscommunications, and New York was like its own character too.

Finally Nathaniel came to a stop in front of the American Museum of Natural History. Banners advertising an exhibit on biodiversity flapped violently in the wind (which was funny, because the banners had butterflies and birds all over them, and it looked like the wings themselves were flapping). On the front steps, the huge bronze statue of Theodore Roosevelt riding a horse stared bravely into the park, as if he was about to ride off into the apocalypse.

Nathaniel wasn't sure what to do with Wild Blue Yonder, so he locked the brakes on the carriage wheels and gave her a carrot he found under the front seat. "Be good, girl," he said, petting her nose. She nipped him playfully.

See? He could be social when he wanted. The horse liked him.

They all ran two at a time up the massive majestic front steps of the museum. Someone had tied white and silver balloons to the handle of the front doors, and they were bopping around in the wind.

"Weather balloons," Nathaniel said knowingly.

"Actually," said Tiny, "I bet the balloons are for the wedding."

A security guard just inside the door stepped outside and stared them down. "We're here for the Swanson wedding," Will said, jumping in before Nathaniel could stop him from lying. But Nathaniel was impressed. Will looked and sounded like the epitome of cool. "We were inside earlier; we just stepped out for some air." The guard looked down at his clipboard.

"Name?"

"Cleo Wasserman," Juliet stepped in. "I was hired to perform some classic works of the Bard for the Swansons in honor of their special day." The guard leafed through the pages on the clipboard. He eyed Lu's Shakespeare T-shirt and black skinny jeans. "And them? There's a dress code."

"Hello," Lu said. "It's storming out here. Can you just let us—"

"They're my stage crew," Cleo said quickly. "My acting partner is already inside." She smiled coyly. "He's the Romeo to my Juliet."

"Go on," the guard said, smiling.

Nathaniel smiled back. Maybe the facts didn't matter so much. Maybe he was too focused on the answers, and not enough on the questions. They were awake in the city in the middle of the night, and they were alive. And though they hadn't made it to their real destination yet, the journey itself was proving almost worth it.

For the first time in a long time, he was out in the world, and he was living.

3:00 A.M.

(5 Hours Left)

Creatures of the Deep

Lu

In the main lobby, a gigantic skeleton of a barosaurus stared down at them. A raptor skeleton tagged along at his side. They looked like pals. It made Lu feel kind of nostalgic for the way things used to be, with Tiny.

Music wafted through the hall from somewhere else in the museum.

And there, standing under the majestic creature from the late Jurassic period, was Jasper.

The *real* Jasper.

"Bae!" Cleo cried, leaping across the great hall like she might take off and fly. Lu watched her fling her arms around Jasper and open-mouth kiss him in front of one of the most majestic creatures to ever roam the earth, like it was no big deal.

"That takes balls," Will said appreciatively.

The couple turned around. "Thank you for helping me find my other half!" Cleo smiled at them. "Thank you, especially, Will."

Will blushed. "I'm just glad you two found each other."

Jasper stared at him. Will stared back. It was like looking into a mirror. "Uh. Cool hair, man," Jasper said.

"Thanks," said Will. "But I'm thinking of changing it back."

"Good luck tonight!" Cleo said, taking Jasper's hand. "I really owe you guys. And I hope you find a way to fix whatever is going on with you." She smiled. "But if you ask me, I think you're pretty cool as you are."

"Thanks," Lu said, and, weirdly, meant it.

"And if you decide to apply to Tisch, I'll show you around!" She and Jasper waved, and ran off through the great hall.

"Want to hear a cool dinosaur fact?" Nathaniel said. He was staring up at the giant skeleton. "Did you know the brontosaurus is no longer considered a legitimate scientific classification? What scientists have always classified as brontosaurus is actually the apatosaurus."

The four of them looked at him.

"What?" he said. "I think it's cool."

"That's a barosaurus," Tiny said.

"I know." He blushed. "It just made me think of that."

Lu studied Tiny. Did she look a little less transparent than she had before she threw her poems to the wind? She even looked less ghostly than she had back at the Plaza. Maybe Tiny was right—maybe she could stop disappearing just by being herself.

Lu tried to piece together what that meant, but it was three a.m. and she was tired. She yawned. She had been awake for a lot of hours. They all had.

"You want to know what else is cool?" Nathaniel continued. "The first dinosaur I ever learned about was the megalosaurus. But I used to think it was called a megasaurus."

"Maybe you should be a paleontologist instead of a geophysicist," Tiny said. Their voices got fainter as they moved on to another dinosaur.

The sounds of high heels clicking on the shiny floor echoed from somewhere far off. "Hey." Lu tugged on Will's arm. "Come on."

"What? Luella, are you trying to sneak off with me?"

"Yes," she said. "Now let's go before I change my mind. Or Nathaniel makes us go to school." She made a face.

"Want to find the wedding?"

"Uh, yeah," said Lu. "I am wearing my wedding finest, after all." She flashed her neon Band-Aid. Will grinned and dusted off his—well, Jasper's—hoodie. He held out a hand to her. She hesitated a beat before taking it.

"You're not going to catch cooties, you know," Will said.

"Can you not ruin the moment, please?"

"I'll try my best, but I can't make any promises."

As they walked down the hall, their shoes clicking against the marble floors, Lu couldn't stop thinking about how weird it felt to be holding Will's hand. Weird, but good, too. Weird and good on the inside, because Lu still couldn't feel anything on the outside.

For the first time in a long time, she felt like someone was looking out for her. Like she wasn't in it alone. Will had fought Owen for her. He had led them all on a detour across town just to reunite two people who had lost each other. Will was a good guy. He had always been good. She wished he could see that too, instead of being so confused. Will's hand was big and wrapped perfectly around hers. She let herself hold it just a little bit tighter. Will glanced at her out of the corner of his eye but said nothing.

They made their way past the barosaurus and his raptor buddy, and through the main entrance, where they saw a sign that said, FOR THE SWANSON WEDDING, PLEASE FOLLOW THE SIGNS TO THE MILSTEIN HALL OF OCEAN LIFE.

"The whale room," Lu said excitedly. "It's my favorite room in the whole museum."

"You used to hate it."

"Yeah, well, I grew up."

They ran down the stairs to the first floor and followed the signs to their left. Adults in black tie roamed the hall, glittering and tuxed.

"Fancy," said Lu.

"We fit right in," Will agreed.

They stopped under a scattering of giant fireflies glowing in a diorama that hung from the ceiling. "Bioluminescence," Lu said quietly.

"Bio what?"

"Bioluminescence. It means the biochemical emission of light from living organisms. My dad used to take me here when I was little. We always stopped at the fireflies. I could say *bioluminescence* before I could say *dog*." Lu swallowed. "We could stand here for hours. I kept trying to make my butt glow. If the fireflies could do it, why couldn't I? Why couldn't I be bioluminescent too? But I couldn't glow. I was just a normal, nonglowing kid. I wasn't special. And my dad"—Lu's voice quavered—"he would just wait there with me while I kept trying. He never told me I couldn't do it." She closed her eyes. "He should have stopped me."

Lu felt the rest of the world fall away, the sounds of the party and the clacking of heels on the tiled floor, and for a minute it was just her and those fireflies, and her hand in Will's, and the sound of his breathing next to her. With her eyes closed, she could just barely remember standing here with her dad, her little hand in his bigger one, feeling like the safest, most loved girl in the world. Like she could glow, like she could do anything. She could almost pretend that the illusion hadn't been shattered six years later, when she'd come home to the moving truck pulling away and the note on the coffee table. A note she still, to this day, had never read. She didn't want to know the reason. Maybe if she'd been able to make her butt glow, he wouldn't have left.

"Earth to Lu," Will whispered. Lu opened her eyes. She pulled her hand away, abruptly, and the sounds came rushing back at her. Will raised his eyebrows. "Want to go in?"

She didn't look at him. Just in case her eyes had gotten all teary or something.

"Yes," she said.

Lu always felt a sense of vertigo when she walked into the Milstein Hall of Ocean Life. It was the one place in all of New York City—even more than standing at the foot of the Empire State Building, or the Freedom Tower—that made her realize just how small she really was. Standing under the massive model of the blue whale, which ran the entire length of the hall's ceiling, the enormity of that other living creature overtook her. Usually she felt too big, too *much* for any one to handle. Here, she felt bitten down to size. There were bigger animals out there than her.

A dance floor had been built across the middle of the hall, and a DJ spinning hits of the eighties, nineties, and today had been set up over by the killer whales. The dance floor swirled with color and light, dresses of all hues twirling under a canopy of twinkle lights.

"It's beautiful," Lu said before she could stop herself.

"Why, Luella." Will flashed her a grin. "Is it possible you're a hopeless romantic after all?"

"Uh, no," said Lu. "It's possible I'm distracted by shiny things." She turned back to face him. "Let's go look at some dead animal dioramas."

She and Will passed the sea lions, frozen forever on their desolate hunk of ice, and the dolphins suspended in graceful arcs beneath a choppy green sea. Lu stopped in front of a sea otter.

"This one used to give me nightmares," she said.

Will raised his eyebrows. "This cute little guy gave you nightmares? Why?"

"On the surface it looks cute and happy, but if you look closer you can tell it's all tangled in the seaweed, under the water where you can't really see. It's stuck there. And it can't get itself out of the mess it's made." She looked at Will. "I know it sounds weird to be so freaked out by a plaster model of an otter."

Will swallowed. "No," he said. "I understand."

Lu shuddered, and they kept walking. They passed the shirtless man diving for pearls, and found themselves in a dark alcove. Above them loomed the giant squid, its tentacles wrapped tightly around the head of a sperm whale. Two great beasts of the deep, submerged in inky blackness hundreds of thousands of feet below the surface.

"Hey," said Lu. "It's us!"

Will laughed. "This is the one that used to freak me out," he said. "You can hardly see what's going on. Just a flash of white where the whale is—a glow of orange over there for the squid. I used to wonder what else was lurking in there."

"Ooooh," said Lu. "Did it give you the heebie-jeebies?"

"At least I wasn't scared of an adorable sea otter."

The dance song that was playing faded into an indie love song. Lu turned instinctively toward the dance floor, but Will grabbed her hand and she stopped short, spinning around to face him. He put his other hand on her waist.

"Dance with me," he said.

"I—"

"Come on," said Will. "You can't say anything snarky in such a romantic setting." Lu closed her mouth. She didn't like being bossed around, but she didn't want to say no, either. She let him lead her to the center of the vast room.

"Do you know why I wanted to come here?" Lu asked.

"I think I can hazard a guess." His voice was serious. She was trying not to look at him. Her eyes wandered across the room, lingering on the other couples, on the little girls in flouncy dresses clustered together, giggling, off to one corner. Anywhere but at Will.

"Lu," he said. "I would take back that night—if it would mean things could be okay between us—"

"I wouldn't," she jumped in.

Will looked surprised. "You wouldn't?"

"No," she said. "Will, that night—I'll never get over it. I'd never . . . I'd never felt that way before." She looked over his shoulder, at the dancers. "I haven't since."

"You really mean it?"

"Yeah, I do."

He caught her eyes this time. "I don't regret that night either," he said. "I regret what came after. I should have been stronger. I was just really . . . confused. About who I was. What I wanted. I think I still am. I don't know why it took me until tonight to fight for you."

"And I was just afraid of getting hurt."

And then, before her eyes, Will morphed again. But this time he morphed into someone she knew. Someone familiar, even though she hadn't seen him in a long time. Instead of the tall, proud, athletic soccer star who ruled the school, who threw massive parties that everyone showed up at, and who girls gossiped about in the back-seats of taxis, the guy who stood there now was a little chubbier, his shirt a little bigger, his jeans a little baggier. Instead of Jasper's cool asymmetrical 'do, Will's hair was brown and rumpled—and not in a cool, purposeful way. More like he hadn't bothered to look in a mirror before leaving home. It was all wrong. But somehow, it felt right.

"Will?" She pulled back.

"Listen," he said. "I—" A little flower girl darted between them, and the DJ spun "Baby Got Back."

"I better see all of you on the dance floor," the DJ said. "They paid me to go all night, and I'm not stopping until the sun comes up and the rain finally comes down."

"I can't think in here," Will grumbled. "Come on."

"Where?" But he was taking her hand and pushing through the crowd without another word.

Together they escaped the whale room, passing the otter trapped among the seaweed, and the squid and the whale fighting, forever in their dark abyss. They ran up the stairs and out the door, past the fireflies emitting their soft light down the hall.

The room they entered was dark, almost pitch black. They were surrounded by large, hulking shadows.

"The meteor room," Will announced. "*My* favorite room." He walked ahead and was soon swallowed up by the dark. "In space, no one can hear you scream."

"Will?" Lu whispered. She picked her way between the shadows, which, when they loomed closer, she could tell were giant meteor rocks, craggy and ancient. "Will?"

"In here!"

She kept going until the room opened up into another room, still dark but dotted with bright pinpricks of color like phosphorescent stars. As Lu's eyes adjusted, she could see that they were tiny minerals and gemstones, fixed in cases on the walls and backlit to shine in the darkness. Glittering rocks of pyrite and geode halves in a rainbow of colors sprouted from the carpeted ground like stalagmites.

In the middle of the room was something Lu remembered well: a big slab of smooth, shiny jade, tilted at an angle against a small set of carpeted steps. She used to play on it with her friends after school when she was a little kid. It had looked a lot bigger then.

Will was sitting at the top, like it was a slide. He was grinning at her.

"Come here!" he called.

"We're not five anymore," Lu said. She rolled her eyes but was already walking toward him. He motioned for her to sit in front of him. She gave him her famous raised eyebrow.

"Oh, come on, Lu. No one can see you. It's okay." Sighing, she took a seat between his legs, facing forward. He wrapped his arms around her waist. "Ready?" Before she could answer, he pushed off. It took them all of a half second to slide from the top to the bottom.

"That used to be a lot more thrilling," Lu said. "Didn't it used to be bigger?"

"I think you used to be smaller."

She started to laugh, and Will started laughing too. He leaned back on the flat green surface, and after a second Lu leaned back against him.

"This is more comfortable," she said, resting her head against his stomach. Her head rose and fell with his breathing. "I wish I could feel this." She meant *this*, as in *everything*. As Lu said it, she realized it was the first time she'd felt that way in a long time. She wanted to feel his arms around her. She wanted to feel his hand around hers. She wanted to feel what it was like to forgive Will. To let herself open up to someone again.

"We'll fix it, Lu. We're going to fix this. We're not going to be this fucked up forever." He looked at her and drew in a breath. She looked up at him. Will took Lu's shaking hands in his so she couldn't stop him this time. She knew her heart was beating. She could sense the rhythmic pressure in her chest. But she couldn't feel it. And then he leaned in. And he kissed her.

She really wished she could feel *that.*

"You make me feel bioluminescent, Lu," he whispered.

"You can't *feel* bioluminescent," Lu said softly. "It's a biochemical mechanism. You just *are.* You can't help it. Fireflies don't think about glowing in the dark. They do it because they were meant to be seen."

"Don't ruin the moment," Will said, and kissed her again. But after a second or two he pulled away. "Are you sure you're okay?"

"No," Lu said, tears pricking her eyes. She couldn't feel them stinging. She couldn't feel that uncomfortable swelling in your throat that happens when you're about to cry. She only knew it was happening because a couple of tears plunked onto Will's T-shirt, forming dark wet spots. She didn't even know why she was crying. "No, I am obviously not okay. This is a really bad time for all this. I have so much to—and I feel so—so—actually, I don't feel anything!"

"Hey," said Will. "Me too. It's okay."

"No, you don't get it. I just don't want to—"

"I'm not going to hurt you. I promise. I wouldn't let us mess this up again."

"Don't be an idiot. You can't make a promise like that. Nobody ever sets out to hurt anyone. It just happens. We as members of the human race are innately selfish. How do you know *I* won't hurt *you*?"

"I don't, I guess." He paused. "You did the first time."

"Then how can you be so calm about this? How can you trust me?"

"I don't know. Because I know you're a good person, I guess, and you didn't mean it. It's just that, if there's even a chance that this could work out, that we could try again, I would risk getting hurt again to see. Wouldn't you?"

"You're so infuriating."

"Lu," Will said. "Breathe."

She swallowed hard. "Do you ever feel like we're like that otter? Trapped no matter what we do?" she asked.

"No," he said, lacing his fingers through hers. "I think we're like the fireflies. We"—he rested his hand on her chest, above her heart—"can't help but glow. We're different. And we've been hiding it for too long." Lu stared at him, his warm brown eyes, and the way his hair was growing just a little too long.

"I guess feeling things isn't so bad," she said.

In that one second she was fourteen again, and she couldn't imagine him belonging to anyone else but her.

THEN

THE LAST DAY OF SUMMER
BEFORE HIGH SCHOOL
THREE YEARS AGO
5:00 P.M.

THE FLOW OF ELECTRONS

Luella

Luella was avoiding going home. Her mom kept texting to ask where she was. OUT WITH TINY was all she wrote back. Eventually her mom stopped texting.

She wasn't out with Tiny. After they left the park, Tiny went home to drop off her school supplies before having a last-night-of-summer dinner with her family. Tiny's family was like that. They actually *enjoyed* spending time together. Like a sitcom family.

So Luella just wandered around from one air-conditioned spot to the next. She popped into Barnes & Noble and read a book on method acting without buying it. She spent four stupid dollars of her allowance on a Frappuccino at Starbucks. Finally she gave in and texted Will.

GELATO FOR DINNER?

Will wrote back immediately.

WHAT ABOUT THE TRADITION? WE HAVE TO WAIT FOR EVERYONE.

I DON'T FEEL LIKE WAITING. COME ON. THEY'LL UNDERSTAND. WE'LL MEET THEM AFTER.

Will paused.

GELATO AND BILL MURRAY MARATHON?

Luella met Will at a fancy gelato place on the Upper East Side that had flavors like blue cheese and basil. Luella got the olive oil flavor, and Will got mushroom, but he threw his out after a single bite and proceeded to share Luella's. "That tasted like feet," Will said.

"This is gelato, not ice cream," Luella retorted. "Your palette is clearly not as sophisticated as mine."

They walked side by side, not touching. Every now and then their shoulders would bump and Luella would leap away like she'd touched an ignited stove. Will had changed a lot over the course of the summer. He was more confident, or something. Now when she looked at him, she wondered if she was starting to think he was maybe, kind of, sort of, well, hot.

Luella concentrated with every inch of her being on not making any slurping or sucking noises while eating her gelato, keenly aware that it looked like she was making out with a dairy product. Which made Luella think of making out. Which made her nervous. Which was not good.

What was happening? Will was her second best friend (after Tiny, of course), and now she couldn't even talk to him!

If Will noticed, he did a good job of hiding it.

It was like some bizarre parallel universe.

So Luella just started saying words.

"I'm thinking of officially going by Lu now, when school starts," she said suddenly. "What do you think?"

"I like Luella," Will said into the dark.

"Yeah, I don't know. All this stuff with my dad. It's been a rough year. I just need to start over. So I thought, you know, new school year, new name. Something different. A change."

"It's okay," Will said. "Yeah, it's cool."

"It *is* cool, right? It sounds kind of rock star."

"You're not even in a band, Luella."

"Lu."

"Sorry, Lu."

"I could be in a band."

Instead of the funny, easy vibe they'd had all summer, the conversation felt tense. It had a weird edge to it, like they were both anticipating something would happen.

"Soccer tryouts are tomorrow," Will said quietly, as if he half expected Lu to not be listening.

"Or as I like to call it, fun with balls."

"Why does everything have to be a joke with you?" He turned to gauge her reaction.

Lu looked surprised. "Everything's not a joke with me."

"It's just that sometimes I want to be serious."

"Er," Lu said. "Okay."

They were standing in front of one of those beautiful old brownstones Lu always passed. She would look in the windows, but she never knew anyone who lived there so never had a reason or an invitation to go inside. She and Will had finished the last of her cone, and their hands were empty and they had nothing left to do.

"So, should we start the Bill Murray marathon?" Will asked, kicking the front step absently with the toe of his sneaker.

"Yeah, okay."

"You have to be quiet though, Miss Talkypants. If my parents knew I was watching a movie with a girl the night before school started, they'd be pissed."

"How big is your apartment? Won't they hear us?"

"Nah, probably not, if they're on the third floor with their door closed. We'll just be stealthy. Come on."

"The *third* floor? Wait—you *live* here?"

Lu realized then, in the middle of everything, that she'd never been to Will's apartment. They just usually met other places.

"Yeah. Pick your jaw up off the floor. A bee might fly in and sting your vocal cords, and then you'll never be able to ask another dumb question for the rest of your life."

Lu clamped her mouth shut and glared at him.

Lu watched him walk up the steps ahead of her. *Watching a movie with a girl.* So Will thought of her as a girl.

They were superquiet until Will tripped on a pair of his own sneakers, which had been lying in the hallway outside his room, and they both tried hard not to laugh, and whispered a lot of *shh*s.

"No, but shh for real this time."

"*You* shh for real!"

"Where the hell are we? A museum? Is that a staircase? Are we in a ballroom?"

"Shut up, Luella."

"How will I know which room is yours? I feel like we're in a hedge maze."

"Well, for starters, you could be quiet and follow me."

Eventually Will turned down a hallway and opened the second door on the right. Lu followed him in, and he flicked on the light before closing the door behind her.

"You have a flat-screen in your *bedroom*?"

Will shrugged. "Yeah, is that weird?"

Lu shrugged. "I don't know. Kind of?"

"Make yourself comfy," said Will, motioning to the bed. "What do you want to start with?" He crouched next to a haphazard stack of DVDs and video games by the TV. "Oh, *I* know!" Using expert Jenga-playing moves, he extracted a case from the middle of the pile, popped the DVD into the player, and hopped up onto the bed next to her. He tossed the case onto her lap.

"Oh no."

"Oh *yes.* Your Bill Murray education commences!"

"This movie looks so dumb."

"*Caddyshack* is not dumb. It's a comedy classic."

Lu jumped off the bed and began inspecting the DVD pile.

"You own *Lost in Translation*?" She raised an eyebrow at him. "I thought you'd never seen it."

"I got it after you told me about it."

"You did?"

"Yeah, I know you don't believe me, but I actually do listen to you, Luella."

"Lu."

"Whatever. Are we watching this or not?"

Lu jumped back onto the bed next to him.

"Fine, but I get to hold the remote." She grabbed it from him.

"Fine," he said.

"Fine." She stuck her tongue out at him.

Will leaned in really fast and kissed her. Closed mouth, no tongue. Lu reared back, her eyes wide.

"I— What?"

"Sorry. That was unexpected."

"No kidding."

They sat in silence for a minute, staring in shock at the TV as the antipiracy warning played.

"Besides, that wasn't even very good," Lu mumbled.

"Oh really? And you're some expert?"

Lu shrugged. "You're not supposed to keep your lips so stiff. And, like, you can use your tongue."

Will stared at her blankly. Lu sighed and rolled her eyes.

"Stay still. Like this."

She leaned in. Will closed his eyes, but she kept hers open. When her lips touched his, she opened her mouth and let her tongue graze his. Then she pulled away.

"Uh," said Will. "Okay, your version wins."

Lu leaned back and crossed her arms, smiling, satisfied. "I know." She selected play on the movie menu.

"Wait." Will turned to her. "That's it?"

"I thought you wanted me to watch *Caddyshack*."

"It suddenly doesn't seem that important," Will said. He leaned in again, and when his lips touched hers, she felt goose bumps all along her arms. This time she closed her eyes. Their mouths were open. He tasted like olive oil gelato. At least it wasn't mushroom.

Will's hands moved up her body, tracing her nonexistent curves, pushing her back onto the bed. He was heavy on top of her, but she didn't mind. It felt kind of nice, actually. Against every conceivable rule of logic, Lu found herself pulling him closer. She felt this sudden inescapable chasm between them, like if she let go, she might never see him again. She might lose him. High school was starting the next day. Their lives were about to change forever. He was going to join the soccer team and become one of those soccer guys. But none of that had happened yet. Tonight he was *hers.* She had to mark him so that no one else would ever be as special to him as her.

"You can take my shirt off," Lu whispered.

Will pulled back and stared at her.

"I *can*?"

"Do you need me to ask you twice?"

"Hell no," said Will. Her shirt went fluttering to the floor. He stared at her bra in dismay.

"Need some help?" Lu asked.

"Why are you even wearing one of those? It's not like you need it."

"Shut up, Will!"

Will fumbled to unhook her bra, like if he waited even a half a second longer, Lu, her bra, and the entire room would melt away into a third dimension and he'd have missed his chance forever. Lu thought maybe that had even happened, that they'd gotten sucked into a time warp or something and she'd missed it, because the next thing she knew she was completely naked, and so was Will.

"It's cold," she said. Will covered them with a blanket. His skin was warm against hers. "Have you ever, like, done this before?"

"Have you?"

"I asked you first."

"Do you always have to win? Can't you just be, like, honest and real with me for, like, two seconds, Keebler?"

It was kind of hard to joke around when you were flat on your back, naked.

"No," she said. "It's my first time."

Will looked relieved. "Mine too."

Will smiled and then so did Lu. He kissed her very, very gently.

"Good."

"Good."

"So," said Lu, because she talked when she was nervous. "I guess, we're probably going to have sex."

"I guess."

Lu reeled back a little, mostly at her own surprise. She hadn't intended to say it out loud, but now that she'd heard herself say it, it sounded crazy. Obviously she knew everything about it from health class—even how to put a condom on a banana. But the idea of actually doing it with another human being felt like light-years away. Like, *Star-Trek-Enterprise*-going-into-hyperspace far away. She suddenly felt dizzy.

"Wait!" she said, pushing him off her and sitting up. She clutched the blanket to her chest so he couldn't see anything, which was ridiculous since he already had.

"Hey." Will sat up too. "Are you okay?"

"No," Lu said, realizing as she said it that it was true. "No, I—I can't do this. I have to go." She was already thinking about where her shoes were and how to get to them without Will seeing her naked butt. "Shit, what time is it?"

"Almost ten thirty, I think."

"What? How did it get so late? I told my mom I'd be home, like, half an hour ago."

"Oh." Will looked disappointed. "Okay. But hey, listen, I wanted to say—"

"Can you move over? You're on my underwear."

Will held it up. "These? They're cute." He waggled his eyebrows. Lu closed her eyes and tried to stop the tears from coming. She had no idea why she was about to cry. It was all just too much. She needed to put some clothes on and sit in her bedroom, alone, and process what had almost just happened.

"Stop," she said. "Please just give them to me."

She fumbled to get dressed under the blankets. Will looked like he wanted to ask her something but was too afraid to spit it out.

That was the moment Lu realized just how much this meant to her, everything they'd spent the summer building, every weird and kind-of-wonderful moment. It meant so much to her and she had been about to do this huge life-changing thing that could risk everything. And what if it didn't mean as much to Will? What if none of this did? Everything was suddenly coming crashing down around her.

What if he didn't feel the same way about her that she felt about him? They'd been friends for so many years, since they were little kids, basically. And this summer everything had changed so quickly. And high school was about to start, and things were about to change even more.

Besides, Lu didn't believe in love anyway. It always ended. Just look at her parents.

Her heart still hurt so much from her dad leaving. She didn't think it was strong enough to handle getting hurt again. It would break into a thousand pieces, and it would be impossible to put back together.

She had to get out of there. She knew, in the worst way you can know something, that she couldn't let this go any further. She had to be the one to end it.

"Wait," Will said. "Stop rushing, okay?"

She stood up and yanked on the rest of her clothes. "I really have to go. See you at school tomorrow."

"Okay, I guess. See you, Keebler." Will's voice was soft and rough at the same time, like corduroy. It gave her goose bumps.

It also hurt in a way that she never felt before. Somewhere physical but not at all physical. Behind her ribs but not exactly in her lungs. Somewhere just below it. Where her heart was supposed to be. She never wanted to feel that way again.

Outside, her phone buzzed with its fifth new text message. It was really late.

She'd forgotten all about Tiny.

Will

Wait. What had just happened?

Will jumped out of bed and reached for his cargo shorts. He stopped before he put on his T-shirt, and stared at the full-length mirror. He'd lost some of the weight, right? Was he so hideous that she couldn't stand to touch him? She had flown out of there as fast as if she had been a cartoon roadrunner.

He threw the T-shirt on and fumbled into his sneakers. He ran down the stairs and out the front door.

Luella was standing on the street, staring at her phone.

"Luella!" he shouted. She looked up at him sharply. A dog barked down the street. "Lu. Sorry. Lu."

"What are you doing, Will?"

"I just wanted to . . . Hey, can we talk about this? What just happened?"

Lu looked suspicious.

"Okay. I guess."

"Look, Lu," he said, his voice serious. "I was thinking—"

"Stop," she said, "just stop." Lu was smiling a weird tight-lipped smile. Will stared at her in surprise. It didn't look like her at all. Something had changed really quickly, and Will had no idea when or how or why. He just knew that it was his fault. He had done something to make her run away. Maybe it was something he didn't even realize. Maybe it was just . . . how he was. Maybe she was running away from *him*. "We all know what's going to happen when we start school. You have a whole new life ahead of you. You're going to be on the soccer team and leave all your mathlete friends behind, and you're never going to want to be seen with a theater girl like me. And I'm going to try out for every play and hang out with super unbearably artsy kids and go to indie concerts and probably start smoking cloves."

"Cloves?"

"Yeah. Cloves. And my friends will judge guys like you, and your friends will probably talk shit about me and my friends. So why don't we just cut our losses and quit while we're ahead? You go your way, I'll go mine. No hard feelings—it'll save you the trouble of doing it later. Okay?"

"What?" Will's face crumpled. She was lying. He knew her lying face so well.

"Really," Lu said. "No hard feelings. It was a great summer. But it's over now."

Will clenched his jaw.

"That's what you were going to say, right?"

It didn't matter now, what he was going to say. She had said enough for the both of them. And then his face hardened into something tighter, colder. Everything was so messed up, and it had happened so quickly. Everything that had made this summer the best summer of his life was slipping through his fingers. All he had wanted was to impress her. He was changing himself for her. The whole reason he had wanted to join the soccer team was for *her*.

And she was throwing it all back in his face. How could she do that to him? What kind of person *was* she?

Lu could never love him the way he loved her. She was cold. She was heartless. Where her heart was, there was nothing but a gaping black hole. She felt nothing.

Will could be that way too. He could show her. Suddenly he didn't want to be himself anymore. He wanted to be someone different. Someone who didn't care about anyone.

"Sure," he replied. "If you say so."

Something had changed inside him. It only took a moment.

Lu pursed her lips. "All right then."

Will looked at her. There was more he wanted to say, but he didn't. "Enjoy high school." Then he turned and jogged up the steps of the stoop, past the red tin mailbox, and through the black lacquered door of the brownstone that stood between two potted cone-shaped shrubs.

The next day was the first day of the rest of everything. Will would make sure of that.

NOW

4:00 A.M.

(4 Hours Left)

The Topography of a Memory

Will

The minerals and gems sparkled around them in the dark. Lu's head was on his chest, and the dark wet spots on his shirt had grown into one big teary wet patch.

"Lu"—he took a deep breath—"when you left that night, did you do it because you were embarrassed to be with me? Did you think—did you think I was gross?"

Lu reared back. "What?"

"You know. Because I looked like . . . this. Because I wasn't ripped like the guys on the soccer team. Or some cool band guy like Owen. Because I wasn't, like, hot, I guess. Someone you would want to be with."

"How do you know who I want to be with?" Lu said.

"But why do you like me? I'm messy and complicated. I have so many *issues* and I need everyone to like me. You should be with someone like Owen, or Jasper. Someone cool and easy."

"Right." She snorted. "Because I'm so uncomplicated? I like you because you're you, not in spite of it."

"Really?"

"Of course. I liked you that summer because you were there for me when I needed someone. You made me laugh. You let me be me."

Will shook his head. "Even though I was ugly."

"You know what, Will? I didn't think that. I thought you were cute. I still think so! And this may come as a shock to you, but I've never thought Jon Heller was cute. I've never wanted to be with someone like him. And Owen is too obsessed with himself, and I don't even *know* Jasper. I like you for you, Will. I always have."

Will's heart expanded in him, like one of those capsules you put in water that expands into an animal-shaped sponge. He wondered if his heart looked like an elephant, or a koala. He shook his head. "That's so crazy."

"Why is that crazy?"

"Because you're the whole reason I wanted to change." He sat there, imagining his tiny capsule of a heart expanding into a big orange gorilla. "So why did you do it, then? Why did you leave? Why did you say all that stuff?"

Lu twisted. "I'm messed up. I really, really liked you. I was just afraid you didn't like me back in the same way."

"Wow. We were real idiots at fourteen."

"Seriously."

"Do you think we've gotten smarter since then?"

Lu let out a big breath. "Man, I hope so."

Lu opened her mouth to say something else, but Will moved in fast, kissing her before she could say a word. She resisted at first, but soon she let her hand rest on his cheek.

"Even though we didn't do it, you'll always be my first everything, Will Kingfield," she whispered.

They sat next to each other, their backs against the wall, surrounded by sparkling rocks and gems.

"Will," Lu said, "if you change back tonight, or if you don't, you'll still be you. You know that, right?"

They sat there quietly in the dark, thinking.

"Do you remember when you said that thing about not knowing what it feels like to be really happy?" Will nodded. "Well, now," said Lu, "is the perfect opportunity for a happy dance."

Will jumped up and grabbed Lu's hand, and together they did the happy dance, lit by the glowing minerals and gems in the darkest room of the Museum of Natural History. It was the best happy dance he'd ever done.

How could you rewrite the wrongs of the past? The past was behind them, and they could never go back. Maybe it wasn't even about the past anymore. Maybe it was just about trying not to do the same stupid things in the future. They could forgive each other, but they would never forget what had happened. It was too important. It was too important to them now.

The four of them stood on the front steps, facing the wilds of Central Park. The wind blew furiously through the trees.

"The next time you guys decide to disappear like that," Nathaniel said, "can you please do it on a night where all our lives don't depend on it?"

"Oh, you know you loved getting to see all those fossils after hours," Lu said.

"Listen, Nathaniel." Will spoke up. "Before we go back to school, there's one more thing I need to do. Everyone has been really brave tonight, and confronted their fears, and I just want to tell you guys something. Lu and Nathaniel and Tiny." He took his phone out of his pocket, held it up to his face, and hit record. "And, everyone else at school and maybe even the world. I gave up a lot three years ago. I gave up a really brave, really smart, really funny, and really weird girl. Weird in the best possible way. I should have fought for her; I should have made her see that she could trust me and that I wasn't going to leave her. I shouldn't have let my own fears and my own insecurities stand in my way. But it was hard, and there was an easier option, and I took it. And I'm sorry. I'm sorry, Luella Jane Austen."

"Ugh." Lu put her head in her hands, but Will wondered if it was to hide tears. "My middle name is so embarrassing."

"I gave up my friends, too. Nathaniel, we were buddies; we did everything together. We were like math nerds in crime. I should have fought for you, too. I should have made sure there was still a place for you in my life. I know I only call you when I have to study. I am going to get better about that. It's been really fun hanging out with you tonight, bro."

"Don't say *bro*," Nathaniel said, but he was smiling.

Will bowed. "And, Tiny, you are so cool and funny and talented, and you care more about holding this group together than any of us. You're our glue. We need you, and I can't believe we made you feel ignored. But I get it. The world is tough and loud and crowded, and you have to be really shiny and happy and loud to be seen and for people to like you. I think a lot of people just pretend. But that's not good enough for you. It's not good enough for any of us."

"Thanks, Will." Tiny grinned.

"I don't want people to think I'm this asshole anymore, who just cares about the soccer team and partying and spending my parents' money and getting into the best Ivy League school. I made everyone believe I was who I wanted to be. Even *I* bought it. I'm not the person I used to be. I don't even know if he's still in there. I've been lying and pretending every single day for the past three years, and I'm tired. And no matter how hard I try, none of it is, or will *ever be*, good enough. No matter how much of yourself you give them, everyone always wants more from you. None of you guys can know what it's like to have that kind of secret. And I'm tired. I'm tired of pretending. Maybe I don't want to go back. I'm still me, inside. I just want to be me. And I don't care what anyone thinks."

He hit the record button, and the video ended.

"You'd think you just won an Oscar," Lu muttered. "We should have started playing music when you hit a minute and thirty seconds."

"What are you going to do with that?" Nathaniel asked.

"The video?" Will looked down at his phone. "I'm going to post it online."

Nathaniel stood up straighter. "Really?"

"Really?" said Lu, her mouth hanging open.

"Yeah," he said. He tapped away at the phone. "There. It's uploaded. I'm really doing this! And, Lu"—he held out a hand, and she took it and turned to face him—"I want to be with you. Now. I want to walk with you down the hall at school and hang out at the museum again and go out for ice cream—"

"Will—"

"And make out in my bedroom—"

"Will."

"What, Lu? Aren't you happy?"

"I don't know. I mean, I think this is all moving a little fast. I mean, we *just* made up. I don't know, I mean, if I'm ready for all . . . that."

Will stared at her. "What?"

Lu looked uncomfortable. "I just think maybe you should think about this a little more. You're in a really weird place right now. Maybe we could start off as friends again, and see what—"

"Friends?" Will was aghast. "I just posted a video on Facebook that is basically a big middle finger to everyone I know! I thought you had my back!"

"I do!" Lu grabbed his hands, but Will pulled them away. How could she do this to him? How could she leave him all alone on this ledge, standing a hundred million feet above the city? What if he tripped? What if he fell?

What if he had just given up everything—for nothing?

"Nathaniel?" Will spun around to his former best friend. "What about you?"

"Uh, I want to be friends again. I do. But I don't know. She's kinda right, Will. I mean, you don't know anything about my life now. All this stuff that you're saying, it's awesome, but you don't have to give everything else up for us to be friends again, you know?"

Will was livid. Every dark thought, every dark fear he'd ever had came boiling up in him.

"You think you're smart, Nathaniel? You think you're some brilliant scientist? Then how come we're still like this? How come I'm still morphing? And Lu's still numb? And you're still some superfreak of nature? And Tiny—" He pointed at her. "Oh shit," he whispered.

Everyone looked. His blood went cold.

Tiny was gone.

Either she had run away again, really, really fast when they weren't looking—

Or it had happened. She had finally disappeared.

Tiny

She hadn't. Not yet.

But time was running out, and she had a plan. She needed everyone to stop fighting, and to work together.

She needed one more grand gesture.

Tiny could feel something in her changing. It had started after she'd thrown her poems off the top of the Empire State Building. She got a little bit stronger, a little bit more solid. She came back—a little bit. And again, after the ghost incident at the Plaza.

And again, when she ran off while Will was talking.

Before she knew what she was doing, she'd turned around and was running away, down the steps. She was taking out her cell phone. She was dialing.

Nathaniel and Lu were right, she realized, as the thunder rumbled beneath the sidewalk and the lightning crackled above her. *Lightning takes the path of least resistance.* This night was magical, but who knew if it would last? Just because she had some cool experiences and had thrown a hundred copies of her poem into the wind, just because she tried to be brave for a night, didn't mean her whole life was suddenly going to change. Would they be friends again tomorrow?

Maybe. Tiny felt a responsibility to make it happen. Will had even said it himself. She was the glue. And it was time to glue them all back together.

The park was wild. It didn't feel like she was in the city anymore. It felt like she was in a dark fairy-tale forest.

She walked farther into the deserted park. Normally, she'd be terrified to be in the park this late at night, alone. This is where people got murdered and attacked when the sun went down. Central Park in the middle of the night was where people went to disappear. But in the dark, amid the trees and shadows, Tiny was already hard to see.

And she was going there for a different reason.

"Hello?" said the voice on the other end of the line.

She was making a very important phone call.

One that she hoped would save them.

Lu

Lu spun around frantically.

"Where did she go?"

"I think—I think it finally caught up with her." Nathaniel looked pale. "She turned all the way invisible."

"But we can still hear her, right? And talk to her? Why isn't she saying anything?" Lu said, gasping. *"Tiny!"*

"Tiny!" Nathaniel cupped his hands around his mouth. "Can you hear us?" Then he put his hands on his knees. "Oh god. This is my fault."

"No!" wailed Lu. "It's my fault. I let this happen. She's my best friend and I let this happen."

"Lu, what are you talking about?" said Will.

"She's so good to me and always taking care of me and making sure I don't do stupid shit. She was there for me throughout my parents' divorce. And she's also the only person I can go on adventures with and who I trust with my secrets and who . . . just gets me.

She's the only person I can be strange with. What did I do? I let her disappear."

"It's okay, Lu." Will took her hand and squeezed. She didn't feel it. "We'll find her."

"We have to find her. We *have to*. Without Tiny, I'm . . . alone. I have no one."

"You have me, Lu." Will looked hurt. "You have us."

"But you don't understand. Tiny is my *best friend*. And I took her for granted. We have to find her."

She wheeled on Nathaniel.

"Nathaniel, help, please. Use your superpowers. No! Use your superbrain! You get all this science stuff! You can figure it out! We have to find Tiny, and then we have to get to school, to normal, for real, before . . . it's too late." She gulped. "If it's not already too late. I can be numb for the rest of my life, I can handle it, but Tiny can't disappear. I couldn't handle *that*."

"Okay," said Nathaniel more to himself, it seemed like, than anyone else. "Okay. Where could she go?" He looked up. And his face fell.

Lu followed his gaze, and her heart sank. The museum was across the street from Central Park. At four a.m., it was the place to go if you didn't want to be found. Maybe if you never wanted to be found again.

Did Tiny *want* to disappear? Or was it possible . . . she was *leading* them someplace?

If she were Tiny, where would she be?

Then she remembered. That picture. The one of the four of them sitting on the giant *Alice in Wonderland* statue in the middle of the mushroom. Tiny had given one to each of them that summer, the photos in pretty wooden frames she'd gotten on Etsy. Traditions were Tiny's favorite thing—or had been, once. Lu had a lot going on that summer. She'd thrown it in her desk drawer with her movie tickets, concert stubs, stray Post-its with random ideas scrawled on them to be completed at a later date.

Alice in wonderland. A normal girl who falls into a bizarro version of her own world. A place where nothing makes sense and the rules have been rewritten by someone delusional without any firm grasp on reality. A place like high school.

Lu didn't know who she was, not really. She had been living in her own delusional world for the past few years. Owen was right. Will was right. She really did push everyone away. She really was afraid of being vulnerable, of getting hurt. She'd pushed Tiny away too. Her best friend. The only one who had been there for her through everything.

She had to find Tiny and she had to let her in. Before she ruined everything.

"This way!" Lu yelled. "Hurry!"

Will

The path was familiar.

The three of them were running through the dark and, frankly, terrifying park.

Will remembered running down this same path with Tiny, Lu, and Nathaniel years ago.

The last day of summer before high school started:

Will was the slowest. He was always the slowest.

"Hurry up!" Lu shrieked gleefully over her shoulder. Nathaniel—always fast, always a little bit super, even then—was so far ahead, Will couldn't see him anymore. Tiny fell back next to him.

"What are you doing?" Will huffed. "You can go faster than that. We both don't need to lose."

"Then you'd be running by yourself," Tiny said, as if it was that simple. "That's no fun."

* * *

It was her idea to have the annual traditions in the first place. It was her idea to take that picture, which he still had. He could never bring himself to throw it away.

He needed to go back to normal now more than ever. If he didn't have Lu, if he didn't have Nathaniel, and if he didn't have Tiny—he had no one. He felt like he was backsliding. Second-guessing everything. The whole night—the past three years, even—started to unravel before his eyes. He was tired. Not just tonight, but of everything. He was so tired of pretending to be happy. Of acting like this new life he'd made for himself was what he wanted.

The picture of the four of them sitting on the giant bronze mushroom, with the giant bronze Cheshire Cat smiling like a big old cat creep above them, was lost somewhere in the tangle of socks and dirty laundry under his bed. He should dig it out. It was a good picture. His old life—his old *self*—was worth remembering.

He'd been so caught up in himself, he didn't realize other people were hurting too. He didn't want to lose Tiny. He wanted her to know that they cared if she got found.

Nathaniel

The path wound around the reservoir and under a series of dark footbridges. He grabbed Lu's hand in one hand and Will's in his other, to keep them close in case the crazies who came out of the woodwork in the park at night made any sudden moves. Nathaniel kept the three of them moving with his superspeed.

The air was heavy. Lightning flashed somewhere up ahead.

What did it mean to be super, anyway? He hadn't acted like it back then, during that pivotal summer that had changed all of their lives. He hadn't made Tiny feel like she was someone worth saving. He'd been the one to pull away. He'd been the one to hide in his desperate attempt to become his brother. Tiny had never asked that of him. He shouldn't have blamed her for it.

He had a second chance to make it up to himself, to her, to all of them, tonight. He had a second chance to be super. And he didn't have to be Tobias's definition of the word. He could make up his own definition of what it meant to have superpowers.

Lu was running alongside him, crying and panting. She was a

total mess. Will was on his other side, his face serious and determined.

They ran down the interwoven paths and under a canopy of leafless trees, their twisted branches like fingers reaching out to them. They ran over a cobblestone bridge, calling Tiny's name.

Lu suddenly screeched to a halt next to him. The path forked in two up ahead. One side was brightly lit with streetlamps. The other was dark and strewn with leaves. A giant tree trunk had fallen across the path, barring their way.

"A tree came down," Nathaniel said, inspecting the branches. "Recently. Like, really recently. Look." The jagged edges were charred and burning in some places, sending smoke up to the dark sky in plumes. The lightning wasn't following them, he realized.

It was following Tiny.

He bent down and heaved the trunk off the path. "Hurry!" he yelled.

They passed along the boat basin, and then, finally, hidden away in a clearing, was the big bronze statue of *Alice in Wonderland.* They'd played up here when they were kids.

Nathaniel had thrown out that picture Tiny had given him of the four of them. After that summer, he couldn't stand to look at it anymore. It brought back too many painful memories. Of everything that happened after it was taken.

He looked up.

Tiny was sitting on the mushroom, her back against the Cheshire Cat. She was grinning. And—was he imagining it?—she looked less invisible than she had before. Everything she did, everything she'd been doing that night, it was working. She was keeping herself from going full-on invisible for as long as she could.

“Oh good,” she said. “You’re all here. Are you done fighting?”

Relief flooded through him. He climbed up the statue and sat down on the mushroom next to Tiny.

Then Lu was climbing up onto the mushroom, and Will was too, and the four of them were sitting there together, on that giant bronze fungus that reminded them of childhood.

Lu wiped away a tear and hiccupped. “Do *not* ever leave me again! I was so worried! What would I do without you?”

“I feel the same way about you!” Tiny squeezed her tight.

Nathaniel was smiling so wide, his face hurt. On his other side, Will said, “I feel the same way about *all* of you!”

“Hey,” said Tiny. “Smile.” She held up her phone and snapped a new picture of the four of them. The flash was blinding. “Now, I have a surprise for you,” she said. “Follow me.”

5:00 A.M.
(3 HOURS LEFT)

PRIMORDIAL SOUP

Tiny

On the street at the entrance to the park was a taxi. *Their* taxi.

Gus leaned out the window. "Hey, you crazy kids!" he called. "You're right back where you started!"

Tiny beamed. "Not quite," she said, turning to her friends. "I promised I'd call him. So, I did."

"I hear you're still trying to get to Chambers Street! Well, get in. And hurry—I promised my wife I'd be home in one hour, and who knows what kind of obstacles will be in our way this time!"

The four of them ran to Gus's cab and squeezed in the back, Tiny riding shotgun this time.

"I was asleep when your friend here called and said she needed a cab and that it was an emergency. She explained everything. Don't know if I believe it, but hey, this is New York. Stranger things have happened. And besides, I liked you kids. Now, everyone, buckle up," Gus said. "It's the law!" He jammed his foot on the gas and they lurched off into the night.

The taxi drove down the West Side Highway. The windows were

open and the sky was alive, the clouds rolling and the air churning in all these different shades of gray and black. The road was empty. The lights glittered across the river. For a moment, sitting there in the cab, there was peace. The night air licked their cheeks and eyes, and their hair all whipped in the wind—except for Nathaniel, whose hair was too short to do anything interesting, though Tiny noticed his curls were all sticking out in even more directions now than they were earlier.

Tiny was thinking.

Lu was thinking.

Will was thinking.

Nathaniel was thinking.

Gus the cab driver was probably thinking too, but he was old and weird and they really didn't care what he was thinking about.

Gus exited the highway at Chambers Street and pulled to a stop at the corner of West Broadway.

"You are safe, where you need to be?" he asked, scratching his beard and smiling. They looked at one another and nodded.

"Thanks, Gus," said Tiny. "We owe you." This time, they all pooled together their money and paid him for the trip—both trips—and gave him a big tip.

"You guys remind me of my own kids," Gus said as he got out of the cab. "They're all grown-up, got kids of their own now. Had a rough go of it in high school. They figured it out. You will too." He put a hand on Tiny's shoulder. Then he got back into the cab, turned off the on-duty light, and drove off in the direction of Queens.

Tiny looked down at herself. She was going to stop fading. If Gus could see it, so could she.

The four of them stood on the sidewalk.

The school loomed above them, all twelve stories, staring down through eyelike windows like some giant multieyed beast. The deserted street was a stark 180 from the usual throng of students. It was weird to look at something so normal in such a totally bizarre context.

Tiny tried the front door. It was locked.

"Amateur," Lu said. "I know the security code to the theater entrance. Come on, this way."

They snuck around the side of the building, to the back door used to load and unload sets from the theater department productions. Lu punched in the code. It beeped twice, and when she tried the knob, it opened effortlessly.

"If that didn't work, I was going to use a bobby pin."

Seconds later they were standing in the darkened scene shop under the stage. They picked their way gingerly over half-painted stools, two-by-fours, and a giant automatic saw.

"Freaky," Will said. "It's like a medieval torture chamber down here."

They walked through an archway and found themselves suddenly on the stage, staring out at the empty house. A sea of red velvet seats stared back at them.

Their phantom audience, witness to all this chaos.

Lu skipped to center stage. "You guys want to hear my monologue from *A Midsummer Night's Dream*?"

The three of them walked out of the theater.

"Aw, come on! Guys? Guys!"

The elevator doors opened onto the darkened twelfth floor.

Tiny could hear thunder rumbling outside in the not-so-distance.

"It looks weird in the dark, with all the lights off," she said. "Doesn't it?" Her voice sounded too loud in the empty hallway.

"The whole school does," said Nathaniel.

"It's like we're not supposed to be here."

"Uh, Tiny. We're *not* supposed to be here."

Tiny shrugged. "Right. Well, according to the law, anyway."

At the end of the hall, they pushed open the doors to the library. It smelled like books and sweat and dust and tears and a little blood.

"I love this place," Tiny said as Lu was saying "Ugh, the library."

"The student archives are in the back," said Nathaniel. "In the sealed-off area where they don't usually let you go."

In the sealed-off area where they didn't usually let you go, student works were bound in leather and shelved alphabetically by the student's gold-foil-stamped last name.

"I can't believe this is it," Tiny whispered. "I hope Tobias knew what he was talking about."

"You don't have to whisper," Lu said. "No scary librarians are here to yell at us."

"Of course he knew what he was talking about," Nathaniel added. "Not just every high school paper is published in *The Journal of Academic Science*."

They made their way down the rows of leather-bound books, to the *S*s, until they reached a slim empty space between two books. It was gone. The paper wasn't there.

"This is it," Nathaniel said. "This is where it would be. Why isn't it here?"

"Maybe there's a reason," Tiny offered.

Nathaniel was hyperventilating. "Where is it? This can't be happening. We came all this way. It has to be here!"

"Maybe someone took it out and they haven't reshelved it yet. Maybe there's another copy somewhere in the school."

"No, no, you can't check out documents from the student archives. You can only access them by special permission, and all physical copies have to stay in the library."

"Maybe it's online too?" Will offered.

"No, the Almquist Foundation is old school, they don't believe in that. Everything is bound in a physical copy." Nathaniel sat down, his back against the stacks. "It's . . . gone."

"I have an idea," Tiny said. She ran to a bank of computers on one wall that were all powered down for the night. She booted one up. "Let's look it up in the library system and see where it is." She keyed around a bit. "Okay, here . . . it says . . ." She read quietly to herself, then looked up at Nathaniel.

"Maybe you should read it for yourself," she said.

So Nathaniel did. He swallowed.

"Well, that's it then," he said. "It's gone. This was all for nothing."

"Where is it?" Lu asked. Tiny glanced at Nathaniel. Nathaniel looked down.

"They took it out," he said quietly. "For his memorial."

The four of them sat there on the uncomfortable standard-issue school library chairs. No one said anything for a long time. The library was dark, and so was the mood.

"What are we going to do now?" Will asked. It was the quietest Tiny had ever heard him.

Nathaniel leaned back in his chair and covered his face with his hands. "I'm so tired," he said. "I'm really tired of trying so hard."

Tiny put her hand on his back.

"Tobias was always the genius in our family. I was just the raptor tagging along at his side."

"I know," she said softly.

"I wanted to be like him so bad. I did everything he did and went everywhere he went. Every decision I've made in my life has been because he made it first. But I know I'll never be good enough to fill his shoes. He left them for me to fill. I owe it to him. In some way, the whole thing is my fault."

"You don't have to fill his shoes," said Tiny. "You don't have to be Tobias. It's been three years since he . . ." She trailed off. After all these years, she still couldn't say it out loud. "Your parents will understand."

"They might. But I won't. I've never been as extraordinary as he was. I thought if I worked at it, worked really hard, I could be. But tonight I realized something."

"What?"

"Tonight I'm more than ordinary. Tonight I have a shot at being extraordinary. I know I have it in me now. Maybe I had it all along. But just because I can, doesn't mean that's how I have to be, you know? I thought I had no choice but to be super. But I do have a choice. I don't have to be perfect. No one is really perfect. No one has to be. The only one who really expected me to be perfect was me."

"Maybe you're afraid of following your own path because it might be *so* different from Tobias's?"

"That shouldn't scare me."

"But it does," Tiny said. "I know you, Nathaniel. It scares you because you've spent so long trying to be Tobias that you don't even know who *you* are. You can be every bit as extraordinary as him. Even more so. In different ways."

"No, I can't. I've spent the past three years working so hard and planning to prove that I can be. I got my whole Anders Almquist application ready and everything. I just . . . I didn't turn it in by the deadline. I was up all night, working on it, and I didn't even finish. I overslept. I missed the deadline." He made a face. "I overslept for my own future."

"Or maybe," Tiny said, "somewhere inside, you knew that wasn't what you wanted. You don't have to be super. You don't have to be Tobias. You just have to be you. Screw being super."

"Screw being invisible."

Tiny smiled.

"Screw wanting to be other people," Will said.

"Fuck wanting to protect myself from feelings!" Lu cried, throwing her fist in the air. "Feelings are fucking great!"

"All these things that happened to us started after we got struck by lightning," Nathaniel said.

"So you really think it was magic lightning." Lu looked skeptical.

"I think I do."

"But that's crazy!"

"Crazier than any other ideas?"

"I guess not," Tiny said. "So, what does this mean?"

"I'm sorry," said Will. "I'm still hung up on the 'lightning changed us' part. I mean, can lightning even *do* that? Nathaniel?"

"Lightning is more powerful than you think," he said. "Some studies even show lightning could have triggered the evolution of the world's first living organisms. Like, lightning maybe caused the Big Bang and woke up all that primordial soup."

"But how is that *possible*?"

"Define possible," said Nathaniel. "I mean, according to Arthur C. Clarke—"

"Who's that?" said Lu.

Nathaniel looked peeved. "He wrote *2001: A Space Odyssey*! And he said, 'The only way of discovering the limits of the possible is to venture a little way past them into the impossible.'"

Will rolled his eyes. "Oh my god, you're such a nerd. Were you always this big of a nerd?"

"Will," Nathaniel said. "Just listen. Have you thought about *how* we've changed? If you think about it, the lightning turned me into the thing I've always been afraid of."

"And the thing you've always wanted, too," Tiny said. "The same thing happened to me. I wanted to be invisible, but I was afraid of it too." Tiny glanced up at Lu. "And, Lu, sometimes I feel like you're the strong one in our friendship. Like you know where we're going and I'm just along for the ride. I'm so scared that if we weren't friends, I'd just . . . disappear. No one would see me at all."

"Tiny—" Lu started to say.

Tiny looked up at Nathaniel, and he felt his heart dip in his chest. "The lightning is turning us *all* into the thing we want—and what we're most afraid of becoming."

Will coughed. "Well, if that's true, I think mine's obvious," he said. "Three years ago I was so self-conscious about my weight. I was so sick of feeling like it defined me, like it was the first thing about me everyone saw. Everyone thought of me as a goofy friend and nothing else. And most of all, I was afraid Luella was embarrassed to be with me. I was so wrapped up in it, I didn't stop to ask if it was even true. All I wanted was to be somebody different." He looked at Lu. Lu looked down at her hands. "I'm afraid I still don't know who I am."

"Well, I'm glad you can admit that, Will," said Lu.

Will looked at her. "What about you, Lu?"

"What about me? I'm fine."

Will looked at her. But it was Tiny who said, "What are you afraid of, Lu? Just tell us. It's okay."

"I'm just . . . It's just that." She sucked in a breath. "Shit."

"Oh," said Will. "I get it." He leaned back and slapped a hand to his forehead. "I can't believe I didn't put it together before now."

"Oh, you think you have me all figured out, huh, King?"

"Actually, Luella, I do. You're afraid of being vulnerable. Of getting hurt. And now. You. Can't. Feel. Anything. Oh my god, I'm an idiot."

"Is that my fault?" Lu said, her voice rising. "People are always leaving me! My mom and I took care of my dad for, like, two years when he was sick. It took over our whole lives! And then the minute he got better, he left us for that stupid cancer nurse. Now they're all shacked up and married, and my mom and I are totally miserable and alone." She sighed. "And Owen was hooking up with someone else, did I tell you that? And it's not like he's the best guy, or that I liked him soooo much or whatever. I just didn't want to be the dumpee. Maybe it was me; I don't know. Like I wasn't all the way in it. I wasn't myself. I wasn't looking for someone who would let me be myself, because then I could be one foot out the door. Because I don't want to get hurt again."

Tiny thought about her best friend, about this philosophy she'd sort of never realized before. Things were always "all cool" for Lu. Tiny never saw her get upset, not really. If everything was all cool for

Lu, she wondered just how much her friend was bottling up. What was going on with Owen that Tiny didn't know about? What had happened years ago with Will, during that last summer before high school? How much did they hide from each other every day? Tiny always thought Lu was the one who never listened to her, but maybe Tiny was guilty of doing it too sometimes.

Otherwise, how could Lu not see how desperate Tiny was to be seen, and how scared she was now that she was going to be lost forever?

She guessed it took almost being forgotten to make you realize how much you want to be memorable.

They were all kind of quiet for a while.

Then Nathaniel spoke.

"I've had enough."

"Enough of what?" Lu asked, her eyes narrowing.

He fingered the application in his pocket.

"Nathaniel?" Tiny prodded.

"We shouldn't have to keep running. Let's show the lightning who's boss."

"How?" Tiny asked.

Nathaniel grinned.

"Let's face it head on," he said.

That was what Tiny had been afraid of.

THEN

The Last Day of Summer

Before High School

Three Years ago

10:00 p.m.

The Luminous Flash

Nathaniel

He watched Tobias pack a backpack, loading up notebooks and pens and some kind of weird electrostatistical apparatus that looked like a magic wand with two wiry prongs sticking up on one end like alien antennae. He was trying not to feel those school's-starting-tomorrow blues. But they were weighing on him. School was starting tomorrow. Things were already changing.

Tobias looked up.

"What?" he said.

"Nothing."

"You're staring."

"I'm just thinking."

"Oh yeah?" Tobias straightened up. He had gotten really tall and really lanky, and his curly brown hair looked even more unruly and Einstein-y than ever. Nathaniel already knew he was following the same trajectory, looks-wise. He already had momentum; it was an unstoppable force of physics. "Whatcha thinking about?"

"Just . . . you know. I'm not ready for school to start."

"Do you have your classes all picked out?"

"Yeah. You're lucky you're heading off to college tomorrow. You got your scholarship. You got into your dream school. You know what you're going to study. You know what you want to be when you grow up. You have your whole life mapped out."

Tobias stopped packing and flopped down onto the couch, next to Nathaniel.

"Listen," his brother said. "You want to know the truth? I envy you too."

"Shut up."

"You shut up! It's true. You have no idea the kind of pressure I'm under." Nathaniel snorted. "Okay. All my teachers. Mom and Dad. My advisers at MIT"—he ticked them off on his fingers—"they all talk about my promise and potential and the bright future ahead of me. They say I'm cut out for NASA, for government research. All I do is work. If I mess up, I'm letting so many people down."

"Yeah," Nathaniel said. "People who worship you."

"Just for once, I kind of want to have some fun. To have a chance to breathe and do something without an end goal in mind."

Nathaniel pretended to play the tiniest violin, for the tiniest tragedy. Tobias crossed his arms and huffed.

"Whatever. You want to know my advice? Think of high school as a fresh start. You have the next four years to do whatever you want. Maybe you'll find out that the way you've always looked at the world is changing. Facts and equations and formulas can only take you so far, Nathaniel. But there's more to life than that." Tobias's face darkened. "There has to be, right?"

Nathaniel studied Tobias. He wondered if they were even still talking about the same thing. "Being so good at something, it comes with a lot of expectations. What if I don't live up to them? What if I don't even want to?"

"Why wouldn't you want to?" Nathaniel said. He literally could not comprehend it.

"I know you want to have it all mapped out like me, but there's no rush. Maybe you shouldn't even be a scientist. Take some time to figure it out."

"What?" Nathaniel reared back. "What, you don't think I'm good enough?"

"No, no, that's not what I'm saying at all. I didn't mean it like that, I just . . . Agh, I'm trying to talk to you like a grown-up, you moron."

Against his better judgment, Nathaniel started to feel his temper rising. "Right, because you're so much more grown up and smarter and cooler and *better than I am*." Maybe it wasn't even all about Tobias. Maybe it was what happened last week with Tiny. Maybe it was just everything.

He was yelling. That was a fact.

"I'm just trying to protect you."

"I don't need you to protect me!"

"I'm your big brother," Tobias said. "That's my job."

"Then you're fired," said Nathaniel. Tobias opened his mouth and then closed it again. He looked almost hurt. Nathaniel wished he could take it back, but it was already out there. He'd never seen his brother look that way before.

Nathaniel's hands clenched into fists. For the first time in his entire life, he truly hated his brother. He wished something bad would happen to him. So he could be free. From living in his shadow. From all of it.

"Come on," Tobias said. "It's getting dark. I have work to do. Are you coming or not?"

Nathaniel turned around and walked out of the room.

"You can go on without me," he said.

Tiny

She stood at the pedestrian entrance to the Brooklyn Bridge. It was getting dark, long after Lu and Will and Nathaniel and Tobias were supposed to meet her, but she was standing there alone.

The weather had been heavy and humid all day, and tonight the air was soupy. Heat lightning flashed above the Queens skyline. It was going to storm. Tiny wondered if she should just pack it in and go home. No one was coming. She felt stupid and embarrassed. She felt like a little kid who still thought she belonged to Science Club.

The last-day-of-summer tradition was the one thing she asked of her friends. It *meant* something to her. She thought it meant something to all of them. Tomorrow was the first day of high school, and everything was probably about to change. But they had each other. If Tiny walked into school the next morning with Lu and Will and Nathaniel, she knew she wouldn't be afraid.

The humidity pressed down on her as the sun slipped behind the buildings and the orange sky burned out into a deep blue. She could only see one star, twinkling faintly far away.

Where was everyone? She tried to call, but no one picked up. No one answered any of her texts. For the first time, she wondered if the tradition only meant something to her. Maybe the others didn't care.

Tiny felt herself slipping away, into the atmosphere like the last fading light of the sun.

Then there was Tobias, pulling her back.

He was biking up the street toward her. When he saw her, he waved. There was the black water churning beneath them, and the night sky above them, full of stars. There was the possibility. The hope.

The *what if.*

"Hey, Tine-O," he said, swinging a leg off his bike and chaining it to a nearby gate.

"Hey, Einstein," she said. Then, looking around: "Where's Nathaniel?"

"Ugh," he said. "Don't call me that. And he's not coming. It's just you and me and the crumbling atmosphere tonight."

Tiny's heart floated out of her body and soared above her like a shooting star, like an explosion of fireworks. She'd always secretly hoped for something like this, one last night, just the two of them.

"Fine," she said, sticking out her tongue. "Don't call me Tiny, then."

"But that's your name!"

"It's just a nickname," said Tiny. "One *you* made up."

They walked along the bridge, watching the water rush below them.

"Actually," Tobias said. "It's just you and me and my massive lightning apparatus."

Tiny laughed. "Your what? That sounds dirty."

"Don't make fun. It's this device I made to record and measure the charges in a lightning strike. It's supposed to attract lightning and parse the charge."

"Erm. Why do you have to do this tonight?"

"When I get to MIT, I'm supposed to submit a proposal for an individualized course of study. I want to study the effects of climate change on lightning in big cities. I just need to collect all the data I can as long as I'm in New York. Then I guess I'll move on to Boston, but New York is bigger." He smiled. "And better." He bent down. "Here—hold this part, and I'm going to plug this in here, and turn this on."

"Is this safe?" Tiny asked. "Are we storm chasers? I know what happens to storm chasers. I've seen *Twister*."

"Heh," Tobias said. "I guess we're lightning chasers." He considered it. "Yeah, it's safe. Basically safe. We'll be fine. Just don't touch it after I turn it on."

Tobias stood back and produced a piece of chalk from his backpack. He used it to draw a box around the apparatus. He drew a bunch of arrows pointing to it and scrawled: DO NOT TOUCH—EXPERIMENT IN PROGRESS.

"Very official," Tiny said.

"Hey, this is a professional operation by a future MIT Earth, Atmosphere and Planetary Scientist. When I work for NASA, I'm totally going to get them to adopt my methods." He held out the chalk. "Want to get in on this?"

Tiny drew a rainbow coming out of a skull and crossbones. She drew some cartoony lightning bolts around it for good measure.

"Nice. Really drives the point home." Tobias put the chalk away and put his backpack back on. They sat down on the walkway and stared out at the water.

It was eight p.m. on a late summer night, and people occasionally walked past them on the bridge. Tiny sat down next to him, dangling her feet over the edge. She tried to push away the feeling that she might fall into the river below.

"Did something happen?" she asked. "Is Nathaniel okay?"

"We had a fight." Tobias lay on his back and looked up at the stars. "Nathaniel . . . he just doesn't get it, sometimes."

"Get what?"

"I don't know. That there's more to life than what he thinks. How hard this all is. All the pressure. The constant work."

"But it's all good stuff, right? This is work you like. And you're really good at it!"

"Doesn't stop me from being scared out of my mind," Tobias said. "I might have had the highest GPA at Daybrook, but at MIT . . ." He stared out at the black water. "I'm not going to be so special anymore." He shuddered. "I'm going to get lost in the crowd there."

Tiny looked up. There were clouds blocking the way in places, but she could see the Big Dipper and the Little Dipper and Orion's Belt. Those were the only constellations she actually knew by heart. "Yeah," she said. "He likes to frame the world in facts."

"Sometimes, the more facts I learn about the universe, the smaller and more insignificant I feel."

"Seriously," said Tiny. "I'm with you on that."

"As far as I'm concerned, deep space gets all the credit for being mysterious. But I think there are enough mysteries down here on Earth to last a lifetime."

Tiny shivered and rubbed her arms to hide the goose bumps.

Tobias turned his head to look at her. "Where's your other half, Lu? I never see you two without each other."

Tiny shrugged. "I don't know. She was supposed to call. Speaking of feeling insignificant . . . I think I got ditched."

"The nerve!" said Tobias. "We'll show her! Come on!" He stood up. "Come on." He held out his hand. "Let's walk."

"What about the apparatus?"

"It'll be fine! Do you not see those warnings? No one in their right mind is going near that thing."

Tiny stood up. "Okay." She smiled. "Let's walk."

They walked the rest of the way across the bridge, and when they got to Brooklyn, they turned around and walked back. It was starting to get really late, but Tiny's parents hadn't called her yet. Lu hadn't called. Neither had Will or Nathaniel. The city lights glittered before them.

"What if I'm not good enough?" he said suddenly.

"What?"

"What if they expect me to know all these things already, and I don't?"

"Tobias," Tiny said. "You're the smartest person I know."

"I'm just . . ."

"What?"

"No. Never mind. It's embarrassing."

"Oh, come on."

"I don't know. I'm just scared of the future, I guess. I worked so hard. I don't want to mess this up."

"You know," Tiny said. "I'm scared of the future too. High school is starting tomorrow. Everything's going to change." She paused. "Everything is already changing. I hate change. I wish everything could stay the same forever."

"No, you don't," he said. "Lots of good things can come from change. The future is yours to write it the way you want. Besides, nothing can stay the same forever. That's scientifically impossible." He threw his arms out wide and grinned. "Make a wish on a goddamn star for something—one thing—to change. And you have to mean it. Go on. I dare you." He pointed. "There's one, peeking out from those clouds."

"I feel stupid."

"No, no, do it. Here—I'll make one too."

They both looked up and closed their eyes at the same time. Tiny hitched her breath and wished. She felt like somebody had seen her, the real her, for the first time. Maybe tonight, if she shone brightly enough in the dark, he wouldn't forget her when he left the next day. He would remember.

She wanted so badly to be seen. To be remembered. She was ready to grow up. She didn't want to be just Tiny anymore. She didn't feel Tiny. She felt huge. She felt massive. There was so much energy inside her, and it wanted out.

Tiny felt like she was about to burst out of her skin. She tilted her face up, waiting, just waiting, for her future to begin.

When she opened her eyes, Tobias had a huge grin on his face.

"Did you make one?"

"Yeah," Tiny said. "I did."

"Cool, me too. Let's go check on the apparatus."

They walked back to the starting point. It was almost midnight, and Tiny still hadn't heard from Lu or Will or Nathaniel. Did her parents trust her so much to be good that they didn't even feel like they had to check up on her? The only person who seemed to care about her at all right then was Tobias. And he was leaving for college in the morning. When he left, she would have no one.

As they got closer, Tiny could tell something was wrong.

"The wind knocked it over!" she yelled, running to it. "All your work!" Tiny bent down automatically and fixed the antennae. "Maybe it's still recording." The metal prongs began to vibrate in her hands. Something beeped. A red light started flashing.

"Don't touch it!" Tobias yelled, grabbing her and pulling her away.

"What? Did I break it?"

But Tobias didn't answer, because suddenly the sky flashed white and bright, knocking them backward.

"What was that?" Tiny asked. "What happened?"

"Oh my god." Tobias sat up. "That was lightning. It worked." His face clouded over. "I shouldn't have done this. You could have been hit. I didn't think this through at all." He stood up, brushing his jeans off. "This was dangerous. What was I thinking?"

"It's okay, I—"

"It's not okay!" he shouted. "That could have killed you, Tiny!" He breathed sharply. "I'm packing this thing up. And then we're going home."

She couldn't shake the feeling that it wasn't his fault; it was hers. That there was so much energy charged inside her, she attracted that lightning all on her own.

Tobias was shoving the apparatus into his backpack and zipping it up.

Tiny thought about near misses and windows opening and closing and how life could change so quickly in the span of just a few seconds. The difference between walking along, minding your own business, and suddenly being struck by lightning.

He swung his backpack over his shoulder and unlocked his bike.

He had a far-off look in his eyes. Like there was something really distracting going on in his brain and he wouldn't be able to rest until he'd worked it out.

"Are you sure you're okay?" Tiny asked.

"Yeah," he said. "Just thinking." He paused, the bike in between them. "Thanks, Tiny. For believing in me. It's nice to know you're out there."

And he leaned across the bike and kissed her.

Tiny felt a small electric shock pass between them.

The hair on her arms stood on end. It felt like—

It felt like—

"Tobias," Tiny said, her lips still pressed against his. "I think you are the only person who's ever seen me the way I want to be seen."

And he said, "For what it's worth, you see me too."

When they pulled apart, it started to rain.

Tobias bent down and wrote something on her sneaker in yellow chalk.

"There," he said. "Words to live by. Get home quick, before this washes off and you forget tonight forever."

"I don't need help remembering." Tiny's heart was pounding. "Tonight was—" *Electric,* she thought.

"Yeah," Tobias said. "I felt it too." He started to get on his bike, then turned and smiled.

There was so much Tiny wanted to say. So much was welling up in her, fighting for space in her head, crowding her mouth with words.

"Later, Tine-O," he said, kicking off. "Get home safe."

The minute he had turned the corner and was out of sight, she bent down to see what he'd written on her sneaker.

Somewhere, something incredible is waiting to be known. —*Carl Sagan*

From down on one knee, she heard tires screeching, a sickening splash, the scrape of metal against metal. The unmistakable spinning of bike wheels in the hot end of summer night.

She looked up.

NOW

6:00 A.M.

(2 Hours Left)

Fate and Other Magnetic Forces

Tiny

It had been three years.

As she'd stood at the foot of the bridge that night, everything had felt beautiful and alive. It was just the two of them and the stars, and the beating of her heart, and her lips against his.

It was just that one moment, but it changed everything. She tried to hold on to it, but it slipped through her fingers no matter how tightly she grasped.

Before she knew what was happening, there were sirens and flashing lights, and a gurney carrying a body into an ambulance. There was so much blood in the street. (She later read a statistic that bike accidents cause the most blood.) She was in the backseat of a cab to the hospital. The driver's name was Gus. She stared and stared at his taxi driver's license. And then she was in the hospital waiting room. And there was Nathaniel, looking pale and awful, and his parents, in shock. And Lu bursting through the doors. And ten minutes later, Will.

And there was this moment, when the four of them just stood

there, staring at one another. Like so much had changed in just one night, they had no idea how to be anymore.

At some point, she realized that the rain had washed the yellow chalk from her shoes.

Tiny's parents made her go to the first day of school, to take her mind off things. She saw Lu there too, and Will. Nathaniel came back a week later. He spent the first semester of school playing catch-up. In some ways, he would always be playing catch up.

And Tiny did the only thing she could do: she got quiet. She got small. She wrote everything down. When her notebook was full of stories and poems, she started a new one. Instead of living out loud, she lived on the page. And then at the end of the day she closed up her notebook and herself with it.

She wrote about everything. How it tore them apart. How Nathaniel retreated from the world, reeling from the loss of his hero. How Lu and Will pushed each other away like oppositely charged magnets, and how they wouldn't speak again until tonight. How Lu never knew how to act around her anymore, didn't know how to ask the right questions, so she pretended everything was fine. How Will joined the soccer team and soon had turned into someone else entirely. How their group of four fell apart.

Tiny was right that no one cared about her after Tobias. There had been someone out there who had seen her, but no one seemed to see her anymore. Or maybe it was that she didn't want to show herself to anyone. It was like Gus the cab driver said. She'd let the bad fear guide her. And it was making her disappear.

For three years she'd kept that kiss bottled up inside her, telling no one. It became part of her, like an organ or something else she needed to live but took for granted. A spleen, maybe. Tobias was like her spleen. She had no idea what her spleen did, but somehow it was vital to her daily existence. She had needed it. She didn't know why anymore, but she did.

But maybe tonight it was finally time to let go.

"The last time I saw him, we had a fight," Nathaniel said. He was blinking really fast, like he might have been trying not to cry. "I wished something bad would happen to him." His voice cracked. "I really miss him."

"Me too," said Tiny.

"Me too," said Lu.

"And me," said Will.

"Why weren't we there for each other more?" Tiny said. "Why couldn't we talk about it?"

Nathaniel shrugged. "We each had so much going on, we couldn't see that everyone else was hurting too."

They all looked at one another.

"What if . . . ," Tiny said. "Nathaniel, isn't your research inspired by Tobias's?"

Nathaniel's face turned red.

"I guess. Yeah." He paused. "I was trying to take it one step further."

"So we'll look at your paper for the answers."

"Mine? No way. It's nowhere near good enough."

"Haven't you been working on it all year?" said Will.

"Yeah, but it's not . . . I don't feel . . ."

"I'm sure it's amazing," said Tiny.

"Besides, we don't have a whole lot of options at this point," Lu added. Tiny elbowed her. "You're lucky I couldn't feel that," Lu said through gritted teeth.

"And we have to reverse the lightning," said Tiny. "I feel it now more than ever. I don't want to be invisible anymore."

"And I want to feel again," said Lu.

"And I just want to be me," Will said.

Nathaniel scratched the back of his neck. "And I don't want to feel like I have to try to be super anymore."

They all looked at one another, then. All four of them. And it felt like it did in the hospital waiting room that night three years ago. Like something was about to happen, and they were waiting to find out what.

"We all believe in you," Tiny said. "If it helps. I mean, we were able to get this far, thanks to you. We can't give up now."

"But I didn't finish it!"

Will blinked. "What?"

"I didn't finish it. I couldn't. I bit off way more than I could chew. I was trying to use Tobias's research as a jumping-off point and take it one step further, but guess in the end I wasn't smart enough. There's a hypothesis, and lots of research. But there's no direction. No focus. I couldn't figure out a conclusive answer. Not like Tobias had."

Slowly, he pulled the beaten-up précis out of his back pocket. He spread it out on the table in front of them.

Tension hung in the air over all of them like a cartoon raincloud.

There was barely any time left. The test was supposed to start right downstairs in the cafeteria in what, a couple of hours?

"What was your hypothesis?"

"It's kind of weird."

"Tell us."

"Well, okay. I guess, um, that big cities, like New York, for example, have their own gravitational pull, and give off their own electric charge. That, combined with the poorer air quality, thinner atmosphere, and increasingly erratic weather due to climate change made me wonder if lightning that strikes in big cities can change the property of matter in unusual or unexpected ways."

"Do you think it can?"

"Yeah," he said. "But I couldn't prove it. Not until all this happened." Nathaniel took a deep breath. He furrowed his eyebrows and studied the page. "E equals MC squared is Einstein's theory that energy is equal to mass multiplied by the speed of light squared. It shows how a small amount of mass can release a big amount of energy. So basically, hidden inside a very small object could be enough energy to wipe out an entire city. But I argue that it can also interact with that city."

Nathaniel wasn't looking at them. It was like the gears in his superbrain were working on high speed.

"Matter can't be created or eliminated. It can't disappear. It can only be redispersed or converted into something else. The amount of energy and mass in the universe is constant."

Tiny was beginning to put the pieces together. She was beginning to understand.

Nathaniel had this superintense look on his face. "I know this is going to sound crazy, but I hope it's not the craziest thing that's happened tonight. What if somehow, when the lightning struck us back on that roof, it, like, reacted with the high electrical charge of the city and the energy we, ourselves, were already emitting, and it . . . well, it reconfigured us?"

He turned to them, finally. There was fire in his eyes. Fire and stars and planets.

"Think about it. It changed all of us. It took who we were, and it redistributed our energy in ways we never could have imagined. It changed our bodies and our brains. It turned us into our fears."

Tiny glanced at Will and Lu, afraid they we going to look skeptical or roll their eyes. But they were hanging on Nathaniel's every word.

He swallowed. "I wonder, if our energy combined with lightning again, I mean, maybe it would convert back into its original form. We've been running from the lightning. It's been following us. Well, actually, it's been following you, Tiny."

It was something, on some level, she'd known all along.

Nathaniel's eyes found hers. "Maybe it's time to stop running."

"What do you mean?" Tiny whispered. But she knew. Of course she knew.

Nathaniel ran his fingers through his wild hair. "You're a small person. But there's a lot of energy inside you. Energy that affected all of us when the lightning struck us the first time. If we let lightning strike us again, there's a chance it would reconfigure us—the matter that makes us who we are, the energy inside us—back to the way we were at the beginning of the night. We'd go back to normal. We could all be happy."

"But we'd have been hit by lightning," Will pointed out.

"Well, yeah."

"Twice."

"Yeah."

"On purpose."

"Yep."

"Do you know how insane this sounds?"

"I'm not saying we should actually *do* it! It's a totally untested theory. Every inanimate object I've ever studied has blown up or been burned to a crisp. It would probably kill us. But in theory, it could work."

Tiny realized something, then. In that moment. That Tobias hadn't been the only person who saw her for her. Nathaniel had too. This whole time. And she'd never noticed.

Tiny watched Nathaniel scan the paper again. His eyes went wide.

"What?" she said. "Did you think of something else?"

Nathaniel coughed. "No. Nothing. Nothing important." She wasn't sure she believed him, but she let it go—for now.

Tiny put her hand on his shoulder. She could feel his heart beating through his T-shirt. He looked up at her. And in that moment she understood how this had to end.

"We have to do it anyway," Tiny said finally.

Lu looked up at her sharply. "Tiny, no."

"We have to, Lu."

"We don't. There has to be another way!"

"There isn't. We have no time left, and no other answers. This is the *only* way."

"But how—?"

"Tiny," said Nathaniel. "All my test subjects essentially *blew up*. There's no scientific proof that this is going to work. It's not worth it. We'll find another way."

"When?" Tiny said, panic rising in her. "When will we find another way? How? I'm disappearing, Nathaniel! I'm almost gone! I'm hanging on as hard as I can, but we're running out of time!

I mean, maybe we don't need scientific proof. We just have to believe that some things can't be explained with facts. The world is big and mysterious. I *attracted* that lightning earlier on the roof."

"How do you know that?"

Tiny thought about that night on the bridge with Tobias, and how it had seemed like she'd attracted the lightning then, too, just because of everything she was thinking and feeling and wanting inside. "It doesn't matter how I know. But I got lightning to strike me before. We just have to believe I can make this happen again."

"I don't know about this," said Nathaniel. "I don't know about this at all."

"Shit," said Will. "This could actually kill us, you know."

"Will, stop," Lu hissed, shooting a glance at Nathaniel.

"Sorry," Will said. "Sorry, man."

"It's okay," said Nathaniel, although it clearly wasn't.

"On the other hand," said Tiny, "it could save us. We won't know unless we try."

"If it works," Nathaniel said, "this will prove everything I've been working on for the past three years, right? Even if I can't win the scholarship anymore. At least I'll know."

"Wait." Lu put her hand on Tiny's almost-gone arm.

"What?" Tiny said. Lu swallowed. She looked at Nathaniel and then back at Tiny.

"How will we know when—*if!*—the lightning is going to strike? How will we be ready?"

"We'll know," Tiny said quietly. "I'll know."

Lu's eyes got watery. For the first time all night, she looked scared.

"What if this doesn't work? Or . . . what if it does, but . . . not in the way we want? What if we go back to normal, and life is just the same as it was?" She paused and then swallowed. "What if you get hurt this time?"

Tiny remembered standing at the entrance to Central Park earlier that night, almost paralyzed by choice. She remembered standing on the Brooklyn Bridge three years ago, making a wish that never came true.

"The thing is," Tiny said slowly, "Tobias was right. The one constant in this world is that things change and nothing stays the same. You change too, or you get left behind. We all have. It's not a bad thing. It's just life. And there's no way to know how it will all turn out until we get there."

They could take the future in their hands and change things. She could make her life what she wanted it to be. Every second, as it unfolded from now until forever, was just a question mark. A whole series of them.

The impossible really could happen. And if it happened once, it could happen again. It could keep happening, every day, as long as they believed it could.

"We'll go to the Brooklyn Bridge. That's a surefire place to get struck by lightning."

"Getting struck by lightning twice in one night," Lu said. "Pretty impossible odds, if you think about it."

"So," Tiny said. "Let's defy the odds."

Lu

Someone grabbed her hand.

"Come on!"

She ran with Tiny down the hall in the dark, Nathaniel and Will right behind them, toward the glowing red exit sign.

Instead of rolling her eyes, Lu couldn't help but smile. Tiny always said Lu was the brave one, that Lu was the optimist who went for the things she wanted. But Tiny was the optimistic one. Lu didn't know how she could think she didn't matter. She mattered to Lu. She mattered so much. She was the most important person in Lu's life, and Lu had taken her for granted. Tiny always made Lu feel lighter, happier, better about everything. She couldn't believe she couldn't see how awesome she was. She would do everything she could from now on to let Tiny know it.

And that was how Lu ended up running down the twelfth-floor hallway at six in the morning, with only the red glow of the exit sign to guide her, screaming into the void of the school.

Their voices bounced off the lockers twice as loud.

Downstairs in the lobby was a stack of boxes labeled COLLEGE BOARD: DO NOT OPEN UNTIL 10/15.

"You guys, stop!" Will said. They came crashing to a stop. "Is that what I think it is?"

"Holy shit," said Lu. "It is. That's the SATs."

Nathaniel walked over and placed a reverent hand on one of the boxes. He placed his cheek up against it and whispered something.

"Dude," Will said. "Are you communing with the boxes?"

"Shhh," Nathaniel said.

Lu put a hand on her hip. "Well?"

"Well, what?" Tiny said. "He's having a moment."

"Should we open it? This is a once-in-a-lifetime opportunity to look at the answers without anyone knowing it was us."

"*Open* it?" Nathaniel was aghast. He stroked the box. "Don't listen to her, girl. We wouldn't do that to you." To the group he said, "Some things are sacred. You can't just go opening every box of SAT booklets you find."

"I don't know," said Will. "I kind of want to open it."

"Me too," said Lu. "I didn't study a whole lot."

"Guys," Tiny interrupted. "If we don't leave now, it won't even matter if you've studied or not, because we won't *make* it to the test." Nathaniel was whispering to the boxes again. "Nathaniel!"

"Fine." He pulled himself away. "See you in a few hours," he said to the boxes. "I hope."

"Come ooon." Tiny dragged them with her. "It's more fun to make the answers up as you go along, anyway."

Lu led them back out through the theater, the way they came in.

The four of them ran down the street. Lightning slashed against the sidewalk just behind them, and the sirens bellowed after. Thunder shook the concrete, set off car alarms along the street, but they kept running. Somewhere along the way, Lu heard a police siren.

"Do you guys think that's for us?" Lu said, her heart pounding hard. "For breaking into the school?" She made a face. "Do you think they know we almost opened the SATs?"

"I don't know," said Will, grabbing her hand and running faster. "But let's not find out."

In the midst of everything, Nathaniel turned to Tiny and grinned. She grinned back. He grabbed her hand, and they ran faster.

Eventually, the sirens receded into the background of the city, blending into the howling of the wind and the car alarms and their feet pounding against the pavement and the beating of their hearts that was the soundtrack to the night. It was like music. One great, big, fucking gorgeous mess of sound. A mad symphony. But somehow it made sense.

"Hey." Lu put a feeler hand out in the darkness as she ran. "Tiny. Where are you?"

"Here," said her friend's voice. A hand slipped into hers. After getting Gus to take them to school, after making them all run to the Brooklyn Bridge and become human lightning rods, Lu could have sworn Tiny was beginning to come back. Not a lot. But bit by bit. It really was in their hands. The lightning would take them the rest of the way.

"Tiny." Lu squeezed. "I'm so sorry. About everything. If I had any part in making you feel ignored. I know"—she gulped—"I know I can be bad at the whole feelings thing. I should have tried to talk to you more about Tobias, about everything after. Looking back, I don't really know why I didn't, except for that I didn't know how, which doesn't feel like a good enough reason, but that's the truth."

"Thanks, Lu," Tiny said. "But it wasn't only you. I have to get better at trusting myself. I ignored myself too. But . . ."

Lu swallowed. "Yeah?"

"You do keep a lot of secrets from me. If you keep doing it, I feel like we're not going to be best friends for much longer. We're not going to be best friends at all. And the idea of life without you as my best friend is—is—*lonely*!"

"And you're not keeping things from me?" Lu said softly. "You could have come to me back then. You could have said you needed me. You could have said you needed someone."

"I know."

"I'm here, you know," Lu said. "Now. It's a little late, but—"

Tiny looked around. The boys were out of earshot.

"We kissed," she blurted.

"What?"

"We kissed that night."

"Are you kidding?" Lu was trying so hard to keep it together. "That counts more than anything! Why did you go along with my Josh Herrera plan if you'd already had a first kiss with the guy you really wanted to have your first kiss with? I was just trying to make you feel better!"

"I don't know," Tiny said. "I wanted to believe it, I guess. I wanted to try to move on. It didn't work, though. Josh Herrera is kind of a jerk."

"What! No. But those soulful eyes! And that hair!"

"I know!"

"What a waste of good hair."

"I missed you so much, Lu. I felt so alone."

"I know this is going to sound weird, but so did I. There was so much I wanted to tell you!"

"We can start now. Right?"

"Okay, here's the truth," Lu said, and then the rest just came pouring out. "That summer before high school, Will and I . . . I think we were kind of in love, or whatever. That last night, instead of coming to meet you, I went over to his place and I guess we kind of ended up . . ."

Tiny's jaw dropped about five feet. "You and Will? I knew it!"

Lu rolled her eyes. "Yeah. And it was really weird and embarrassing."

"Lu." Tiny gasped. "Did you have sex?"

"No! But almost. Like, really almost. I freaked out."

Tiny's mouth opened involuntarily. "What happened?"

Lu sniffed. "It was sooo awkward. I wanted to talk to you about it, but, Tiny, I felt *so* guilty for ditching you. And with everything else that happened that night, I just felt like it wasn't as important. I was afraid he didn't like me as much as I liked him. So I told him it was a mistake. We never spoke again. Until tonight."

"Oh, Lu. I'm so sorry."

Lu smeared black mascara gunk across her cheek with the back of her hand. "It was a bad summer. The worst of my life, maybe. There was my dad, and then Will, and then Tobias—and then after that, you and I . . . I mean, it's never really been the same. I never wanted to feel so torn on the inside again. I promised myself I would never get so attached again. To anyone. So I would never let myself get that hurt ever again. . . ." She trailed off and looked at her shoes. "Or whatever."

"How could you not tell me any of this? There's this whole gaping backstory of your life I didn't know. I'm your best friend. Or at least, I was."

"No," Lu said. "You still are. You'll always be."

They walked along the dark sidewalks, punctuated every now and then by the orange halo of light from the streetlamp. The boys were still up ahead. "I don't know why I brought us to the party tonight. I just felt like it was calling me. Like it was time. Maybe it was the lightning. Maybe I just had things I needed to say and I finally couldn't keep my mouth shut anymore. I don't know."

"Do you need a reason?"

"I guess not."

And then Lu threw her arms around Tiny's neck and hugged her so hard, Tiny almost couldn't breathe.

"You're the best fucking friend in the world. I love you, Tine."

"I love you too, Loozles."

They crossed under a streetlamp, into the light.

Will

Will and Nathaniel walked side by side. Will looked up at the sky, then down at his watch. The edges of the sky were beginning to fade. The sun would rise soon.

His phone chimed with a notification. He'd forgotten all about the video.

He opened the link.

There was a stream of comments on the video he'd posted. Not very nice ones. He couldn't blame them.

The last one was a video.

A door swung open; a vast dark living room stretched out before the camera, like the set of an abandoned movie.

It was *his* living room!

There were empty and half-empty red plastic cups scattered across the floor like grass seeds, flipped on their sides, perched on end tables, the mantelpiece, the coffee table, like they were struggling to grow. They were lined up along the hall credenza, single file. A sticky film covered the hardwood floors.

The place was *trashed.*

On the wall above the couch, someone had written LOSER in something brown and sticky. Will was officially an outcast now. Everything he'd worked so hard for had been for nothing.

He didn't know whether to be angry or relieved.

"Gross," Lu said over his shoulder.

"Wow," said Tiny, on his other side. "I can't believe people would do that to you. They were supposed to be your friends."

"People are the worst," Nathaniel said.

"Wow," said Will. "My parents are going to kill me dead."

"They never have to know," said Nathaniel. "I'll come over Sunday, help you clean. Just like I was going to come over tonight and help you study."

"Let's hope Sunday goes better."

Will started down the street again, then stopped, and turned around. "Thanks," he said. "For coming over. Sorry things got so out of hand. Tonight, but also in life, too."

"It wasn't your fault," said Nathaniel. "We just went separate ways."

"It *was* my fault. I should have been there for you after . . ."

Nathaniel looked down and didn't say anything.

"I just got so wrapped up in my own shit. I don't know why it was so important for me to join the soccer team. I just wanted to be . . . different than I was."

"I get it. Trust me."

Will looked up at Nathaniel. "You know, you're really brave."

"I am?"

"Yeah. It's not just tonight, Nathaniel. You've always been braver than I am."

Nathaniel let that sink in. "Huh."

"You know," Will said, huffing as they walked quickly down Chambers Street. "You were really good at explaining that science stuff."

Nathaniel grinned. "I was really good, wasn't I? I've had a lot of time to study the last three years."

"I bet you really could have won that same scholarship Tobias did. You deserve it. I think you do, anyway."

"Thanks. But you know, I don't know. I've been thinking. Maybe it's a good thing I missed that deadline. Maybe it's time to find my own path. One thing I realized tonight is I have a choice in all this. I don't have to be the best just because my brother was. I'm going to be okay with just being myself."

"Well, if you did apply, obviously you would win. It'd be some *bull*shit if you didn't."

"If I do, just make sure your idiot friends don't talk too loud in assembly, okay?"

"Eh, I don't think they're going to be my friends after tonight. That video's going viral."

"I'm glad you don't want to be someone different anymore," Nathaniel said. "Welcome back, Will."

Will was thinking about how Nathaniel was a good friend, and about how you don't know what the path will look like until you walk down it—or run down it, in the middle of the night. There's no way to know if the path you choose will be the wrong one. But sometimes you just have to choose, and trust that both paths will lead you back to where you're supposed to be, eventually.

Nathaniel

A few blocks away, a row of Citi Bikes came into view, shiny and blue and locked firmly in place. "Nathaniel," Tiny said. "Can you use your superstrength to steal us a couple of bikes? We'll get there faster."

Nathaniel grinned.

They rode across town through the night, the four of them. The wind howled around them. It still hadn't rained, but the sky pressed down on them like a fist, making it hard to breathe.

Every few seconds thunder roared, angry, like a lion descending from the sky. And then the lightning would crack closer, closer, ever closer.

Nathaniel kept turning around to check on Tiny.

"I'm still here!" She would say. "Stop checking on me. I'm fine!"

"Good! Hang on! Don't disappear yet—we're almost there!"

"How much farther?" Will groaned.

"A couple of minutes!"

Nathaniel pushed on through the atmospheric pressure and the wind. At this point the streets were nearly deserted. The subways were boarded up. The buses had stopped running. All the cars had made their way home. Everyone in the city was inside, waiting for the flooding rain to come. Waiting for Stormpocalypse.

The city was shut down.

They had the road to themselves.

That was when the sky lit up, and the first bolt of lightning came crashing into the street itself, zapping down just behind Nathaniel's bike.

He heard Tiny scream, and whipped around in time to see her veer automatically to the curb and onto the sidewalk to avoid the seared black hole now smoking in the street. He narrowly missed another bolt of lightning as it came shattering down just ahead of him.

"Ohmygodohmygodohmygod!" Lu yelled. "We're all going to die!"

"No!" Nathaniel called over his shoulder. "This is a good thing! We need the lightning!"

"That's crazy, Nathaniel!"

He threw a wild smile over his shoulder.

"Good crazy, or bad crazy?"

"There's only one kind of crazy!"

"Lu!" Tiny called. "The lightning is our friend, now!"

Sparkling phosphorescent light was streaking down around them on all sides.

"Keep going! We're almost there!"

They wove together and apart in the street. Sometimes Nathaniel lost sight of Tiny amid the streaks of too-bright light.

"Nathaniel!" Tiny called. "It's following us. You were right!"

"Is it bad that I wish it weren't?" He dodged another bolt of white heat.

Up ahead was the on-ramp to the bridge. A big flashing road sign said: CLOSED TO TRAFFIC DUE TO STORM.

They all dropped their bikes in the street.

Nathaniel couldn't help but wonder if it was the same place where his brother had dropped his own bike, three years ago.

He stopped.

"Guys," he said. Tiny turned around, then Lu, then Will. Nathaniel looked at his bike lying on its side. He looked up at Tiny, who came over and laid her bike in a right angle against his. Then Will did the same thing. Then Lu. Their four bikes formed a square at the base of the bridge.

"To Tobias," Nathaniel said. "Thanks for everything, brother."

"To Tobias," the others echoed. The wind blew between them, rattling the bikes, pushing their hair in their faces.

They turned to the bridge.

"Here goes," Nathaniel said, and took the first step.

It was the superpowers talking, he knew. But maybe it wasn't. He had been brave before tonight. Just maybe in his own, slightly weird, Nathaniel-ish way.

The wind was blowing so hard, they had to hold on to the bridge cables so they didn't get blown away. Thunder shook the pavement, and lightning sprayed across the sky, brighter than the city lights below. Ahead of them, through the twin arches of the bridge, was Brooklyn. To their right, the glittering lights of downtown Manhattan. To their left, the famous Midtown city skyline. Below them, the black water of the East River churned furiously, spitting up white caps of foam.

They were the only living, breathing things standing on that bridge.

His heart was pounding.

It was pounding for his genius brother, who tried so hard to understand the unexplainable. It was pounding for what they were about to do. It was pounding because there was something he knew—something he'd realized back there in the library at school—that he hadn't told anyone yet.

The thing he hadn't been able to stop thinking about since then.

The lightning would course through them. It would change them. The charge in lightning had changed the properties of the subjects he studied drastically—sometimes unrecognizably. If the lightning was following them—following Tiny, really—and if it struck them, however impossibly, again, it was true that there was a chance what happened earlier would work in reverse. Every particle would realign, every cell would go back to the way it was. They would all go back to normal.

But here was what bothered him about that.

If their cells were completely reconfigured to revert back to their starting state, then everything about this night would rewind. To the way things were before they got hit. It would be like a time machine, basically. Everything about them would go back to the way it was. *Exactly* how it was. Their bodies—and their minds.

Their memories.

They would forget this night had ever happened.

If this really did work—if it proved Nathaniel's research right, everything he'd been working so hard on—if he surpassed Tobias—if it did change them back—

He wouldn't remember it.

What's more, Nathaniel didn't want to forget the rest of the amazing things that had happened to him tonight. The things and people that had led him to stop believing so much in facts and to learn to finally believe in magic.

To learn, really, to start believing in himself, instead of trying so hard to be someone he wasn't.

But he was maybe beginning to realize something. There were some things from your past you couldn't hold on to. Tobias was one of them. Tiny was another.

You had to let go of the past in order to keep trekking forward in your hiking boots into the future.

He didn't want to forget about this night. But he didn't want Tiny to disappear. And he didn't want Lu to be numb forever. And he wanted Will to be himself again.

So which was worse? Was it worth it?

Maybe, if he wanted it bad enough . . .

Nathaniel grabbed Tiny's hand tighter in his.

If he willed hard enough . . .

"Whatever happens," Tiny said, looking into his eyes, "this night was worth it."

He could make himself remember . . .

"If we have to go, we're going out in a blaze of smog and electricity."

He could hold on . . .

They stood there. Waiting.

He looked down at Tiny, almost completely part of the darkness now. He needed to believe that life could be different if he let it. He needed to believe there were some things in this world that couldn't be explained with facts and research.

He needed to believe that some things were just magic.

He couldn't promise that everything would turn out the way they wanted. He couldn't tell her that they were going to fix things. He couldn't ask her why she'd felt so ignored for so long—so desperately invisible that she attracted the most powerful energy force out there. He reached out, trying to pick her hand out of the night. Near-invisible fingers squeezed his. She was still there. She was still there. And maybe if he believed they could find each other again, he could finally let go.

Tiny

She looked up at the sky, which was now growing light. It was always darkest right before the dawn. And dawn was here.

She was back on the Brooklyn Bridge. The last time she'd been here was the beginning of everything. For so long Tobias had *been* everything. He was her bright star. Her compass. But letting go of Tobias had been like trying to forget the direction you were walking in.

At least, until now.

"I lived tonight," she said to herself. "I really lived." Then she started talking louder, turning around to face her friends. "I took risks, real risks, in the real world. For the first time in so long I know what it's like to show people the real me. To be seen. I'm not ready to give up on that." She looked at Nathaniel. Real life didn't have to be a letdown. It didn't have to be any less than you imagined it could be. You just had to give it a chance to prove you wrong. You had to go out on that limb alone, even if it scared you half to death. And if you were lucky, if you were really lucky, maybe you would find you weren't out there alone. And if you fell, someone would be there to catch you.

"Me neither," said Lu.

"Me too." Will took her hand. "We've come this far."

Tiny turned to Nathaniel. "Nathaniel?"

Nathaniel took her hands in his. They were shaking. "This whole night. You wanted to be seen so badly you caused a lightning storm to follow you around the city." She was laughing and crying like a crazy person. "I was a superhero tonight because of you. You've already lit up the sky for me."

There were so many *what ifs*. What if the real world took them in different directions? What if grief and longing followed them wherever they went? What if they applied to different colleges? Wanted different things in life, went different places? What if they cared about where they were going in life more than they cared about one another? What if this was over before it even had a chance to begin? What if they started out all great and then somehow messed it up?

Lu was right: you had to ask the *what ifs*.

But she was wrong, too.

Sometimes you had to ignore them.

You can't expect someone to see you if you can't even see yourself.

Thunder began to rumble again, deep and ancient and all knowing. Thunder that knew everything about you. All your terrible secrets, and your good ones too. Tiny looked around at Lu, at Will, at Nathaniel. She'd known them her whole life, but she felt like she hardly knew them at all before tonight. She had always been quiet. She'd always been shy. But she had always believed in magic. And now, because of her, they did too.

She had trusted them with parts of herself she couldn't with anybody else, and they had done the same. She wouldn't give that up for anything. It was important. It was the most important thing. This night had changed her life, and she never wanted to forget it.

"Let's not get hit," she said. "Let's stay this way. We don't need magic or science to be okay. Maybe if we believe hard enough, we'll be fine."

At first they all looked at her like she was crazy.

"Maybe the answer isn't in the lightning. Maybe it's in ourselves! If we believe, we can make all of these strange things superpowers, not burdens. We don't have to let them weigh us down. We can use them to make us stronger. They're part of us now—part of what makes us who we are." She looked around them. "Will," she said. "You can choose to be you. Lu, you can choose to let the right things in. Nathaniel, you can choose to forge your own crazy superpath in life." She smiled. "I can choose to be seen."

They were all quiet for what felt like a long time.

"Okay," said Will. "What the hell? I'm in."

"Me too," said Lu, grabbing his hand. "Those *what if*s. They're important, you know."

Nathaniel looked at her. "You're sure about this?"

"If I am—are you in?"

He reached out and took her hand.

"I'm all in." He grinned. "It's all just one big science experiment, anyway, right?"

Will helped Lu to stand, and Lu grabbed Tiny's hand, and Tiny grabbed Nathaniel's.

The sky was purple, black, and gray. The wind wipped around her, threatening to draw her up into the clouds with it.

Life, she realized, was kind of like lightning. Sometimes you had to go out into the storm and risk getting struck.

And then, the clouds burst as if they just couldn't wait any longer.

For the first time that night, finally, finally, it began to rain.

For a minute they just stood there. All four of them, their heads tilted to the sky, letting the rain wash over them. After twelve hours of waiting, it had finally come.

Tiny began to laugh. And then so did Nathaniel, and then Lu, and then Will. They were all laughing hysterically, their heads thrown back, the water running into their eyes and mouths and soaking their hair and their clothes.

Tiny felt something swell up in her that she'd never felt before. She was alive in this world and she had been quiet for too long.

So she started to dance. She jumped up and down in a circle. Then Lu joined in, laughing, throwing her arms up in the air and jumping up and down, kicking her feet. "Why are we dancing?" Lu called.

"I don't know!" Tiny called back.

"Come on, Will!" Lu shouted.

Will grinned, his hands in his pockets. "No."

"Come on!"

"Definitely no."

"Chicken," said Lu.

"There isn't even any music."

"Then you're not listening! Come on. Show us your happy dance."

Will shook his head. He looked away. But slowly, his feet started to move. He did the Charleston, then the hand jive.

"That's it, Kingfield," Lu said.

Will jumped into a puddle, splashing Lu.

"Hey!"

"It needs some work," said Will, "I'm still getting the hang of it." He grabbed her and lifted her off her feet.

"Ow, put me down!"

And Tiny felt the laughter bubbling up inside her with no way out. She just wanted to laugh and laugh and laugh until she was crying and screaming and there was nowhere else for her to go other than staight ahead without thinking. Just charging forward into the night and straight on into the rest of her life.

"Come dance with me, Nathaniel!" she called. She reached for Nathaniel's hand. "Come *on*!" she said. "Dance!"

He took her outstretched hand and he started jumping up and down with them too. She grabbed Nathaniel's hand and spun him around, and he laughed and spun her back. He dipped her so low that the invisible ends of her hair probably grazed the concrete and came away dirty with soot at the ends. It was a good thing no one could see it.

In the midst of everything, Tiny felt something stirring and crackling inside of her. She looked down at herself. For a strange, surreal moment, she could make out small pinpricks of light extending from each of her fingertips. Now that she was envisioning all that energy roiling inside her, she couldn't shut it off.

Tiny thought about the energy flowing through that first lightning bolt of the night, her body dissolving from solid mass into some form of crazy, psychotic energy—the energy of chaos.

And then she threw her hands to the sky, flattened her palms against the air above her, and pushed forward with all her might, unleashing this crazy electrostatic magic into the world.

All she wanted was to be seen. That was all she'd ever wanted.

And it was at that exact moment, as the others were dancing and laughing, not expecting it, not expecting a thing, that lightning came forking through the sky, right in their direction, and the blinding white light eclipsed everything else.

Saturday Morning

7:00 a.m.

A Brief Theory of (Relatively) Everything

Tiny opened her eyes.

Her face was wet, her clothes and hair were soaked through. It was morning and she was standing on the Brooklyn Bridge.

She raised her arm over her eyes and blinked.

It took her a second or two to remember what today was.

The SATs.

The wind was still blowing, and it was raining. But the world hadn't ended.

The last time she had stood here was three years ago, with Tobias. But now she saw she was with her three childhood best friends. They hadn't been together like this since that night.

No—they'd been together last night, on Will's roof. It had been just last night, hadn't it?

How had they gotten here?

Lu looked around at Tiny, Will, and Nathaniel. The last thing she remembered was fighting with Will on his roof. A door slamming shut in the wind. The big orange moon rising above them. And then—

And then, nothing.

She couldn't remember the last eleven hours. But she had the weirdest memory of a taxi driving down empty streets. Of life, all across the city, suspending because of the threat of water. She had heard music. She—

Owen! Had she made it to his show? She took out her phone and then wondered something. Did she care? She texted him.

I DESERVE BETTER THAN YOU.

That was all it said.

Lu felt a familiar restlessness well up in her. Some force of emotion pushing up through her chest like the trunk of a tree. The roots wrapped around her heart, gripping tight. But for once it didn't feel like too much. It just felt.

She looked up, and there was Will.

Will was confused. "Either the party took an unexpected turn, or the studying did," Will said. He remembered the party getting loud and out of control. His apartment had been full of people he hardly knew. He had been wondering who they were, and why he had invited them.

He had been wondering who *he* was.

And there, across the crowded room, there was Lu. And suddenly he remembered himself again.

Now, the rain blew into his face, and he wiped it away with the back of his hand. He looked at Nathaniel. "I don't think we got much studying done," he said. "I'm sorry."

He meant it too.

Not that he was super pumped about studying or anything. But maybe because standing here, on the Brooklyn Bridge with his three oldest friends and the rain pouring down around them, just felt right.

He had known all along that the world wasn't going to end.

"You know," Nathaniel said, "I think I need a break from all the studying anyway." For some reason, a Carl Sagan quote popped into his head. *Somewhere, something incredible is waiting to be known.* He thought about eating his lunch alone, and the Anders Almquist Earth Science Scholarship that was folded into quarters in his back pocket, and oversleeping for his future. And he thought about how many years of his life he'd spent working toward a dream that was never his. But maybe it was time to find out what else there was out there in the universe.

He took out the application, crunched it into a ball, and then threw it over the edge into the gray river below.

Tiny smiled as Nathaniel pushed his glasses farther up his nose, and turned to look at her. She had missed him. She couldn't help but notice that his hair was curly and unruly, and looked more and more like Einstein's every day. And then she said something to Nathaniel that she'd never said before.

"I miss him."

Nathaniel wiped the water out of his eyes.

"Me too," he said.

"But I miss being friends with you more."

Nathaniel took her hand, and they stared out together over the city and the first reaches of sunlight rising above it.

* * *

Lu felt a shoulder bump against hers.

"Keebler," Will said. "I have to tell you something."

"Me too," Lu said. "I had this dream, or something. It was about you. I think. I wanted to say—"

"I'm sorry," they said at the same time. "You are?" they said at the same time.

And at the same time, they laughed.

Nathaniel looked at his watch. "Crap, you guys, the SATs. We have to go. The test starts in less than an hour."

"The test," said Will. He looked up hopefully. He hadn't gotten any studying done. "Do you think it's—"

"Canceled?" Lu answered. "I doubt it." She realized, in that moment, that she didn't want it to be. It was the weirdest feeling. She actually wanted to make her mother proud.

No, it was more than that, she realized. It was so much more than that. She wanted to make her*self* proud.

"After all that," said Tiny. "It was just a big thunderstorm after all." She felt like she was standing on the edge of something. It was raining outside, and even though the news had predicted that the world would end that night, there she was. Still living. And there was the world. Still spinning.

Lu grinned and flung her arm around her. "Hey, Talulah," she said. "Do you think maybe it's time to start some new traditions?"

Will nudged Lu with his elbow. "Yeah," he said. "Maybe one that doesn't involve mushroom-flavored gelato."

"Or the SATs," said Nathaniel. "Or partying. Or thunderstorms."

Tiny smiled. "Yeah," she said. "I think it's time." Something floated past her on the wind, and she reached out and grabbed it. A sheet of notebook paper with handwriting on it. *Her* handwriting.

Suddenly she had a memory of being at the top of the Empire State Building, throwing sheets of paper into the night sky.

As Lu turned to go, she could have sworn she had the balcony scene from Romeo and Juliet stuck in her head.

Will went to scratch his beard. But wait. He had never had a beard—had he?

Nathaniel took one last look at the view from the bridge. The view his brother had once looked out on. For a minute he felt super. He felt like he could fly.

And then he let it go.

"Guys," Tiny said. "What happened last night?"

Something passed between the four of them. A glimmer. Of the past. Or maybe it was the future.

Maybe she *would* mess things up. Maybe they all would. Or maybe, maybe, they wouldn't. Maybe, just maybe, they were holding on to something real, struggling against the current not to let it slip away.

"I have no idea," Lu said. "But come on. We're going to be late."

Nothing traumatic had to happen for Tiny to grow up. It could happen just like that, on a cold, rainy morning in October. All those little things would change her, though. Just the act of living in this world was enough to do it.

She wanted to be seen. And remembered. There was so much energy inside her, and it wanted out.

The four of them turned and started walking.

Maybe nothing was wrong with her. Maybe everything was. Maybe there was a whole life ahead of her, waiting to be lived. And she was going to be okay.

8:00 A.M.

They made it just in time.

ACKNOWLEDGMENTS

In case you are wondering if any of this is scientifically possible: I don't know. I haven't gone out into a lightning storm and tested it—and I don't recommend you do that either! What I do know is that it is a work of fiction. Real scientific theories provided the foundation for Tiny, Nathaniel, Lu, and Will's story, and I took it from there. Many thanks (and maybe apologies) to the brilliant minds who inspired my own imagination:

Albert Einstein, for the epigraph at the beginning of this book, and for the theory of relativity, with which I took many creative liberties.

Arthur C. Clarke and Carl Sagan, for their beautiful ideas about the infinite possibilities of the universe, quoted on page 306 and on pages 325 and 365, respectively.

Patricia Lawler Kenet gave me a copy of *Physics: Why Matter Matters!* by Dan Green and Simon Basher, which reminded me of most of what I'd forgotten from Mr. Condie's high school physics class. I am forever thankful that a book with so many amazing science puns exists, and to Patricia for giving it to me.

The MIT Department of Earth, Atmospheric and Planetary Studies website provided inspiration for Tobias's fictional academic interests. *National Geographic* and the National Oceanic and Atmospheric Administration provided useful information about lightning.

Though he was not a scientist, thank you to William Shakespeare, for so many things, but in this case for the quotes on pages 138, 141, and 236.

The odds of writing a book without any help at all are virtually impossible. Thank you, thank you, thank you, to:

Writing teacher extraordinaire and all-around publishing guardian angel Micol Ostow, in whose YA novel workshop I wrote the first full draft of this book. And to my classmates Darci Manley, Shani Petroff, and Anna Hecker, for insightful notes and hearts in the margins, without which I might never have made it past that first workshop.

Jessica Regel, my amazing agent, for *getting* this book from the first read and continuing to champion it for all the reads after that. I'm so lucky to have you in my corner.

My magical editors at Simon Pulse—Sara Sargent, Liesa Abrams, and Nicole Ellul—whose guidance pushed me to write the book I'd been trying to write all along. To Karina Granda, for designing the actual cover of my dreams.

The generous editors and friends who have given me notes along the way, especially Tara Weikum, Jen Klonsky, and Katie Bellas.

Sarah Barnard, for going on random ill-advised high school adventures with me, and for giving me the copy of Ned Vizzini's *Be More Chill* that made me want to be a YA writer.

Jillian Schlesinger, for sharing my brain and knowing what it's like to have a crazy idea and then see it through to completion. Alissa Weiss, for always asking, always listening, always being up for talking it through. The whole story is long and complicated.

BP, for fifteen years (and counting!) of lunchtime chats.

The Batesies: I can't remember what life was like before we were friends.

My writing pals, Anne Heltzel, Leila Sales, Rebecca Serle, Lexa Hillyer, Jess Rothenberg, Jackie Resnick, Danielle Rollins, and Alyssa Sheinmel. Knowing we're all in it together makes the hard parts less hard and the fun parts way more fun.

My incredible family: Shelby Davies, for being the most special bug; Jody and Lee Davies, for teaching me the importance of imagination; and Sandra Messler, for displaying everything I've ever written on your coffee table and for buying me my first issue of *Seventeen*.

Jeremy Kestenbaum, for being the cocreator of the world's best pizza, but most of all for being you.